SWAN SONG

Even in that crippled condition I was still going 55 when I reached the pond and I realized with absolute certainty that, barring a miracle, I wouldn't make it around the curve. I pressed both feet on the brake pedal, sending the car fishtailing across the centerline. As I pulled back into my lane, I was vaguely aware that the dark van was still with me, but I was too busy to think about much more than slowing the car down. *Hold on, Hannah! Here we go!*

My car sailed over the ditch, shot through a hedge, ripped through a barbed-wire fence, and plunged, nose first, into the murky water of the Baxter's pond. The last thought I had before everything went dark was not of my husband or daughter or the fear of dying but *Oh, damn, I'm going to ruin Connie's scarf....*

PRAISE FOR **SING IT TO HER BONES**

"Hannah Ives is a welcome addition to the mystery landscape—smart, brave, wonderfully human, the kind of woman you want for your new best friend. *Sing It to Her Bones* is an impressive, polished debut from a writer to watch." —**Laura Lippman, Edgar Award–winning author of *Butchers Hill***

"Scenes of Annapolis and the Chesapeake Bay area add an authentic tang of sunlit salt air to this suspenseful debut novel. Hannah Ives is an appealing, believable heroine." —**Margaret Maron, author of *Home Fires Burning***

For Barbara
I enjoyed meeting
you at Magna, & hope
you enjoy meeting Hannah

SING IT
TO
HER BONES

A Hannah Ives Mystery

Marcia Talley

Marcia Talley

A Dell Book

Published by
Dell Publishing
a division of
Random House, Inc.
1540 Broadway
New York, New York 10036

The trademark Dell® is registered in the U.S. Patent and Trademark
Office.

ISBN: 0-440-23517-0

Printed in the United States of America

Published simultaneously in Canada

August 1999

10   9   8   7   6   5   4   3

OPM

In Memoriam

Paul Pierre Nash
1950–1993

Acknowledgments

WITHOUT THE HELP OF MANY GENEROUS PEOPLE, THIS book would not have been possible. Any mistakes made are mine alone and should not be attributed to the individuals mentioned below.

To my husband, Barry Talley, for his love, unwavering support, and unflagging fondness for Chinese carry-out food. To Quentin Kinderman, the other sailor in my life, who would be a dangerous man should he turn to crime. To my daughters, Laura and Sarah, who were with me when Emily was born and know her better than I do. To BM3 Christopher Wellington of the U.S. Coast Guard station at Thomas Point in Annapolis for valuable information about rescue at sea. To Dr. Anthony Massey and Dr. Charles Kinzer for hypothetical glimpses inside a doctor's files. To friends at the Naval Academy, especially David, Charles, and Bill, for whom no question was ever too off-the-wall, and my colleagues at the Naval Academy library who listened patiently to Hannah's adventures over countless lunches.

To the Malice Domestic Conference for awarding me their grant for unpublished writers in 1998, I am everlastingly grateful. Thanks, too, to my editor, Jacquie Miller, for her perceptive suggestions and to my miracle-working agent, Jimmy Vines.

To my writers' groups, who read every word of this manuscript, sometimes more than once—Sujata Massey, John Mann, Janice McClain, and Karen Diegmueller in Baltimore; and Janet Benrey, Ron Benrey, Carolyn Curtis, Ray Flynt, Mary Ellen Hughes, Trish Marshall, and Sherriel Mattingly in Annapolis—1,000,000 thanks. There's a bit of each of you in every Hannah novel.

To my dear friends Kate Charles and Deborah Crombie, who read the final manuscript and offered constructive criticism and encouragement, and to Sara Ann Freed and Linda Sprenkle, who nagged, thanks for being the best cheerleaders a girl could ever have.

To Dr. Stanley Watkins for saving my life and to the 2,599,999 other breast cancer survivors now living in the United States from whom I draw my strength and inspiration.

I cannot bid you bid my daughter live;
That were impossible: but, I pray you both,
Possess the people in Messina here
How innocent she died; and if your love
Can labour aught in sad invention,
Hang her an epitaph upon her tomb
And sing it to her bones. . . .

—**William Shakespeare,**
Much Ado About Nothing,
Act 5, Scene 1

chapter

1

WHEN I GOT CANCER, I DECIDED I WASN'T GOING TO put up with crap from anybody anymore. I would have quit work right then, too, but even with Blue Cross/Blue Shield paying 75 percent, the surgery and the chemo treatments cost me too much to ditch the job.

I thought about it, though. I imagined walking into her cubicle and announcing, loud enough for everyone in the office to hear, "Fran, I quit!" Just like that. And she'd look hurt and confused and go, "Buh-buh . . . " and I'd say, "As of *right now*!" Then I'd strut right out, past all of them standing in a line behind their desks. I imagined they'd be smiling at me and clapping.

My husband thinks it's the job that made me sick. "All that stress," he says. "It can't be good for you, Hannah." One morning while I was sitting at the kitchen table hugging a bowl of cornflakes and trying not to throw up, he handed me an article he'd torn out of a magazine in the doctor's office, "Stressed to Kill." Families can be so helpful. My sisters are always sending me stuff like that. "The Anticancer Diet," "Superfood for Women," "Cancer: Facts vs. Feelings." I keep it all in a manila folder by my bed, so when they visit, they think I'm reading it.

The truth is, I was born stressed. The pediatrician told my mother he had never seen a kindergarten kid with ulcers before. In first grade I went hyper when Mom brought home college-ruled notebook paper. "It says wide-ruled," I wailed. "It says so, right-here-on-this-list." And I fussed and whined and carried on until she drove out to the 7-Eleven after dinner and bought me exactly the right kind. I stopped having stomachaches after the second grade, so I suppose I learned to cope. You have to stay in school, don't you? So you manage. You work it out. The same goes for jobs. And bosses.

I'm not sure when my boss, Fran, started acting like a fruitcake. She was always a little weird, kept her desk locked up tight even while she was sitting at it. Once she attended a two-day seminar at an executive hotel outside the Beltway and came back all fired up about Total Quality Management. Right away she selected six of us to form a group to meet during lunch hour for weeks in order to come up with four or five suggestions to improve our service, like making a telephone training video, installing a second fax machine, and hiring a stress management consultant. When we submitted our list to Fran, she studied it for a long time, then grabbed a black Magic Marker from the ceramic mug on her desk and drew a heavy line through the "stress management consultant." "We don't have stress here," she said. We all gasped, and I swore to everyone in the lunchroom afterward that I saw the papers on her desk flutter.

So this is how I'm dealing with the stress we don't have at our office. I tell myself I'm in it for the benefits and the money, the paycheck that lets me get on with my life. I have hopes! I play the lottery when I think about it, and every year I order a magazine or two by licking and sticking those itty-bitty picture stamps. But face it, the Prize Patrol from Publishers Clearing House is not going to knock on my door with a check for ten million dollars. So I show up at the office, day after day, or visit the doctors when I have to, like an actor in a long-running play who knows his lines and doesn't have to think about them much anymore. It's a show, one act following another.

Emily Jean, in an uncharacteristic display of pragmatism, thought that one up. "Look, Mother," she said to me one day when I was feeling particularly exhausted and depressed because my hair was thinning out. "It's like you've got these two missions. *Re*mission, that's one, and you're working hard on that. Then *inter*mission. Those are the good times between the acts that make all of this other shit bearable."

"God, yes!" I agreed, but all the time she was talking I was thinking, *The way I feel right now, I'd have to rally to die.* I didn't tell her that, though. I didn't want her to worry. "You're absolutely right, pumpkin," I said instead. "Let's get to work on those intermissions."

I had been contemplating a weekend at Virginia Beach or a two-week cruise in the British Virgin Islands. England, maybe. As it turned out, that cute little cottage in the Cotswolds was going to have to wait. Like I read somewhere, life is what happens when you're making other plans.

It's called downsizing or rightsizing. Reduction in force. A RIF. Whatever. It means you're fired. A quality management team somewhere on the tenth floor had been throwing darts at our organizational chart, pinning a major portion of Whitworth & Sullivan's Technical Support Department to the wall, smack dab through the *o* in *Support.*

Fran, we heard later, had gone all glassy-eyed and sullen when they told her, refusing to believe that half her staff was about to be tossed onto the street. "It's a business decision," they explained, and gave her two days to get with the program. She stonewalled, so they called in the managing partner, an ex-marine named Cooper, who had no qualms about summoning us individually to the firm's best conference room, offering coffee or juice—the charming, disarming, oh-so-personal touch—and then, whack! kneecapping us with the news.

When it was my turn, I chose an upholstered chair opposite Fran with about as much enthusiasm as a candidate for a root canal. Nobody said anything at first. While Coop thumbed through the papers stacked in front of him, as if trying to remember my name, I settled uncomfortably into the chair, attempting to blend inconspicuously into the gold damask, a little hard to do when you're wearing a red plaid dress. I crossed my right leg over my left, then, because I was nervous, tucked my right patent leather toe behind my left calf. It's a bad habit I picked up somewhere. It makes me look like a pretzel.

Outside that window in Washington, D.C., two floors down, I knew K Street would be alive with lunch-hour traffic. Attorneys and secretaries, bankers and lobbyists, folks who still had jobs would be heading out to drop a small fortune at Charlie's Crab or a few bucks over at the Lunch Box. It was a day to take your lunch to Farragut Square and sit in the sun. Let it soak through your skin and warm your bones, bones like mine, which had been sucked cold by the air-conditioning.

Inside, while Coop oozed on about severance pay and maintenance of health benefits, I stared at Fran, who sat straight-backed and immobile, like an ice sculpture. I willed her to look at me, but she focused on his reflection in the tabletop. If Jones of New York had issued shotguns along with its suits, I thought, Old Cooper's shirtfront would have been a sodden mass of red and we would have been picking bits of lung and rib out of the oriental carpet. I concentrated on the way his yellowish hair sprouted from his upper forehead in spiky clumps and how his earlobes wobbled when he talked. Frankly, when he laid the news on me, I didn't know whether to run out and hire a lawyer to sue his ass or fall down and kiss his feet.

The first week, though, I was mad as hell. Poor Paul learned to lay low at home. He'd nursed me through all five stages of grief when I lost my breast, and he told me, in a good-natured way, that he wasn't sure he could face starting all over again at stage one. In the evenings he would retreat to his basement workshop, where he'd bang away with a hammer or cut wood into curious shapes, coaxing hideous screams out of the table saw and claiming between trips upstairs to the refrigerator for a cold beer that the job didn't matter. Even after the unemployment checks stopped coming and my severance pay was exhausted, even then, he insisted, if I hadn't found another job, we'd manage. I knew we weren't anywhere near qualifying for food stamps. Paul was a full professor, after all, with tenure. He taught math at the Naval Academy.

One evening several weeks later, as I was sulking in front of the TV—watching some gawd-awful made-for-TV movie and plotting some fantastic but improbable revenge involving Coop, Fran, handcuffs, cockroaches, hidden cameras, and the FBI—Paul's sister, Connie, called. "The next time you need a wig, Hannah," she complained, "call the Cancer Society first and get a recommendation. You have no idea how many shops I had to call before I found one that didn't specialize in wigs and accessories for the transgender community!"

Mentally I smiled and added leather collars with studs to my revenge.

Connie wasn't really as put out as she sounded. "Thanks awfully, Connie," I told her. I could hear ice clinking in a glass as she drank. Her usual, I suspected, a diet Coke with lime. If she'd had what she called a Good Art Day, there'd be rum in it. "I really appreciate your help. I just wasn't up to it, and I'm damn tired of wearing this stupid turban."

"I thought you looked kind of cute in that psychedelic hat I gave you. Whatever happened to it?" The ice clinked again, and I could hear the TV in the background. She was watching the same movie as I was. While I was struggling to remember what I had done with that hideous hat, she went on. "It's at Tysons Corner, this shop I found. A place called Brighter Day. We'll go there tomorrow, then have a blowout lunch at the food court. That should cheer you up!"

How shopping for wigs could cheer a body up, I couldn't imagine, especially when underneath one would still look like a nuclear accident victim. But when we got there just as the shop opened, Brighter Day turned out to be a friendly place, with racks and racks of special bras and swimwear, attractive head wraps on wall pegs, drawers of breast prostheses, and a large selection of bangs and wigs. You could practically build a woman out of all the body parts on display. It also had a private room to try it all on in. The saleswoman escorted us there, then left us on our own with a double quartet of heads. I sat on a bench covered with flowered chintz and tried on a cute blond number that, except for my brown eyes, made me look alarmingly like Eva Gabor.

"It's discrimination," I complained, half to Connie and half to Eva in the mirror. "Ageism, plain and simple. Or maybe the cancer."

"They didn't deserve you, Hannah." She draped a shoulder-length pageboy bob over the tips of her fingers, smoothed out the bangs, then rotated her wrist until the too-black hair swung crisply back and forth.

"Twenty years of my life I gave them, Connie! Twenty effing years! I clawed my way up from lowly paralegal to head of Archives and Records. And this is the thanks I get? I even chaired the United Way Campaign, for Christ's sake!" I snatched a halo of Orphan Annie curls off my head and arranged them crookedly on a styrofoam head that stared back at me, eyelessly.

"You've got a great résumé. You'll land another job eventually." Connie handed me the wig she was holding.

"I don't have a résumé. I haven't written a résumé in years! I don't even *want* to write a résumé!" I studied myself in the mirror and decided I looked like I was auditioning for a part as an extra in *Miss Saigon.* I had to laugh.

Eventually I chose an ash brown, Princess Di-ish sort of do that looked very much like my own hair, back when I had some. Combed and styled by the saleswoman, I felt more normal than I had in weeks. With my turban stashed in a wig box, we left the store and headed for California Pizza Kitchen.

I had my mouth all set for the artichoke pizza, but Connie surprised me by walking right past the familiar doorway, forcing me to hurry after her, leaving my favorite pizza lying forsaken and unassembled in the kitchen. Connie was being beckoned by an elephant, serenaded by a tree, inexorably drawn by steam rising from a tangle of jungle vegetation outside the Rainforest Café.

"Well, this is certainly different," I remarked as Tracy the Talking Banyan Tree delivered a sober report on the harmful effects of deforestation. I wondered what Lord & Taylor thought of its new neighbor.

I pointed to a snake, its tongue flicking in and out. "It's like a bad drug trip! Are you sure you want to eat here with all this, ah, wildlife?"

"C'mon, it'll be fun," she said. "I expect Tarzan will come swinging through on a vine any minute!"

I ordered a Rainforest Rickey while Connie went for Sheba's Jungle Juice, an unlikely mixture of yogurt, coffee, and Oreos.

Later, over a grilled portobello mushroom sandwich served on an oversize platter—everything must be bigger in the jungle—I was trying Connie's patience again by talking, half-seriously, about a lawsuit. Behind her, a huge reef tank was set into a pillar, the glass distorting its contents so that the fish swam around like fun house fish. "Oh, what's the use?" I moaned. "They've got all the money and time in the world. I'd probably croak long before the case ever came to court."

"You're *not* going to croak! Besides, you have an obligation to spoil your grandchildren, whenever Emily and what's-his-name get around to producing any, that is."

I took a sip of my fruit juice. "Oh, Connie. Whatever am I going to do? No one wants to hire an old woman like me. Not with my medical history."

Connie put down her cappuccino and touched my arm. "Your medical history is none of their goddamned business." She leaned close, her breath sweet with cinnamon. "Give it a rest, Hannah. Take some time off to consider your options."

"Gawd, Connie, you sound just like Fran." I smiled to let her know that I was just kidding.

She ran her finger around the inside of her cup and licked off the foam. "Why don't you come stay with me for a while? Hang out at the farm?"

The waiter had put a Chocolate Diablo on the table in front of me, and I had just taken a bite. "On the farm?" I mumbled through a mouthful of devil's food. "What would I do there?"

"You could help me with my paperwork, Hannah. I'm useless at it. One day the IRS is going to catch up with me."

"I never thought I'd be seriously considering working for my sister-in-law."

"Well, the pay isn't great, but the food is wholesome. I don't do desserts like this, though." For the next few minutes, we ate in silence, except for the twittering mynahs and the snarling leopards.

Eventually I stood, lifted my sweater off the back of the chair, and picked up the wig box. "Thanks awfully for lunch, Connie, but I'd like to go home now. I need to think, and I can't do it in here with all those damn birds and monkeys chattering away."

While Connie took care of the check, I watched the room darken as it had every few minutes since our arrival with the flashes and rumbles of a mock thunderstorm. A toddler waiting in line with his father cowered, clinging, to his father's leg. I thought about Connie living all by herself, with no one to cuddle up to when the weather got bad. Connie had been married to a Prince Georges County police officer. Ten years ago they had moved back to the family farm near Pearson's Corner, an old fishing community on the Truxton River in southern Maryland, to be with her ailing father. Then the old man had died, and Craig had been murdered by a fugitive bank robber following a routine traffic stop on Route 301. Connie had been a widow for almost a year, turning her grief inward and focusing on her art, all the while playing good Samaritan to me.

We walked out of the restaurant past a young man with a pair of macaws perched on his arms. The colorful birds were obligingly doing tricks for three small children who stood off to one side in a little huddle, apparently afraid to approach the birds any closer.

"I feel like crap most of the time," I complained as we reached Connie's car. "I'm afraid I wouldn't be very good company. And what about Paul?"

"Paul's a big boy, Hannah. He can fend for himself for a few weeks."

"And my doctors? What about them?"

"Pearson's Corner isn't exactly the dark side of the moon, Hannah. You'll be only a two-hour drive from Johns Hopkins."

Connie had an answer for everything.

I had to admit that the offer was attractive. A quiet place to go where no one would bother me and I could wait, peacefully, for my hair to grow out.

Several hours and a long, hot bubble bath later, I'd convinced myself to do it. Paul could hardly object. Connie was his sister after all.

chapter

2

PAUL DIDN'T SEEM TO MIND AT ALL. "SOUNDS LIKE A good idea," he said with enthusiasm. Too much enthusiasm, if you ask me.

"You could at least pretend some reluctance to see me go." I was standing in front of the stove, stirring oatmeal. He wrapped his arms around my waist from behind and rested his chin on the top of my head.

"I'll manage fine for a while." He kissed my neck, then gave my bottom a friendly pat.

I turned and pointed the wooden spoon, gooey with oatmeal, at him. "You're not exactly the world's greatest cook, you know."

"Trust me, I'll manage. I can eat in the hall with the mids if I get tired of hot dogs and hamburgers." He opened the cupboard over the microwave and pulled out a box of Kraft macaroni and cheese. "This is always good."

I laughed and ruffled his graying hair with my free hand. "Paul, you're a prince."

"Not really. Connie called and twisted my arm. Hard. She threatened to tell you all about Theresa Jane Delaney if I didn't agree to let you come."

"Who's Theresa Jane Delaney?"

"The love of my life . . ." He paused just a fraction too long, long enough for me to pull a dish towel off the rack and snap it at him. He feinted to the left. "When I was sixteen! Long before I met you, sweet cakes."

I kissed him firmly on the mouth. "I just love it when you talk dirty."

On the long drive down Route 2 from Annapolis to Pearson's Corner, I tuned the radio to WETA-FM and, between classical selections, listened with smug satisfaction to the traffic reports. An overturned tractor-trailer on westbound New York Avenue near Kenilworth at the District line had Route 50 backed up all the way to the beltway. Not my problem anymore!

As I drove, sipping McDonald's coffee through a red stirrer straw I had jammed through the plastic lid, I recalled the time Paul first brought me to his family's farm, in 1973, the year we were married. I was thinking that not much had changed in Chesapeake County since then, although yuppies from nearby Baltimore and Washington, D.C., were beginning to discover the area, seeking decent schools and a quiet, relatively crime-free place to raise their children. The friendly communities, verdant fields, lush forests, and unspoiled water views that had drawn them to this quiet part of the county in the first place were still to be found in abundance. For the time being at least.

At Milford, just past the Maryland State Environmental Research Station, I slowed at the flashing yellow light and waited for a delivery truck to pull out of the 7-Eleven and onto the highway. At the next intersection I turned left on Pearson's Road and left again almost immediately at the high school, where the road forked. I slowed to ease my car around the curve that skirted a pond, then accelerated past the old Nichols place. Within minutes, I spotted Connie's mailbox, which had at one time been beautifully painted with irises á la Vincent Van Gogh and her name, C. Ives, in black gothic letters. Unfortunately the mailbox had been battered, almost beyond recognition, in a drive-by whacking. Rust was developing where the paint had been chipped away by the vandal's bat. So much for low crime, I thought.

After the first long day getting settled in at Connie's, it felt strange to crawl into bed alone. I missed Paul and remembered how odd it felt when we first slept together in the bedroom he had used as a child, right there on the plaid bed sheets surrounded by the memorabilia of his youth: his *Hardy Boys* books and old school texts, seashells from a class trip to Ocean City, a second-prize bowling trophy so ornate and improbably tall that it barely fitted on the shelf and made me wonder what on earth the first-prize trophy had looked like. Like now, it had been spring, and we left the window open. I remember lying in his arms, listening to mournful owls, frogs clearing their throats, and the constant creaking of the crickets, sounds that kept his city bride from Cleveland wide awake.

Now most of those youthful trappings were gone, replaced by Laura Ashley curtains and matching bedclothes, the bookshelves full of art books, knick-knacks, and family photographs. This time the night sounds that drifted into the window on a soft, sweet-smelling breeze soothed me like a lullaby, and I fell asleep almost instantly.

I awoke refreshed with the sun on my face. I lay quietly for a while, listening to the birds argue in the tree outside my window and studying the shadowy, shifting patterns cast by the leaves on the wallpaper. The steady hum of a tractor drifted in from the Baxter farm just to the east. I plumped my pillow and sandwiched it between my back and the tall, carved headboard while considering the picture on the wall nearest my feet, an aquatint of Paul and Connie's great-grandparents, looking severe. The first time we'd made quiet love in this room, Paul had turned their picture to the wall.

A few moments later I heard a toilet flush and the sound of running water. I lay lazily in bed until the sounds died away, then padded downstairs in my nightgown. The pine floors felt smooth and warm beneath my bare feet and creaked comfortingly in all the familiar places—the third step down from the land-ing, just inside the dining room as you pass the buffet, the first board as you step over the threshold into the kitchen. Connie had the radio tuned to WGMS, where Pachelbel's *Canon* was playing softly, but she wasn't anywhere in sight.

"Connie!" I called.

"Out here!" she replied.

The water in the coffee machine on the counter had just finished burbling through the filter, so I poured myself a cup and one for Connie. In the refrigerator I found some half-and-half. Connie drinks her coffee black with sugar, so I checked the sell-by date before pouring any of it into my mug, just in case this carton was left over from the last time I visited, over three months ago.

Carrying both mugs, I passed through the utility room into Connie's studio, which had been cleverly converted from a derelict screen porch.

Connie was working, sorting through a pile of dried ornamental gourds of all colors, shapes and sizes. On the workbench in front of her, pots of paints and brushes waited, lined up in orderly rows. The room smelled of oil paint and shellac.

Connie squinted critically at the gourd she had been painting. She had turned a plump butternut squash into a whimsical farm boy in blue overalls, his face dotted with freckles.

I chuckled. "How you do it is beyond me, Connie. You see beyond the vegetable exterior right into its very soul."

I picked up a crooked neck squash and turned it in

several directions. "They all look like ducks to me. Or swans."

Connie laid the farm boy down on a sheet of newspaper and began work on another figure. It was clearly a French schoolgirl, her beret formed by the curling stem end of the gourd. Connie dabbed a spot of pink onto each of the figure's cheeks.

I passed her the coffee.

"Thanks, Hannah."

She took a sip, then held up a graceful sandpiper, its neck bent as if caught in the act of picking clams out of the sand. "What do you think of this one?"

"I think they're all wonderful. Where are they going?"

She waved her arm in a wide arc, including in its scope most of the shelves on the wall behind her. "I'm sending this lot up to New York at the end of the week." The shelves were full of gourd soldiers and gourd musicians. Whole gourd families—boys, girls, mamas, papas—smiled out at me with twinkling eyes. There were scores of ducks, geese, swans, roosters, and other fanciful figures.

"You've come just in time to help me pack up." Connie pointed to another corner of the room where flattened cartons, rolls of bubble wrap, and bags of plastic peanuts were stored. "I haven't had much help out here since Craig died. Except for Colonel, of course."

Hearing his name, the old dog raised his head from where it rested on his paws. Until then he had been sleeping comfortably on a braided mat in front of the screen door that opened out into the backyard.

I put my coffee down on Connie's workbench, knelt down, and called to him, patting my knee. "Come here, boy. Come on, Colonel."

Colonel slowly unfolded, stretched, and staggered stiffly over to lick my face. I grabbed both his ears and scratched behind them, the way he liked.

Colonel was a short-haired, white and brown mixed breed, half German shepherd and half fox terrier. Fortunately for Connie, who wanted a watchdog, the part that barked was German shepherd.

"You're looking pretty good for an elderly dog." I scratched vigorously down the bumps along his spine. "Joined AARP yet?"

Connie laughed. "He's got arthritis so bad he can sometimes barely move. But let him catch sight of a squirrel, and he's a pup again."

Colonel rolled onto his back and offered me his stomach. As I rubbed, his back legs quivered in ecstasy. I thought about all the times I had considered adopting a dog. But we live in downtown Annapolis, where you've got to fence the yard and walk your dog on a leash. Not much fun for a dog or its owner.

Colonel had been a companion to my father-in-law during his final illness. He'd been named after a Korean war buddy of Paul's father, and though at first the dog had been called Colonel Sam, it wasn't long before it was shortened to Colonel.

"Want to take Colonel out for a walk while I fix breakfast?" Connie rinsed out the brush she had been using and set the schoolgirl figure on a shelf to dry.

"Sure. Soon as I get dressed."

Back in my room, I changed into jeans, pulled a sweatshirt over my head, and slipped into my jogging shoes. As I tightened and tied the laces, I was reminded that I hadn't been doing a lot of jogging lately, just exercises like spider-walking my arm up a wall. This was supposed to keep the damaged muscles on my chest and under my arms from tightening up. I didn't bother with any makeup and didn't feel like putting on my wig. Instead, I rummaged in one of the plastic grocery bags that passed for matched luggage when I'm in a hurry to pack. This one was full of hats friends had given me: a hat dripping with sequins, one with cat ears, a navy cap from the USS *Ramage* DDG61. Sequins weren't exactly appropriate for dog walking, I thought, and certainly not the cat ears! After a few moments I selected a Baltimore Orioles cap with my name, Hannah, stitched on it in elaborate sewing machine script and settled it snugly over the soft brown stubble just beginning to reappear on my head.

As I paused through the kitchen again, Connie was frying bacon. I left my mug in the sink—Connie didn't have a dishwasher—and returned to the studio.

"Come on, boy." I unhooked the screen door, and Colonel loped happily through.

Connie's backyard was a square of grass the size of a tennis court, closely mowed. It grew rich and green where the shadow of the maple trees protected it from the hot sun, more yellow where the grass was exposed. To my right a gravel driveway led up to the barn that

Connie used as a garage. Beyond the barn a fence marched off into the distance, dipping now and then as it followed the gently rolling fields that sloped down to a large pond just visible on the horizon. Colonel trotted ahead, his tail in a tight C curled smartly over his back.

Near the barn I opened the gate and passed through, remembering to close it behind me. It was a habit I'd got into when there used to be cows around. A stick leaned crookedly against the gatepost, and I picked it up, mostly so I'd have something to do with my hands.

Behind the barn we passed Connie's kitchen garden, where neat rows of young plants were just beginning to push their way up through the soil. In the field beyond, nearly an acre of hills and poles was devoted to the business of cultivating her ornamental gourds. Colonel and I skirted the planted fields and walked through the tall grass, following the fence line. The farm to the west of the fence belonged to the Nichols family, but they had moved to Florida long ago, abandoning their farm.

When we reached the pond, Colonel planted his front paws at the water's edge, took a long drink, then chased a frog into the water. He sat alert, ears erect, studying with hopeful eyes the ripples where the frog had submerged. When he panted, his clean, pinkish purple tongue hung out, dripping saliva onto the ground.

He probably would have sat there forever, but I

raised my arm to distract him and threw the stick as far as I could into the nearby woods, the scar on my chest stretching and stinging with the effort.

Colonel bolted off through the trees. He returned in triumph a few moments later, carrying the stick in his mouth. He trotted over and laid it at my muddy feet. I retrieved the stick and continued walking as Colonel danced and circled around me, urging me to toss the stick again, but I was already tired of the game.

Once the fence had been a continuous line of posts and barbed wire. Occasionally, to save posts, Paul's father had nailed the wire to the trees that grew naturally along the property line. After many years the trees had grown around the wire, engulfing it. It now appeared as if some magician had pulled the wire right through the trees. In other places where it was not adequately supported, the wire had rusted through and separated, leaving gaps.

For some reason I was profoundly happy. I found myself singing "Zip-a-Dee-Doo-Dah," whacking the stick against my leg to the rhythm of the song as I walked. Colonel grew bored and ambled on ahead, sniffing at fence posts and tree roots, lifting a leg every so often to mark his territory.

Suddenly he began to root around, poking his nose into a pile of leaves that had blown up against the fence last fall. I heard a frantic rustling; then a rabbit bolted out of the leaves and dashed easily through the fence into our neighbor's field. Colonel raced off in joyful pursuit.

"Colonel! Colonel! You get back here!" The beastly dog ignored me.

I wasted some time searching back along the way we had come for a break in the fence, then gave up. Risking a tear in my "Smith College—100 years of Women on Top" sweatshirt, I held down the lower strand of barbed wire with one hand and carefully squirmed through. I ran after the dog, yelling, "Colonel, come!" and waving my stick impotently.

Colonel had disappeared behind the house.

I had never seen the old Nichols place up close. The once-white siding on the ancient two-story dwelling was pitted and stained gray-green from the woodsmoke that used to pump out of the chimney night and day. Dark green shutters, missing most of their slats, hung crookedly from an insufficient number of nails. Nearly all the windows were broken—juvenile delinquents in training were responsible for that, I was sure—and most had been boarded up. Shingles torn from the roof by the wind littered the ground.

Colonel had apparently cornered his rabbit. As I rounded the side of the house, I saw him guarding an old cistern that had been used to collect rainwater back in the days when wells weren't so easy to dig. The cistern was a concrete cylinder about five feet in diameter, set deeply into the ground and topped by a cover of wooden boards joined together with wide metal straps. Two large, flat stones rested on top.

Colonel continued to bark, but I couldn't see the rabbit. Perhaps it was hiding in the bushes that had grown

up, lush and green, around the foundation of the house
back by the cistern where water was plentiful.

When I was still about twenty feet away, Colonel
trotted over to me, circled twice, then returned to his
duty station by the cistern. He barked, then looked at
me expectantly. He barked again.

"Are you trying to tell me something, dog? Who do
you think you are? Lassie?"

As I got closer, I could see that the cistern's cover
was cracked.

"Did your rabbit go down the well, Colonel?" I
peered through a gap in the cover but could see only
a sliver of light on the water below that reflected the
blue sky above me and a dark shape that must have
been the shadow of my head.

"Well, boy, if your rabbit's down there, he better be
a damn good swimmer."

With both hands, I pushed one of the rocks to the
ground, then the other. It took more effort to wrestle
the cover itself aside. This done, Colonel, ever helpful, placed both paws on the lip of the cistern,
hunched his shoulders, and peered in.

The cistern was fed from a pipe leading into it from
the roof of the house. It was impossible to tell how
deep it was because of all the water it contained. After the recent rain the water level was fairly high, only
four or five feet from the place on the rim where my
hand rested. A rusty automobile axle jutted out of the
water at an angle, wrapped in a tangle of baling wire.
Like the house, this cistern clearly hadn't been used
in years.

"No rabbit, Colonel, old boy. Just a lot of junk." I grasped his collar and pulled until his front paws touched the ground. Before I could turn to push the wooden cover back into place, however, Colonel was leaning into the cistern again, howling pitifully. "For heaven's sake, Colonel! I told you there's nothing down there!" Using both hands, I tugged on his collar again, but Colonel refused to budge.

While my hands were occupied with the stubborn dog, a sudden gust of wind lifted my Orioles cap and snatched it from my head. I watched helplessly as it sailed into the cistern, revolving slowly like an autumn leaf. It floated on the surface for a few seconds, then began to sink beneath the stagnant water.

"Now look what you've done, you stupid dog!" I picked up my stick and used it to poke around in the floating debris, trying to fish up my precious cap before it sank and was lost forever. I had no intention of walking back to the house bald. I leaned into the cistern as far as I could with safety and used my stick to push aside some deteriorating blue fabric, an old milk carton, and what looked like a white plastic garbage bag.

But it wasn't a bag. Something solid was floating there that responded to my gently prodding by turning over lazily. Not a plastic bag at all, but a pair of human buttocks, with what looked like part of a leg attached.

"Oh, God, Colonel! Let's pray I'm seeing things. Let's hope it's a dead deer or a small calf down there." I felt ill. But I couldn't convince myself, let alone the dog, that I was seeing anything but the sad remains of a human being.

I ran the mile or so back to Connie's at record speed, although everything conspired to delay me: the barbed wire fence plucking at my clothes, the muddy field sucking greedily at my shoes. After what seemed like hours, I burst into the studio, the screen door slapping shut behind me. I found Connie in the kitchen, slicing a grapefruit.

"What happened to your hat?" she asked.

"Connie, I think there's a body in the cistern over at the old Nichols place!" I paused to catch my breath, bracing my arm on the kitchen counter. "Who do I call out here? You were married to a cop! Who would you call?"

Dear, unflappable Connie looked up at me, then laid the knife down with elaborate care on the cutting board. "Nine-one-one," she said. "Just like everyone else."

YOU'VE GOT TO HAND IT TO THOSE FOLKS AT 911.
While I stood at the kitchen counter panting, my
heart pounding in my ears and feeling as if a live,
leaping thing in my chest had swollen to twice normal
size, crowding out my lungs, Connie made the call. Almost as soon as she hung up, we heard the firehouse
sirens in town kick in, wailing long and loud, the old-
fashioned way, to call in the volunteers.

Connie led me back to her studio. There the windows offered a panoramic view over the fields as far as
the next ridge where the road into town and a scattering of houses lay.

"Watch that road. Once the trucks round the corner at the light and head out Church Street, we'll be
able to see them."

"Why are they sending the fire department?"

"I'm not sure." Connie draped my shoulders with a mohair afghan she had lifted from the back of a barrel chair that sat in front of the wood stove that made it possible for her to work in her studio in the wintertime. "I told them you found a body. Maybe they think it's possible to revive it."

A chill began just behind my ears, slithered down my neck and spine, and radiated out into my limbs until I was shaking uncontrollably.

"It was just pieces, Connie. They can't revive pieces!"

Connie, who was standing behind me at the window, reached out to rub my arms up and down briskly. "Better?" She pressed my coffee mug, which had been mysteriously refilled, into my hands. I had time for only a few perfunctory sips before the fire truck went screaming by.

I don't know why I thought the police couldn't begin their investigation without me. "Should we go over now?" I turned to look at Connie over the rim of the mug, the image of her face slightly distorted by the steam rising from the hot liquid.

"Not yet, silly. They know where to find us when they need us."

A few minutes later an ambulance streaked by, sirens wailing, a blur of yellow and white against the green fields. A tan and black county patrol car followed at a more sedate pace, with a single officer inside. We could see him talking on the radio.

Connie took the half-empty cup from my hands and set it on the workbench. She pointed to my torn sweatshirt and muddy shoes. "You might want to wash up and decide whether you want to greet the police like that. . . ." She pointed to my scruffy head. "Or are you thinking about putting on some hair today?"

I hugged her, and we stayed that way for one long, comforting minute while Connie rubbed my back. I pulled away first, managing a halfhearted smile. "Let's go for the hair." I was still shaking and drew the afghan around me a little closer. "Just give me a few minutes to get myself together."

"Sure, honey. If anyone shows up, I'll keep them busy with my gourmet coffee and dazzling repartee, but you'd better hurry." She turned and pointed out over the fields. Two cars passed, taking their time, followed within a minute by someone in a blue Volvo station wagon. "See those cars? The vultures are gathering already. Picked up the police call on their scanners, I'll bet."

I watched as a red Miata caught up with the Volvo, a caboose on the slow-moving train. I had little patience for ambulance chasers. "You'd think they'd have something better to do with their time." I ran a hand over my head where thin, pale wisps of hair lay, plastered with cold sweat to my skull. I felt like hell and probably looked like it.

"Can't say that I blame them. It's probably the most exciting thing that's happened in Pearson's Corner since old Mr. Meadows blew his wife away with a shotgun blast in 1952. Folks say she deserved it, too!" Connie turned me by the shoulders and shoved me gently in the direction of the bathroom. "Off you go!!"

I smiled, for real this time. "Yes, Mother."

*   *   *

It took ten minutes to run a warm washcloth over my head, face, and neck and to dress in clean tan slacks and a burgundy turtleneck. With my wig in place, I looked almost presentable. I was haphazardly brushing a bit of blusher on my cheeks when Connie appeared in the bedroom door. She studied me critically. "Much better." Connie had changed out of her jeans and into a pair of crisp white shorts and a red striped T-shirt that, I had to admit, seemed more appropriate for a tennis game than a crime scene, but I was hardly an expert in these matters. With her copper curls brushed, she looked much younger than her forty years.

"Anyone show up yet?" I asked.

"Not yet. But judging from the cars that have passed by, I'd say over half the town is over to the Nichols place by now."

"Well, I'm ready to join them."

A look of concern crossed Connie's face. "Are you sure you haven't had enough excitement for one day, Hannah?"

I looked at the wall clock which Connie had decorated with gilded seedpods. "I can't believe it's only eleven o'clock. I feel like I've lived a hundred years since this morning."

"Maybe you'd prefer to wait here? I'm not sure I'm prepared to see any of that . . . well, whatever it is."

"Come on, Connie. Let's walk over. I'm sure the police won't be letting anyone anywhere near that cistern. They've probably even called in reinforcements to help hold back the mob."

I returned the blusher to my makeup bag and zipped it shut. When I tossed the bag carelessly on top of the dresser, it skidded sideways and toppled a picture of Paul taken at Camp Letts the summer he turned twelve.

"Gosh, Connie! How could we have forgotten to tell Paul? Just give me a minute, okay?"

I dialed Paul's number at work but got his voice mail. "There's been some excitement down on the farm," I told the recording. "Give us a call."

Rather than take the long way across the fields, Connie and I walked together down the driveway, the gravel crunching pleasantly beneath our sandals. At the end of the drive we turned right onto paved road. It was early May, and the sun had warmed the pavement so we could feel the heat through the soles of our shoes. Grass and wildflowers grew in high hedges along both shoulders. The plants absorbed the sun, seeming to convert it into sweet, spicy perfume that washed over us in warm waves.

Several cars passed, followed by a small white Isuzu pickup that honked and slowed. The driver, a ruggedly attractive, ruddy-faced fellow I guessed to be in his middle fifties, rolled down his window.

"Hi, Con. I heard the news down at the marina office. Someone said you found a body at the old Nichols place."

"Not me, Hal. My sister-in-law, Hannah, here."

Hal nodded in my direction. "Wonder who it is?" he inquired.

"Hard to tell." She lowered her voice and rested her arms against the window of the truck. "Hannah said it looked like it had been there for quite a while."

Hal shifted into park. In the silence between them, I could hear WTOP, all-news radio, blaring over the noise of the air conditioner running full blast.

"You gals want a ride?" Before Connie could answer, Hal twisted sideways and struggled to move a huge sail bag which fully occupied the passenger seat. "Genoa #3" was stenciled on the canvas in black letters. It refused to budge.

"Thanks, Hal, it's a nice thought, but where would we sit?" She gestured toward the back of his truck, where several plastic buckets and four striped lawn chairs lay, folded up. "Should we set up those chairs and ride in the back like queens in the Fourth of July parade?"

Hal chuckled and saluted with his left hand. "Suit yourself! Guess I'll catch up with you in a few minutes." His face gradually disappeared behind the tinted glass as the window rolled up, and he sped away, taking the curve at the bottom of the hill at least fifteen miles over the forty mile per hour speed limit in a squeal of steel-belted radials.

"Who was that?" I asked Connie as the smoke from his exhaust dissipated in front of us.

"Hal Calvert. He owns the marina where I keep *Sea Song*." She pulled a pair of sunglasses out of her pocket and put them on. "His family's lived in Chesapeake County for centuries. Old Mr. Calvert's still alive. Walks down to the boatyard from the family compound every day. Keeps his hand in, too, refinishing teak. He varnished *Sea Song*'s toe rails this spring. Eighty-eight years old and he still has a steady hand with the brush."

Another car approached and tooted its horn. Connie waved as it passed.

"You take the boat out much?"

"Oh, about once a month when I can find someone to sail with me." She turned to look at me. "That's something I was hoping we could do while you're here."

I groaned. I had taken a course at the Annapolis Sailing School several years ago just to please Paul, but I wasn't especially good at it. I knew port from starboard by remembering that *port* and *left* had the same number of letters. I had memorized a whole book full of nautical terms; living in a sailing capital like Annapolis, I didn't want to embarrass myself by calling the mast a pole or by referring to the bow of the boat as the pointy end. As for the mechanics of sailing, though, if anyone fell overboard with me at the helm, he'd better resign himself to drowning.

"I'm afraid I've forgotten everything I ever learned in sailing school, Connie."

"Nonsense! It's like riding a bicycle. It'll come back to you."

"Let's hope."

"I thought about selling *Sea Song*, you know, after Craig died. But he loved her so much! He must have said it a million times: 'That Tartan's a good, sturdy bay boat, Connie. Should last us for years.' That's why I don't think he'd have minded my paying off the loan with part of his life insurance settlement. Sometimes I wonder, though. You know what they say about sailboats: It's a hole in the water where you throw your money!"

By then we had reached the Nichols farm, where trucks and cars were parked higgledy-piggledy along both sides of the road, their tires half on the asphalt and half on the grassy shoulder. A crowd of approximately twenty people had gathered, and I noticed Connie's friend Hal, still in his truck, deep in conversation with three firemen clustered in a disorderly huddle outside his window. Yellow crime scene tape stretched from the battered Nichols mailbox to the telephone pole at the foot of the drive. A uniformed officer stood nearby. He was young and trim; the sleeves of his uniform strained against the muscles that bulged in his upper arms. He looked perfectly capable of discouraging anyone from wandering too close to something he shouldn't. Farther up the drive, next to the house, sat a fire truck, an ambulance, two Chesapeake County patrol cars, and a dark silver Ford Taurus.

"What do they need the fire truck for?" I asked the officer, whose name tag said "Braddock."

"Routine."

I stepped closer. "And the ambulance? I found the body, Officer Braddock. I don't think an ambulance is going to help much."

"Also routine." He smiled a straight, white, gap-toothed grin, causing the deepest dimples I'd ever seen to appear suddenly in his cheeks. He looked about twelve years old. "I'll need to get your names," he added.

Braddock wrote our names at the bottom of a long list.

"What's happening up there?" I asked.

"Nothing much. We're waiting for the medical examiner and the ECU."

"What's the ECU?"

"Evidence Collection Unit."

While we were busy distracting the talkative Officer Braddock, a young boy seized the opportunity to slip under the tape. "Hey!" Braddock was on him in two steps, catching the youngster by the waistband of his jeans. "Out you go, young man!" The kid smiled and shrugged as if to say, *Well, it was worth a try!*

Connie and I stepped back then to join the others milling about on the road, creating a significant traffic hazard. A heavyset woman in a flowered dress had just emerged from a car parked a short distance away. When she caught sight of Connie, she waved and struggled up the hill.

"Ellie Larson," Connie informed me. "She owns the Country Store with her daughter, Angie. Angie must be minding it today."

Ellie arrived, wheezing and out of breath. She dabbed at her forehead with a crumpled tissue, leaving specks of white behind. "Just driving by and saw all the cars. Someone having an auction or a garage sale?"

"Hannah was walking the dog this morning and thinks she saw a body in the old cistern out back."

Connie turned to me, and I got to tell my story all over again, concluding, because I knew Ellie would ask, with "No, I don't know who it is!"

Ellie looked thoughtful. "Not many people have disappeared around here in the past few years. Some teenage runaways is all, but they always turn up. Except . . . well, except for the Dunbar girl."

"What about her?" Connie asked.

"She disappeared about eight years ago. It was after the homecoming dance at the high school. Hasn't been seen since. A pretty, curly-headed girl. Looked like a cherub. Do you think it could be Katie Dunbar?" Ellie looked at me expectantly.

I felt the chill returning. "If she's been dead for eight years, it'd be a little hard to tell, don't you think?"

Connie took off one sandal and tapped it on the side of her leg to dislodge a stone. "I remember her now. Pretty, yes, but not terribly bright. I used to see her down at the Royal Farms convenience store. She worked as a cashier evenings and weekends." She lowered her voice. "Gosh! There's Katie's parents now." She jerked her head to the right.

I turned in time to see an older man in denim overalls climb out of a battered red Ford 4 × 4. A toolbox was bolted across the back of the cab; plastic buckets and miscellaneous pieces of lumber with red rags tied to their ends protruded over the tailgate. A woman I took to be Mrs. Dunbar sat in the passenger seat, but she seemed reluctant to get out. As if to persuade her, Mr. Dunbar held out his hand. Mrs. Dunbar slid across the seat to the open door on the driver's side, took his hand, and alighted from the cab clumsily. I could see she had been crying, and she kept wiping her eyes with a huge white handkerchief. Wet splotches dotted the front of her quilted jogging suit, and she seemed to be having trouble walking in the thick-soled shoes she wore. Mrs. Dunbar's hair was so pale it was hard to tell if it was white or blond. It was clamped high at the crown with a fluorescent plastic butterfly clip, and strands had escaped and fallen in a disorderly way around a face that was as pink as her outfit and almost as puffy. The Dunbars stood together next to their truck, looking lost. I had seen that look before. It was the haunted look of a shell-shocked veteran, the same look that had stared out at me from my own mirror in those tortured days after Emily had run away from home for the first time and I thought we'd lost her forever.

"It's Katie. I know it's Katie. Who else could it be?" Mrs. Dunbar clung to her husband and continued to sob hysterically, tears falling too fast to wipe away. After a bit she returned to the pickup and, leaving the door open where any passing car would knock it off, sat in it, her ungainly feet dangling out the side.

Mr. Dunbar patted her knee. With one motion he took off his hat, scratched his head, and stuffed the hat into his back pocket before approaching Officer Braddock.

"My daughter's been missing eight years, Officer.

She disappeared eight years ago last October. Is that her? Is that her you found?"

"We don't know yet, sir. We don't even known if it's human remains." He was distracted for a moment by a late-model dark blue Crown Victoria that pulled up to the drive, its turn signal flashing. "Here's the medical examiner now, sir. Maybe we'll have news for you soon."

Braddock untied the crime scene tape and trailed it across the drive so that the doctor could drive through.

"Dr. Franklin Chase," Connie said. "Junior. His father delivered Paul and me umpteen years ago. Took over the practice when his father retired."

"What's an obstetrician doing identifying bodies?"

"He's a GP, Hannah. We elect our medical examiners in this county. Probably the last county in Maryland that hasn't switched over to forensic investigators. No special qualifications needed for medical examiners, either. Hell, *you* could be a medical examiner if you could muster enough votes."

I watched the doctor climb out of his car. He looked to be in his thirties, handsome in a baby-faced sort of way, and prematurely bald. "He looks competent enough."

"He is," Connie told me. "Although I don't think Frank entirely approved of his old man. Frank is all modern equipment and newfangled remedies. Goes off to medical conferences all the time. His father was more old-fashioned; he mixed modern medicine with herbal remedies and homeopathy. Even kept a herb garden behind his house." She waved at Dr. Chase, and he saluted in return. "Of course it's sadly neglected now."

After Dr. Chase's arrival the scene throbbed with renewed activity. The police evidence unit and photographers moved back and forth between the cistern and their vehicles. Dr. Chase disappeared for a long time behind the house, then reappeared carrying something in his hand. He knelt down and bent over an object on the ground, then made a call on his cellular telephone.

Meanwhile, the fire department had rolled out two lengths of hose, coupled them together with some other equipment, and dragged the whole awkward contraption up the driveway and behind the house. At a signal from a fireman stationed at the rear of the house, an engine sputtered to life and gallons of greenish brown water began cascading down the drive.

"They're pumping out the well." The reedy, high-pitched voice came from behind me. It belonged to the same towheaded boy who, moments before, had tried to slip by Officer Braddock.

"They are?"

He met my gaze with a directness unusual for someone his age, which I guessed was about nine. "They're looking for clues. There'll be rings and clothes and things at the bottom. And body parts." He grinned at me, ghoulishly.

I tried not to give the boy the satisfaction of looking shocked. "Why aren't you in school?" I asked instead. "Don't they have school on Wednesdays anymore?"

"I come with my cousin over there." He pointed toward the fire truck, where a young man in a tattered yellow slicker leaned negligently against the bumper. "He's running the pump." The boy rolled a stone around on the blacktop with the toe of his tennis shoe. "I'm 'sposed to be home sick. But I'm better now." With a swift kick, he sent the stone skittering across the pavement and into the ditch. "Bye!"

"Bye." I watched as he dashed across the road and joined his cousin, who was mopping his brow with the back of his hand.

It was nearly two o'clock, and the temperature had climbed into the high eighties. Reporters from the local weekly appeared, trailed closely by the *Washington Post* and the *Baltimore Sun*. They stationed themselves along the fence line, camera bags slung carelessly over their shoulders, screwing on, switching and adjusting various telephoto lenses. I watched while one hapless reporter in shorts stepped with exaggerated care through the high grass of an adjoining field, pausing every few feet or so to massage his exposed legs. The day had turned into a carnival. I expected a concession truck would arrive any minute and start selling coffee, hot dogs, french fries, and Coca-Cola.

An attractive man in a dark gray suit, his sandy hair receding slightly at the temples and combed straight back, strode down the drive, keeping far to the left to avoid the water. *Where had he been hiding?* He spoke briefly to Officer Braddock, lifted the yellow tape, and ducked under it. His eyes took in the crowd; then he surprised me by coming up directly to Connie and giving her a kiss on the cheek.

"Hi, Connie. How's it going?"

"Fine, Dennis. Considering."

Dennis extended his hand. "Hannah, isn't it? You probably don't remember me, but we met at Craig's funeral."

"Of course I remember!" I didn't, of course. The funeral had been a merciful blur. I doubt I would have noticed if Ronald Reagan had happened to stop by to offer his condolences. With Nancy.

Dennis smiled, revealing even white teeth. "I'll be back with you in a minute." He turned to address the crowd. "There's nothing to see here, folks. Why don't you just go on home now and read all about it in the papers tomorrow?"

Connie came to my rescue. "That's Dennis Rutherford," she whispered. "He and Craig went to high school together, then joined the police force at about the same time. Dennis is a lieutenant with the county's criminal investigation division. He must be in charge here."

The crowd retreated slightly, but only to keep their feet dry and to clear the way for the recent arrival of a hearse with "Sterling's Funeral Home" elaborately etched on the side windows. We observed in silence as two officers emerged from behind the house, carrying a white body bag. They deposited it on a waiting stretcher, then helped the driver lift the stretcher and slide it into the hearse. Officer Braddock climbed into the passenger seat and watched carefully in the side view mirror as the hearse backed down the drive, turned, and disappeared up the road. Dr. Chase followed in his own car. It would be a long ride from Pearson's Corner to the State Medical Examiner's Office up in Baltimore.

"What did Dr. Chase say?" Connie asked Dennis when he reappeared at her side.

"He thinks it's a woman, but the body's badly decomposed. It began to fall apart the minute we tried to move it."

I shuddered. "Was she murdered?"

"Murdered? Well, I'm no expert, but people don't usually shoot themselves in the head, then strap cinder blocks to their waists with baling wire before flinging themselves into wells."

Connie closed her eyes and took a slow, deep breath. "Everyone thinks it's Katie Dunbar."

"I don't know, Connie, but if it is, I have a hunch we won't have to look very far for her murderer. We did a thorough investigation when she disappeared back in '90. That Lambert boy is going to have a lot of explaining to do."

Dennis touched Connie's elbow and hurried us both up the drive. He unlocked the Taurus on the passenger side, opened both doors, and motioned us inside. "I'll give you a lift home, but you'll need to hurry. Unless I'm very much mistaken, that's the Channel Thirteen Eyewitness News team just cresting the hill, and I'd rather not deal with them just now."

In one smooth motion, Dennis folded his long legs into the driver's seat, pulled the seat belt across his chest, and started the engine. He turned to look at Connie. "You still make a mean cup of tea?"

chapter

4

WE ELUDED THE PRESS BY THE SIMPLE EXPEDIENT OF taking Dennis's unmarked Taurus and driving it hell-bent for leather in the opposite direction. We whizzed past the folks from Channel 13 as they rounded the curve near the pond, sending ducks and chickens squawking and flapping from the grassy berm and into the muddy water.

Twenty minutes later I was standing in Connie's kitchen, holding the lid on the teakettle with one finger while I poured hot water into Dennis's cup. "What was that you were saying earlier about the Lambert boy?" He ignored my question, and Connie shot me a sudden sideways glance that said, plain as day, "Hannah, do shut up."

I tried to act grateful. Lieutenant Rutherford had, after all, saved me and my butt from a cold, hard plastic chair in the Chesapeake County Eastern District Police Station by deciding to interview us late that same afternoon in Connie's bright kitchen, where the sun, low in the sky, slanted through the decorative shutters Paul had installed for her last winter.

Connie served butter cookies out of a Tupperware container she kept on top of the refrigerator. Dennis held a cookie between this thumb and forefinger, dipped it into his cup, let it soak for a few seconds, shook it slightly to make sure it wouldn't drip, then popped the cookie, whole, in his mouth.

He watched me watching him and seemed amused. "I learned to drink tea in England," he explained. "On a Fulbright scholarship."

I wrapped my hands around a mug of Earl Grey and watched while Dennis stirred milk into his tea. I like that in a man.

The good lieutenant seemed in no hurry to leave.

I repeated my story—I was getting good at it by now—while Dennis listened thoughtfully and jotted down bits of what I said in a pocket-size notebook.

Dennis must have regretted his earlier burst of candor because he volunteered no more information about Lambert. In fact, he seemed more interested in what Connie could tell him about recent activity at the Nichols farm than anything I had said about finding the body.

"The Nicholses moved to Florida years ago, Dennis. Long before I came home." She rested an elbow on the table and stirred her tea absentmindedly while holding the spoon loosely between her thumb and forefinger. "If the body turns out to be that of the Dunbar girl, though, I realize I must have been here when . . . whoever . . . dumped her in the well. It gives me the creeps."

Connie licked her spoon, then waved it in the general direction of the window. "You can see that although we share a fence, I'm not exactly within sight and hearing distance of that house."

Dennis studied her, his greenish brown eyes intent. "Have you seen anything recently? Trucks or cars going by? People who don't live here or have business out here?"

"Uh-uh."

"Someone may have attempted to repair that cracked cistern cover or come back to check on the body, just to make sure it stayed hidden."

"No, nothing like that, Dennis." She poured more hot water into his cup. "I'm not sure I would have noticed anyway. I'm usually engrossed in my work."

Dennis stood, pushing his chair back with his knees. In three long strides he covered the length of the hallway leading into Connie's studio, still carrying his cup. He ducked slightly to keep from hitting his head on the doorframe. When he spoke again, his voice was slightly muffled. "You've always had a good view of the road from here."

"True, but I've usually got my back to it."

I stood in the doorway and watched while Dennis wandered around the studio for a few more minutes, looking but not touching. When he returned to the kitchen, Connie said, "I'd ask you to stay for supper, Dennis, but I don't feel much like cooking tonight."

"I couldn't stay anyway, Connie. I have to get home to Maggie. She'll be wondering where I am." He peeked under his cuff to check the time.

"Whew. It's later than I thought." He extended his hand. "I'll be in touch." For Connie he had a hug. "Take care."

While Connie stood at the sink with her back to me, rattling the crockery, I watched from the window as Dennis backed up his Taurus, eased it skillfully around my Toyota, turned, then headed down the drive. It was with considerable self-restraint that I waited until he reached the road before I pounced. "Okay, Connie. Out with it! What's the story with you and Dennis?"

"We're friends. Just friends."

"Ha!"

She turned to face me. "No, really! Wipe that cynical, suspicious look off your face! Dennis was very supportive when Craig died."

I thought about the way Dennis had moved about Connie's house with easy familiarity. He knew where Connie kept the cups and that she stored sugar in the refrigerator. I was betting he knew where the toothpaste was, too, and which side of the bed she slept on.

"Ha!" I repeated. Connie's mouth turned up slightly at the corners; then she returned her attention to the dirty dishes.

"And who's Maggie?"

"Maggie is Dennis's daughter."

I was surprised. I'd assumed Maggie was his wife.

"She's twenty-two but still lives at home. She hasn't been very well lately, Hannah."

Connie read my mind, which was thinking *cancer.* "No, not that! It's bipolar disorder. Manic depression. Whatever we call it these days."

Wet dishcloth in hand, Connie began to wipe down the stove top. "They've had her on lithium, Depakote, Wellbutrin, and something called norepinephrine, but nothing seems to work for long. One minute she's chartering buses and organizing pro-life marches on the White House; the next she's locked herself in the bathroom, threatening to commit suicide. It's a big worry."

"She must be a handful for her mother."

Connie draped the dishcloth over the oven door handle to dry. "Dennis's wife died suddenly last Christmas."

Open mouth, insert foot. I was curious about how she died, but the look on Connie's face said, *Don't go there,* so I changed the subject.

"I wanted to ask Dennis more about 'that Lambert boy,' but you kept shooting daggers at me. What's the big secret, Connie?"

Connie looked baffled. "No secret. I just sensed that Dennis thought he had spoken out of turn, and I didn't want to put him on the spot." She joined me at the table, where I was refolding the napkins—Connie always used big, checkered cloth ones—so we could use them again in the morning.

"I don't remember much about the Lamberts. Dad

was pretty sick, and I didn't pay much attention to the news. I'd be so exhausted by the end of the day I'd just fall into bed. The Lamberts still live down on Princess Anne Street, though, right behind the nursing home. Their son, Chip, was a big athlete back in the late eighties. He went to the University of Maryland on a basketball scholarship, I think. He got married and moved to Baltimore, last I heard. He and Katie were high school sweethearts, so naturally he'd be asked about her disappearance."

"I would certainly hope so!"

"Let it rest, Hannah! I can't believe you're still standing up asking silly questions after the day you've had. It makes me tired just to look at you. Do you want dinner?"

We agreed to let tea substitute for dinner; then I tried calling Paul. When I got the answering machine again, I left him a grumpy message, then collapsed in the living room to watch the seven o'clock news. After Tom Brokaw bade us good night, I let Connie have dibs on the tub because I was too weary to get up. I lay in front of the TV, like a lump, my feet propped up on the arm of the sofa and in sole, proud possession of the remote control. I used it to graze through the channels. Earlier Connie had poured us each a glass of heart medicine: red wine. The stem of my glass rested on my stomach so that the ruby liquid sloshed from side to side as I breathed.

Connie wasn't much for modern gadgets; she had owned an answering machine once, but could never figure out how to program it. While she soaked in the tub, I lay on the sofa and grumbled to myself about Connie's aversion to electronic devices. If she had had an answering machine, I complained, there might have been a message on it from Paul when we returned from the Nichols place. At eight-thirty I switched from a mindless network sitcom to a biography of Shirley Temple on A&E. Surely he'd be calling me soon. I drained my wineglass and settled in for the wait. The last thing I remember was Shirley and her bouncing sausage curls dancing up the steps with Stepin Fetchit.

How I got myself into bed is a mystery. I awoke to the sound of gravel crunching. Socks were still on my feet, and my mouth tasted like old navy soup spoons. I drew aside the lightweight chintz curtains and peered out the window. My green Toyota was rolling down the drive with Connie at the wheel. I had blocked her in. Downstairs a note stuck to the door of the refrigerator with a plastic magnet from Pizza John's informed me that she'd gone to get a newspaper and that she'd be "back in a few."

I took the opportunity to bathe. With the tub half full and steam already clouding the mirror, I settled into the water, first resting my back against the cool porcelain, then sliding down until I was lying almost flat. I adjusted the hot-water tap to a trickle and watched as the water level slowly rose to cover my thighs and arms, my feet, my chest, and finally, my breast. The right one had once been small, round, and perky like the left one until cancer and a surgeon's knife had reduced it to a rough, red rope across my chest. I ran a finger gently along the knotted scar and thought about the reconstructive surgery I was considering.

I sat up, soaked a washcloth in the hot water from the tap, wrung it out, and placed it over my face, covering it completely, breathing in the hot, moist air, breathing slowly, evenly, feeling my body melt into the water. Under the washcloth scenes from yesterday played and replayed behind my closed eyelids. I tried to clear my mind, but images of that white, floating thing kept swimming to the surface. I flung the washcloth aside and tried to concentrate on Connie's elaborate floral wallpaper, following the wandering vines as they snaked over the medicine cabinet and curled around the light fixtures, but even that didn't banish the visions. So I meditated, focusing on my mantra instead.

A knock on the bathroom door jolted me awake. "Hannah, are you all right?"

"Sorry, Connie. I must have fallen asleep. I'll be right out."

I emerged, wrapped in an oversize terry-cloth bathrobe I found hanging from a hook on the back of the bathroom door, my skin flushed with the heat. Connie sat at the kitchen table surrounded by paper cups of fresh coffee plus a box of assorted doughnuts she told me she had picked up at Ellie's.

I peeked inside. "Crullers!" My favorite. I took a bite and mumbled, "You *are* a doll."

Connie finished the last of a chocolate-covered

doughnut, sipped her coffee, then wiped her mouth with a napkin. "Gawd, just think of the calories!"

"Crullers don't have any calories," I said. I showed her the hollow core. "See, they're full of air."

"Dream on, Hannah. You might as well just paste it on your thighs."

Connie had purchased three newspapers and spread them out on the table. "I knew you'd be interested in seeing these." The *Washington Post* didn't mention our murder at all, at least not that we could find. The *Baltimore Sun* had a small article in the Maryland section, but we had made it big in the *Chesapeake Times*, with pictures. There it was, solidly occupying the treasured spot on the front page usually reserved for marijuana busts, boat fires, fatal traffic accidents, or farmers who had grown misshapened vegetables resembling Newt Gingrich. "Here." Connie moved her mug aside and smoothed the paper out.

"What does it say?" I leaned forward, still licking the sticky glaze from my fingers.

In the *Sun* I was described as "a woman visiting from Annapolis," but the *Times* mentioned my name and my hometown and had a small picture of me and Connie, talking to Ellie. I peered at it. "Connie, why didn't you tell me I looked so dreadful? My wig is crooked."

"Don't be silly. It's your imagination. You look fine."

"Liar!" I tossed my empty cup into the trash. "Does it say anything about Chip Lambert?"

Connie adjusted her reading glasses and leaned over the page. "Let's see. 'The partially calcified body of a young woman' blah-de-blah-de-blah. Oh, here we are. 'Katherine Dunbar was last seen on October 13, 1990, leaving a dance at Jonas Green High School with her date, Charles "Chip" Lambert, also sixteen. Police are awaiting a positive identification of the body before reopening the case.' "

I turned the paper slightly toward me. BODY FOUND IN CISTERN, shouted the headline, and in smaller type below, FOUL PLAY SUSPECTED. Another photograph filled most of the page below the headline: Mrs. Dunbar gazed out from the window of her husband's truck with sad, unfocused eyes. He stood outside the door, holding her hand.

"I think that image will haunt me forever, Connie. It's the personification of grief. Even though it's been a long time since Emily put us through hell on earth by running off after that rock band, one doesn't easily forget. I know exactly what is running through that poor woman's mind." I pushed the newspaper back toward my sister-in-law. "It could have been Emily lying down there at the bottom of that cistern." My eyes stung with tears. "Eight years she's been living this nightmare, Connie. Eight years." I touched the photograph of Mrs. Dunbar. "But by the time this is all over, at least she'll know, one way or the other."

While Connie did the laundry and painted, I spent the rest of the day trying to make sense out of her accounts, which consisted of a spiral-bound notebook full of nearly indecipherable scribbles and a shoe box stuffed full of invoices, check stubs, and receipts. I was so caught up alternately worrying about Connie's slovenly bookkeeping habits and the poor Dunbar family that I forgot to worry about why Paul still hadn't returned my call.

chapter

5

IT RAINED ALL THE NEXT NIGHT. GREAT EXPLOSIONS
of thunder rattled the windows, followed before I
could finish chanting "one one thousand" by zigzags
of lightning that sliced through the dark and scented
the air with ozone. When I awoke at eight, the rain
had stopped, but clouds still plastered the slate gray
sky and patches of fog hovered over the low-lying
fields. I breathed in the sweet, damp air and felt im-
mensely content. Until I remembered. Rain. The cistern would be full again.

I had planned to spend the day lounging around
the house reading one of the paperbacks I had brought
with me. A dozen mysteries lay under my bed, jumbled
up in a plastic grocery bag. I never dreamed when I
packed them up in Annapolis that I'd be walking right
into a real-life mystery a few days later. I was sitting

cross-legged on the floor, browsing through the pile, trying to decide whether to revisit a favorite Dick Francis, *Reflex,* or to launch into the latest Sue Grafton when Connie tapped lightly on the door.

"Hannah? You up?" The door eased open, and Connie's tousled head appeared.

"Just picking out the day's reading material." I waved the Sue Grafton at her, *N Is for Noose.* "What do you suppose she'll do for titles after she gets to the end of the alphabet?"

Connie plucked the book from my outstretched hand and scanned the blurbs on the back flap. "Oh, I don't know. How about starting over? AA is for Alcoholics Anonymous, BB is for Gun." She set the book down on top of the dresser. "I gave up on Grafton somewhere around the letter *J,* I think." Connie turned apologetic. "Hannah, I was wondering. Could you help me pack up my gourds this morning?"

I saw my nice, quiet day sliding down the tubes. I shrugged. "Sure. Why not?" I tried to sound enthusiastic about helping prepare the shipment, but I really just wanted to get it over with.

A few minutes later, in the kitchen, I grabbed a bagel and a cup of coffee and tried to call Paul at home. I got the message you get when the line is busy, which meant he was either talking on the phone or logged on to the Internet. I suppose the phone could have been off the hook, too, or out of order, but my bet was he was slogging through his E-mail. So what the hell was going on? Paul might have missed seeing the article in the

Sun, but there was no way he could have missed my messages. I was becoming seriously annoyed. Too bad Connie didn't have a computer and a modem. I could have E-mailed my husband a nasty-gram.

In the studio I lounged against the workbench for a few minutes, munched on the bagel, and watched Connie work. My gawd, the woman was disorganized! She'd unfold a box, tape it up, then get distracted by something on one of the pieces she was packing, take it over to the window, turn it from side to side, squint . . . it drove me nuts.

"You won't finish until sometime in the next century if you keep checking everything like that. You need to set up an assembly line." I unfolded six boxes, taped down the flaps, lined them up, and filled each with a layer of plastic peanuts. Then I rolled each precious object in protective bubble wrap and snuggled it down into the bed of peanuts. After an hour of this I was decorated in peanuts. They clung by static electricity to my sweatshirt and jeans and dangled from my chin, but we had ten packed boxes and left a wall of empty shelves.

Colonel, who had been observing all this activity with one eye open, head resting on his paws, a plastic peanut stuck to his right ear, followed us outside and trotted behind Connie as she went to the barn. Connie swung the barn door wide, while I tried to brush the peanuts off my clothes, but they clung stubbornly to my hands and fingers. As I shook my hands vigorously, I heard a door slam and a reluctant engine grind, sputter, and cough into life. I just had time to think, *Don't tell me Connie is still driving my father-in-law's old Chevy truck* when the familiar vehicle, scaled with rust, emerged from the barn. Connie's head protruded from the window of the ancient truck, looking back over her left shoulder because the side view mirror was long gone. She backed up to the studio door, dismounted, and unhooked the tailgate.

"Isn't it a mess? I have to keep a trickle charger on the battery."

I had to agree it was a sorry heap. Once bright red, the finish had faded over the years to a dull pink, and the chassis sat crookedly on four tires, all completely bald.

It took only a few minutes to load the boxes into the back of the truck—they were bulky but quite light—and lock up the house. Soon we were bouncing down the drive—the shock absorbers also belonged in a museum—and I kept looking through the rear window to make sure the boxes were still with us, hoping I'd used enough bubble wrap. As Connie turned right to follow the road into town, I slid sideways on the dry vinyl seats. No seat belts, either.

Just past the Baxter farm, the narrow road curved sharply right and widened into Church Street, named for St. Philip's Episcopal nearly a half a mile away, at the stoplight where Church Street intersected with High. Church Street wound through a pleasant, tree-lined, residential neighborhood, dominated by large family houses built in the twenties and thirties. About halfway down, Connie slowed and pointed to a modest gray dwelling on our right, with a wraparound porch and neat white trim.

"That's the Dunbars'," she said.

A familiar truck was parked at the head of the drive, and behind it sat a black Lexus with Virginia plates. "Wonder who that is?" I asked. Connie shrugged.

At the stoplight Connie turned left on High. Just past the cemetery she spun the wheel sharply to the left and pulled into one of the unmarked parking spaces in front of Ellie's Country Store.

I hadn't been there for several years, but I was pleased to see that Ellie had made an effort to retain the old-fashioned cracker barrel atmosphere of the place. Outside, a wooden porch extended across the front of the building, decorated with turn-of-the-century farm implements, milk cans, and painted metal signs advertising Nu grape, Dad's root beer, Norka ginger ale (Tastes Better!), Glendora coffee, and various brands of chewing tobacco. Inside, Ellie had added a wood-burning stove since the last time I had stopped by and had scattered a few solid-looking wooden crates about, sturdy enough for customers to sit on. Between two of the crates sat an old nail keg that served as a table for a well-worn chess set. A modest selection of groceries and sundries occupied shelves that ranged out to the right of the door, and on the left a counter ran the length of the room. Behind the counter double doors led to the kitchen. I heard the chink and clink of dishes and glasses being washed.

Ellie had an alcove in the back where she handled

UPS. When we came in, she was standing there with a customer, weighing a large box.

"It's going all the way to California, Mrs. Foster. That's why it's so expensive. They go by zones."

Mrs. Foster, a scrawny woman wearing blue jeans and a turtleneck shirt, simply said, "Oh," and opened up her wallet to extract two new ten-dollar bills.

We were almost up to the counter before Ellie noticed us. "Oh, hi, you two."

"I've got some boxes for you, Ellie."

"Okay. I'll be with you in a minute." She leaned over the counter and shouted toward the kitchen, "Bill! We need your help out here unloading some boxes!"

Bill, whom I took to be in his mid-twenties, appeared immediately. He wore khaki bermuda shorts, a T-shirt covered in food stains, and a five o'clock shadow. "No problem," he grunted. A man of few words.

While Bill slapped back and forth in his cheap rubber sandals, helping Ellie and Connie get the boxes ready for UPS, I selected a bottled iced tea from one of the upright glass-fronted coolers standing near the window. I took it to the cash register just as a heavy-set woman I assumed was Ellie's daughter, Angie, emerged from the kitchen, wiping her hands on a towel that she had tucked into the waistband of her jeans. She had Ellie's unruly light brown hair, and I noticed a certain resemblance around the eyes and mouth.

"Hi, there. Can I help you?"

"I'm just waiting for my sister-in-law over there." I pointed with my drink.

"Oh, you must be Hannah." She squinted at me. "Sorry! I didn't recognize you at first."

I noticed her checking out my wig and decided I'd make it easy for her. "I've lost some weight lately."

"Lucky you!" Angie, who had a good thirty pounds on her mother, gathered up a roll of fat at her waist and pinched it between her thumb and index finger. "I could stand to lose some myself."

I wasn't sure what I was supposed to say to that. *Darn right?* I covered the silence by examining the candy bars and packs of gum displayed prominently near the cash register. I selected a Milky Way Dark, one of my vices, and laid it on the counter. "Want a candy bar, Connie?"

Connie didn't even turn around. "After those dough-nuts? Are you nuts?"

"Just having a fading spell. You work me too hard."

"Why don't you order us some lunch?"

Angie took our order for two crab cake sand-wiches and a single order of fries on the side—they were for Connie—writing it down with a nubby pen-cil on a green order pad. She tore off the page and shoved it into the kitchen through a square window that had been cut in the wall, where Bill, who ap-parently served as cook as well as UPS assistant, picked it up.

While I gulped my iced tea, Angie rang up a bottle of dish soap and a box of raisin bran for a bearded sailor who looked as if he had just returned from a round-the-world cruise. After he left, letting the screen door bang shut behind him, she perched behind the counter on a tall stool.

"My mom tells me that you found that body yesterday."

I nodded without taking my mouth from the bottle.

"Mom thinks it's Katie Dunbar."

"That's what everyone thinks, Angie, but that's because she's the only person who ever went missing from Pearson's Corner. It could certainly be somebody else, you know. Anybody could have dumped a body out here."

"I hope it isn't. Katie, I mean. I'd hate to think of her lying all alone down there in that cold, cold water." She stared at her hands, which lay folded in her lap. "Course I'd hate to think of *anyone* ending up like that. But Katie . . . well, she was my best friend."

"She was?"

"Oh, yes! We were on the cheerleading squad together. Everyone said we looked like twins."

I studied this doughy young woman who was sliding into middle age far too early and tried to reconcile what I saw sitting before me with a perky blond youngster shaking pom-poms and shouting "Gimme a J, Gimme an O!" I couldn't do it.

Angie began twisting the towel. "I still remember Katie at the homecoming dance. She was so happy! She couldn't sit still. Just flying around the room in a gorgeous satin dress, blue like the sky. It cost the earth, too. Three hundred dollars! Katie showed me the receipt." Her voice was a husky whisper, as if she were sharing a great secret. "She danced with all the guys on

the basketball team, even though she came with Chip."
Angie reached behind her to rearrange a tin box of
crackers that must have been cutting into her back.

"After she disappeared, I kept thinking about that
night. Playing it over and over, trying to remember
if I missed anything." She leaned back against the
shelves and closed her eyes. With one graceful hand,
she beat out a slow, imaginary rhythm in the air. Suddenly her eyes snapped open, and she stared at me.
"We had real bands then, you know, not disk jockeys
like they have today who just sit on their duffs all
night and play CDs."

She let out a long sigh. "I broke a strap on my gown
that night, and when we went to the rest room to pin
it back together, Katie told me she was the happiest
girl in the whole, wide world. Later I saw her standing
near the punch bowl, holding Chip's hand. Chip just
smiled that sweet, closed-mouth smile of his and
looked mysterious."

"I read in the paper that he was the last person to
see her before she disappeared."

"That's right, except for whoever . . ." She shivered.
"But Chip could never do anything like that."

"Maybe they had a fight and something got out of
hand."

"Oh, no! Chip was crazy about Katie. Besides, he's
way too religious, one of those born-again Christians.
He attended that all-glass megachurch over near Lan-
ham; still does, for all I know. You've probably seen it.
It's the one that looks like a humongous greenhouse."

I shook my head. Episcopalians like me aren't

usually up on the location of churches with TV min-
istries and parking lots the size of RFK Stadium. I
changed the subject. "I keep thinking about the Dunbars and how tragic it would be for them. Was Katie
their only child?"

"Oh, no. They have another daughter, Elizabeth.
She's four years older than Katie. Now that she's working for some hotshot law firm in D.C., though, she
doesn't come home very often." She leaned toward me
confidentially. "To tell you the truth, I think Liz is a little ashamed of her parents, her father just being a
handiman at the local nursery and all. They don't call
him a handiman, or course; he's head gardener or
deputy horticulturalist or something."

The phone rang, and Angie took a minute to write
down a carry-out order for four Italian subs and hand
it through to Bill.

While Angie scribbled, I stared at a poster hanging
crookedly on the wall and wondered how Katie's parents could have afforded a three-hundred-dollar dress.
I know we couldn't. For her junior prom, Emily had
selected a red leather skirt with a slit from here to
Christmas and a strapless black plastic bustier with
spangles that cost the earth and would have looked
right at home in Madonna's closet. I absolutely put
my foot down, insisting it made her look like a tart.
There had been a terrible scene in the dressing room
that sent the sales associates scurrying for cover and
ended with both of us in tears and not speaking to
each other for a week. Shortly after that Emily had

run away again, and I tried to convince myself that it hadn't been my fault.

Angie hung up the phone and stuck the pencil she had been using behind her ear. "Sorry about that. Where was I?"

"You were telling me about Katie's sister," I prompted.

"Oh, yeah. Liz is a lot older than Katie. She was a sophomore at the University of Maryland when Katie disappeared."

"It must have been hard on Liz, too," I said.

"I suppose." Angie paused. "But they were never very close. Katie was prettier and more popular than Liz." She leaned forward, and her folded hands disappeared into her lap. "One time when Katie was a freshman and Liz was a senior, they had a knock-down, hair-pulling, rabbit-punching fight in the girls' locker room just because Katie got asked to the senior prom by one of Liz's old boyfriends." She wiggled off the stool and turned to fetch our sandwiches, which had just appeared in the pass-through window. "I'm sure the police filed that interesting fact away in their little notebooks," she added. "They talked to Liz, too, you know. She was home that weekend."

Connie chose that moment to join us and demand what she claimed was a hard-earned lunch. Angie returned to the kitchen, and Ellie busied herself with the UPS delivery truck. Connie and I sat on the wooden crates and balanced our paper plates on our knees. "Gawd, these are good!" Connie mumbled through a mouthful of succulent backfin crab lumps.

She offered me some of her fries, but she had ruined them with catsup, and I told her so.

"Picky, picky." She waggled one under my nose, just to taunt me.

I had finished my sandwich and was standing at the cooler, selecting a fruit drink for Connie, when the screen door slammed and a familiar voice boomed out, "Hey, hey!" Dennis. He made a beeline for Connie. "I knew I'd find you here." He gestured toward the front porch. "That decrepit heap you're driving is a dead giveaway. I should give you a ticket just on general principles."

Connie popped a french fry, loaded with catsup, into her mouth. "I had to put my boxes in something, Dennis. What brings you here?"

"I'm dying of thirst." He joined me at the cooler, where he picked out a bottle of cranberry juice, twisted off the cap, and finished it in three long gulps. I simply stared.

Dennis put the empty bottle down on the counter and fumbled in his pocket until he found three quarters, which he laid on top of the cash register. He pulled up a crate and sat down next to Connie, his arms resting on his knees. "I've just come from the Dunbars." He looked up at me. "I had the unhappy task of telling them that the body you found has been positively identified as Katherine Louise Dunbar and that she had been murdered."

From the kitchen came a long, high-pitched wail and the clang of something metallic hitting the floor and rolling, rolling, rolling.

IT WAS A MARX BROTHERS MOVIE.

Dennis, Connie, and I reached the kitchen door simultaneously, a confusion of legs, colliding shoulders, and bumped elbows. Dennis straight-armed the kitchen door, but it moved only a few inches, stopping with a hollow thud against some inert object on the other side. When we finally squeezed through, it turned out to be Bill's broad behind as he stood with his arms around the sobbing Angie, comforting her in the narrow space between the door and a stainless steel counter strewn with chopped vegetables. Angie rocked back and forth, moaning, using a soiled dish towel as a handkerchief, pressed hard against her eyes and completely covering her face.

Bill moved to one side so that Ellie could sidle by and join her daughter. Ellie fussed and cooed while escorting Angie to a folding wooden chair just to the left of the door. Angie sat down heavily beneath a wall-mounted telephone near the spot where a copy of the menu, sheathed in plastic, was tacked to the wall. While Connie and I hung back, leaning against a sink, I could hear Dennis's voice, deep and reassuring, talking to Angie, arranging an appointment for an interview later in the day. Angie nodded mutely while dabbing at her swollen eyes with the crumpled towel.

"I feel like an intruder here," Connie whispered. "The worst kind of eavesdropper."

I, on the other hand, was inclined to stay, even though I could feel that water from the edge of the sink I was leaning against had soaked through the back of my slacks.

Connie tugged at my sleeve. "There's nothing we can do here. Let's sneak out the back." She pointed to a screen door near the french fry cooker. I followed reluctantly, but as we reached the door, I hung back, gazing across the kitchen at the sad tableau: Angie seated, still sobbing; Ellie leaning solicitously over her, rubbing her back; Dennis squatting in front of the two, forearms resting on his thighs; and Bill, looking helpless, wiping the stainless steel counter over and over, even though it was by now thoroughly clean. As far as they were concerned, we were no longer there.

We drove to the farm, sitting in silence most of the way. I thought about all the problems of my own that should have kept me from saddling myself with somebody else's.

One, I had had cancer. Maybe I still did. Who knew how many microscopic malignant cells had survived the chemicals and were even now cruising around my bloodstream, scouting out a comfortable spot to set up housekeeping?

Two, I was unemployed.

So why did I care so much about these people I had just met and a dead girl I never knew at all? Were they simply a distraction from my own troubles or was it the realization that Emily had been just Katie's age the night she flounced off to a Phish concert in Washington, D.C., and we didn't see her again for over three weeks? But unlike the Dunbars, we'd been lucky. Somewhere between Durango and Albuquerque, Emily and her rat-tailed, pierced-eared boyfriend had run out of money and decided to hitchhike home.

I need to go home, too, I told myself. *Get some perspective. Sort through my mail, print out my résumé, find some envelopes, and, last but certainly not least, give Paul a sizable piece of my mind.*

By three o'clock I had thrown my toothbrush and a few necessities into the car and told Connie I'd call, promising to see her again in a few days. I settled into the driver's seat and breathed deeply. The overnight rain had cleared the air, leaving it fresh and smelling of clean, damp earth. Plump clouds scudded across an otherwise clear blue sky, and the sun warmed my face as I drove north up 301 toward Annapolis with the car windows rolled down and the wind roaring across my ears, making my gold hoop earrings sing.

Annapolis can be so beautiful in springtime that it

almost breaks your heart. Somewhere before Interstate 97 joins Route 50 bringing visitors in from Baltimore and points north, new construction had widened the highway and money had been found, goodness knows where, to face the overpasses with brick. Wildflowers, in a rainbow of brilliant colors, thrived in the median strips and nestled in the Vs formed by the exit ramps.

On Rowe Boulevard, the scenic approach into Annapolis, the city fathers had planted tulips, and as I waited for the light to turn at Melvin Avenue, I had to admire the red and yellow blooms, heads nodding in the light breeze. Nature was doing its best to cheer me up, but I wasn't buying. It was hard enough to leave Pearson's Corner with the mystery of Katie's disappearance still weighing heavily on my mind, but by the time I passed the new courthouse building near the stadium, I had almost convinced myself that Paul must have interrupted a burglary in progress. I worried that I'd find him sprawled on our kitchen floor with his head bashed in, one arm outflung near the off-the-hook phone.

I was going at least twenty miles over the posted limit when I screeched to a halt at the far end of the boulevard where it dead-ends at College Avenue. Late-blooming fat white cherry blossoms had turned the State House before me into a picture postcard. I thanked God for creating spring, giving me something to hang on to in the face of all that I'd gone through. This was my first spring since cancer had turned my life upside down. For poor Katie, though, there would be no more springtimes.

Our house is an old brick colonial on Prince George Street, tucked between two similar houses not too far from historic William Paca House. On a clear day from our bedroom on the top floor you can see the Naval Academy chapel dome. In the winter, when the trees are bare, we even claim a water view of Spa Creek.

Parking is always a problem in the historic district, particularly in summer when hordes of tourists clog the town, so I sometimes sneak my car into the Naval Academy visitors' lot and walk home. Today I had the luck of a cop in a made-for-TV movie; someone was pulling out of a space just as I circled the block for the second time.

In our entrance hall, ignoring the mail that had piled up—a staggering amount in just four days—I threw my keys on the table and called, "Paul, it's me. I'm home!" I listened, hardly daring to breathe, until I heard his familiar voice.

"Out here!" I found Paul sitting on the patio, a sweating bottle of Coors Light in his hand and the Sunday section of Saturday's *Baltimore Sun* strewn about on the patio table, its pages fluttering in the wind. Paul had anchored them to the table with a flat rock from my garden. He wasn't reading. He was talking on the cell phone. "Later, Murray. Hannah's just here." Murray Simon was an old college friend, a lawyer with a small practice up Route 2 in Glen Burnie, near Baltimore.

Paul punched the talk button with his thumb and turned to smile at me. It was the same crooked grin I loved so well, but today it didn't match his eyes.

"I've been trying to call you for two whole days, Paul. I left messages on the machine. Why didn't you return my calls?"

He set the phone aside, caught my hand, and pulled me into his lap, surrounding me with his arms and squeezing tight. I pulled away slightly so I could see his face.

"Goodness! You'd think I'd been away for a week instead of just a few days." He kissed me on the mouth, and I relaxed into him, savoring the familiar tickle of his mustache as it brushed my lips and trailed along my cheek.

"Missed you," he whispered into my neck. "More than you know."

I leaned back, one hand flat against his chest. "You didn't answer my question, Paul. Why didn't you call me back?" There were tiny worry lines around his eyes. I stood and dragged a patio chair around from the other side of the table and sat down, facing him.

Paul set his beer down on the table and put both his hands together between his knees. He leaned toward me, but before he could say anything, I erupted, words tumbling out of my mouth at one hundred miles per hour, "It's even in the paper!" I pointed to the table. "I needed to tell you that I found a body in the cistern on the old Nichols place!"

Paul's eyebrows disappeared into his hair. A look I couldn't read momentarily lit his eyes. "What? My God. I hadn't gotten to the newspaper yet!"

"Actually it was Colonel who found the body." I described my walk, the headlong dash back to the house, our return to the crime scene, Dennis's visit with Connie, and the disturbing events of this morning. Thinking about Paul's ties to the community, I asked, "Do you remember a girl named Katie Dunbar?"

He shook his head. "Should I?"

"I just thought you might. Small town and all. Connie and I were in Ellie's Country Store mailing some packages when Dennis Rutherford stopped in for a soda. He told us the body was hers. She disappeared eight years ago, Paul. Dennis said she'd been murdered."

Paul opened his mouth, but I'll never know what he was going to say because the phone rang just then. Paul said it was a wrong number.

A few minutes later the blasted thing rang again, but this time Paul ignored it. "Jeez, honey, I feel like an insensitive clod. Sitting here, drinking beer and feeling sorry for myself, after what you've just been through. Are you okay?"

The phone continued to ring—four, five times—making a sound like a strangling turkey—six, seven. "I might be, if you'd pick up the damn phone. Aren't you going to answer that?"

"Let it ring, Hannah. We need to talk."

"I'll say we do. Didn't I just say I've been trying to reach you for days?"

Paul caressed my cheek with the back of his fingers. "I *am* sorry, honey. I should have been there for you." His face took on a look of such infinite sadness that my heart seemed to turn in my chest. Suddenly he was not looking at me, and I panicked.

"Paul, what's wrong?" A cold fist of fear began to form in my stomach. *Mom?* The last time I'd talked to her, she'd had a persistent cough that she'd promised to see the doctor about.

"Not Mother?" I struggled to my feet. "Don't tell me there's something wrong with my mother?"

Paul stood and began to pace back and forth on the slate slabs that formed the patio. "No, it's not your mother." Then, seeing the look of alarm in my eyes, he quickly added, "Or Emily." He ran a hand through his hair and looked at me. "God, Hannah, I don't know how to tell you this."

"What?" I grabbed his upper arms and shook him. "What? For Christ's sake, Paul! Tell me, what?" The knot in my stomach had grown so huge that I thought I would throw up.

Paul took me gently by the shoulders and eased me back into my chair. He sat down, too, and pulled his chair up to mine until our knees touched. I remember thinking that the last time he'd done this was at the doctor's office, the Friday before my mastectomy, a few moments after Dr. Wilkins had told us the results of the biopsy and reported that the fast-growing tumor was already six centimeters long. The doctor had scheduled my surgery for the following Monday, and I was in shock, hardly feeling the molded plastic chair underneath my legs or the warmth of Paul's hands as they cradled both of mine.

Now I sat in my own backyard, rigid again with fear, feeling the gentle pressure of Paul's hands and waiting for him to say something, thinking, *Three*. My mother always said that bad luck comes in threes.

"I'm in trouble, Hannah." Paul cleared his throat. "It could be big trouble. One of my students has accused me of sexual harassment."

I felt the world shift on its axis. Sexual harassment! After the Tailhook fiasco sexual harassment was one of the few things that could get a tenured professor at the Naval Academy booted out on his ear.

Paul studied my face, as if searching it for understanding. "It's not true, of course."

I sat frozen, momentarily unable to speak. My breath came in rapid gasps, and I felt light-headed. "I can't believe I'm hearing this!"

"It may be all right, Hannah. Simon Westlake's this year's division head, and I've been meeting with him. He says he doesn't believe a word of it, but he has to treat her complaint seriously."

"Her?" I repeated numbly. It crossed my mind to be relieved that at least it wasn't a he. "Her who?"

"Jennifer Goodall, a firstie. She told her company officer that we were"—he took a ragged breath—"she says we were intimate and that I promised her a higher grade in Probability Theory if she would—oh, God, Hannah." He covered his eyes with his left hand. "She's failing the course. She claims I'm flunking her in retaliation for her decision to break off our so-called affair."

I didn't know Jennifer Goodall, but I could imagine her: a "firstie," a senior, and, like all midshipmen, a perfect physical specimen. I pictured lustrous blond hair done up in an intricate braid and impossibly blue eyes, a crisp white uniform fitting smoothly and snugly around firm, young breasts. Big tears began to slide down my cheeks and drip, unchecked, onto my T-shirt, a T-shirt I had chosen because it was loose and tended not to emphasis what little there was in the way of breasts underneath.

"Hannah. Hannah." He reached for me. "You know it's not true! Not a word of it! She's desperate, Hannah. As a poly sci major she needs my course to graduate."

I took two deep breaths and tried to think reasonably. This was serious. If Midshipman Goodall were to flunk out at this late date, the navy could send her to the fleet as a lowly enlisted person for two years.

I recalled Paul's grueling teaching schedule, the days at work giving extra instruction, the long hours he spent each night at home grading papers and found the girl's accusation hard to believe. "When is all this supposed to have happened?"

"At the Army-Navy game. At the Sheraton Hotel near the Meadowlands, where a bunch of us were staying."

"But that was last December, Paul! This is May! Even if her story was true, why did she wait so long to report it?"

"I don't know, honey. I can't explain it. The only truth I know is that I spent the night at the Sheraton and that I slept alone."

Just as I had slept alone. Too sick from chemo to attend the annual football rivalry, I had passed that chilly autumn evening alternately watching the game on TV and miserably hugging the toilet bowl.

"What about her roommate?"

"She didn't sleep with her roommate. Apparently they'd had a fight. No one seems to have any idea where Midshipman Goodall spent the night, Hannah, but it certainly wasn't with me." Paul poked at the beer bottle with his index finger, toppling it onto its side. Half a bottle of tepid liquid dripped through the holes in the wrought iron table onto the slate below. "We had one drink together—"

"You had a *drink* with her?" I couldn't believe my ears. "How could you have been so incredibly stupid?"

"I didn't invite her to, for Christ's sake, Hannah. I was sitting alone in the lobby bar, nursing a beer and reading a paperback, when she walked up and spoke to me. I recognized her from Differential Equations her plebe year. She sat down. We ordered a round of drinks. Then, when I realized how drunk she was, I tried to convince her to go back to her room. She refused saying, 'no, no,' she was fine, so I left her sitting in the bar and went back to my room."

"But someone must have seen her! Another mid. A waitress. Hotel staff. Maybe she slept on a couch in the lobby." I shook my head, trying to clear it.

"You could end up in the *Washington Post*," I muttered. "You could lose your job."

"I know." There was a long silence. Wind rustled the newspapers. A blue jay somewhere nearby jeered at the neighbor's cat.

Paul lifted my chin and tried to look into my eyes,

but I turned my head and stared, unfocused, at the stone wall that separated our property from our neighbors, refusing to meet his gaze. "Look at me, Hannah! You've got to believe me! I was never alone with her. Never! Not for a single minute!"

"But it doesn't matter, does it, Paul? In this political climate, who's going to listen?"

"Simon believes me, and I hope you do, too. You are my rock, Hannah. If I lose you . . ." He looked as if he were about to cry.

"Does Emily know?" I whispered, wondering if Paul had called our daughter.

"No, and I'm not planning to tell her, unless I have to."

We sat for a while in silence, each waiting for the other to speak. "What happens now?" I finally asked, after what seemed like hours. "What can we do?"

"Nothing. Simon is handling it, and believe me, he's going by the book. There'll be a formal investigation, of course. Until then it's business as usual. Officially no one knows anything."

I studied the pin oak tree that Paul had planted on our tenth anniversary. Tiny green buds shimmered on the branches, promising spring. What did the future hold for us? Suddenly I saw it plainly. We were living in a cheap one-bedroom condo off Bestgate Road with Paul writing articles for sailing magazines and me working as a Manpower temp. *For richer, for poorer.*

"A job," I heard myself say, as if from a great distance.

"What did you say?"

"A job. I'll need to get a job."

"Hannah, I think that consideration is a long way off."

I shook my head and studied the man who had been my husband for twenty-five years. "Paul, you know I'll support you one hundred percent. I'll take on the secretary of the navy if I have to. But I need some time to take all this in."

I left him sitting in his solitary misery while I shut myself in the bedroom with mine. I lay on the bed and let the tears fall freely. I felt as if some alien from outer space had sucked out all my blood, leaving my bones to rattle around loose inside my skin. I wanted to believe Paul, but I had been so sick. Could I really blame him for wanting a break from all the illness and taking comfort in the arms of a young and healthy woman? Maybe I should have had the reconstruction! The doctor had recommended using a flap of muscle from my abdomen, but I'd decided I could worry about only one thing at a time. "Let's get rid of the cancer first," I'd told him. "Why spend all that money on a patient who's likely to croak?" He told Paul he admired my spunk.

Spunk. That's what I needed. A bottle of spunk. It would give me the backbone I needed to support Paul, the way he had always supported me. *In sickness and in health.* But there was a difference, I argued. I couldn't help getting cancer, for heaven's sake, but he could have avoided sitting around in hotel bars drinking ill-considered beers with creatures named Jennifer, screwing up our lives.

I must have fallen asleep at some point in the night

because the next sound I heard was the front door closing the next morning. Paul's side of the bed was undisturbed. I splashed cold water on my face, hating the woman on the other side of the bathroom mirror who stared back at me with blotched cheeks and swollen eyes. I extracted a pair of shorts and a faded T-shirt from the heap of clothes lying at the foot of my bed, pulled them on, then padded downstairs in my bare feet.

Before leaving for work, Paul had stuck a Post-It on the microwave—"I love you," written with black Magic Marker on the yellow square in solid, bold capitals. A tea drinker, he had made me the gift of a fresh pot of coffee. Overcome by new tears and a growing sense of desperation, I carried my coffee to our basement office, to try to take control of the situation the only way I knew how. I typed up my résumé on the PC, and clicked on the print button. I watched while ten copies spewed out, then printed two more for good measure.

Afterward I toasted a bagel and ate it dry, washed down with orange juice. When the morning paper came, I was half afraid to pick it up, expecting to see a screaming headline, NAVAL ACADEMY PROFESSOR CHARGED WITH SEXUAL HARASSMENT, but there was nothing. Just the shenanigans as usual in the District of Columbia. In the Metro section, though, a small story about Katie Dunbar caught my eye. The medical examiner had released her body. Katie's funeral would be on Wednesday.

Suddenly nothing seemed as important to me as getting back to Pearson's Corner. There was nothing I could do in Annapolis anyway, except brood about my crumbling marriage and my nonexistent career. I would attend Katie's funeral, meet her family, talk to her friends. Who among them, I wondered, could have been responsible for her death?

Figuring Paul would never miss them, I packed up the *Post* and *Sun* classified sections and stocked up on envelopes and stationery and a roll of stamps from Paul's desk. I threw some clean underwear and a simple black dress into an overnight bag.

Tomorrow I'd start some serious networking. I'd call all my friends and let them know I was job hunting. In the meantime I'd bunk with Connie. I wondered how much she'd have to know.

But Paul had already called his sister. I knew that the minute I walked into Connie's studio, two hours later after what seemed the longest drive of my life.

"Hannah," she said. An open-ended sentence. And I was bawling again, in her arms.

WHEN I PURCHASED MY LITTLE BLACK DRESS AT Hechts in Annapolis Mall, the label said it was crush-resistant and wrinkle-free. It also fitted as if it were made for me, or so I had been assured by the plump sixtyish saleswoman, the one who always managed to tap on my dressing room door—"How are we doing, hon?"—just as I had my head caught in the lining of some garment or was struggling, half naked, to zip up a pair of pants one size too small. The perfect travel outfit, she declared when I emerged from the dressing room to check the fit in front of a three-way mirror. If so, the manufacturer had never tested it out on a consumer like me. When I extracted it from the overnight bag at Connie's, that perfect little black dress was a mass of wrinkles, as if I'd spent a restless night sleeping in it or on it. Connie doesn't own an iron, so I hung the dress in the bathroom while I took my shower, marginally improving the situation. A colorful gypsy scarf with an elaborate fringe borrowed from Connie's extensive collection completed the transformation. With luck, everyone would notice the gold, purple, and turquoise flowers and not the remaining wrinkles.

But I didn't think anything could be done about the middle-aged face and puffy eyelids I was seeing in Connie's bathroom mirror. I looked as if I'd been stung by bees. I hadn't given my eyes much of a chance to recover, either, having spent every night since Saturday crying myself to sleep.

On the vanity, Connie had a flat wicker basket of cosmetics to choose from, many I recognized as the free-gift-when-you-buy-fifteen-dollars'-worth-of-our-products variety. I selected a beige foundation and smoothed it on, stroked my cheeks with blusher, then began working on my eyes with a bluish liner. Because of my unsteady hand, I only made matters worse. In addition to puffy, my lower lids were now rimmed with blue and smudged, like bruises. It looked hopeless.

I sat down on the toilet seat and fought back fresh tears of anger and frustration. Connie had reassured me, about twenty times since breakfast, that everything would be all right with Paul. But what did she know, really? As close as we had become, I knew that she was biased in favor of her brother, and who could blame her? Earlier I had overheard her on the phone with him, reporting in some detail on my current condition and reassuring him that everything would be all right with me: "Just give her time."

Time! Why was there never enough time? I checked my watch, made sure my wig was on straight and appeared before Connie in the kitchen, as presentable as I would ever get under the circumstances. I caught her leaning against the sink, drinking coffee, her head tipped way back to get the last few drops, which I knew would be thick with sugar. Over a long-sleeved black cotton dress she wore a stunning vest elaborately embroidered with gold and silver threads.

"You look like the proper mourner," she said, placing her empty cup in the sink. "Love the scarf!" She examined my makeup. "You should let me work on your eyes. You look like a raccoon."

"Too late now. Have you seen my sunglasses?"

Connie pointed to the kitchen table.

I slipped the glasses on. "I just can't stop crying, Connie! People at the funeral are bound to think I'm overreacting. I'm not a member of the family, and I didn't even know Katie."

"If anyone is so rude as to ask, I'll tell them you're menopausal."

"Thanks heaps!" I found myself chuckling in spite of my otherwise grim mood.

Connie picked up her key ring from the kitchen table. I followed behind and waited patiently as she locked the house and backed her Honda out of the barn. Ten minutes later we arrived at St. Philip's Episcopal Church, but even though the funeral wasn't scheduled to start until ten, the parking lot was already full. A young man wearing an international orange slip-on vest with "parking attendant" stenciled on it in black directed us across the street.

Exasperated, Connie backed out of the church driveway, turned, and continued through the light at High. She pulled into the lot behind the Hillcrest Nursing Home, shut off the engine, and set the parking brake with a grinding, upward jerk. As we got out of the car, I noticed three old codgers sitting in plastic lawn chairs on the front porch of the nursing home, deep in conversation, soaking up the early-morning sun. They were dressed in shapeless sweaters in spite of the balmy weather. A male attendant in a green uniform loitered nearby, his eyes on scan.

Connie waved to one of the patients, a silver-haired gentleman wearing a red cardigan. "That's old Mr. Schneider, Dennis Rutherford's father-in-law. He's got Parkinson's, poor thing." Connie shook her head. "I know Dennis would rather be caring for him at home, but it's just too much. Maggie can't cope." She glanced back at the line of old men, sitting quietly in the sun, nodding at the mourners as they passed by the porch on their way to St. Philip's.

"They're a Gilbert and Sullivan chorus," Connie said with a wistful smile. "Always nodding and agreeing with each other, no matter what. In the afternoon when the sun gets too hot, they move around into the shade on the south side of Hillcrest and watch the animals come and go from the vet's instead of paying attention to what's going on along High."

I followed Connie as she headed up the sidewalk. "Hello, Mr. Schneider!" she called.

Mr. Schneider turned in our direction. "Why, hello, Ms. Connie! Say, whose funeral is it today? Not one of us, I know. I checked it out—no empty beds!" He snorted with laughter.

"It's Katie Dunbar, Mr. Schneider. The girl who disappeared a while back."

"Katie Dunbar." He grasped his knee to steady his trembling hand. "I remember Katie Dunbar. Taught her in American history. Not a scholar, by any means, but turned in a fairly decent paper on the triangle trade first semester. Second semester, though, her grades went into the toilet. Squeaked by with a D, as I recall." He shook his head. "Frieda and Carl must be devastated. Devastated."

"I'm sure they are, Mr. Schneider." She patted his other hand where it rested on the head of his cane.

"Send them my condolences, will you?"

"I certainly will."

While we waited for the light at the intersection to change, Connie mentioned that Mr. Schneider had taught at the high school well into his late sixties. "Pity he's now so frail."

"Yes, but there doesn't seem to be anything wrong with his mind or his sense of humor."

As we crossed High Street, Connie explained that St. Philip's Parish was one of the oldest in Maryland, founded in 1697 when a chapel was built by a group of Anglicans on that very spot. The present building dated from 1923 after a fire had destroyed the original structure. The "new" church was of sturdy red brick with an elegant white wooden steeple that seemed to scrape the sky. Stubby transepts hinted at the cruciform shape of the building. From the louvered panels in the bell tower, the somber tolling of a tenor bell rolled out across the town and deep into the countryside, drawing us in. It seemed to resonate on the same frequency as my body, sending chills racing down the back of my neck and skittering along my spine.

Among the last to arrive, Connie and I accepted a printed bulletin from a solemn usher stationed in the nave and made our way as silently as possible to vacant seats he indicated in the back of the sanctuary. The door to our pew groaned alarmingly, and two old dears with stiffly permed hair and hats like fat headbands turned disapproving frowns on us as we eased past an elderly couple rigidly determined to remain seated next to the aisle. I stumbled over a kneeler and, with a mind to the old dears, suppressed an "ouch" as my hand hit the hymnal rack.

Near the front of the church and to the left, an organist with more enthusiasm than talent, her back to the congregation, was halfway through "Jesu, Joy of Man's Desiring," her body swaying from side to side as she played. When the chorale melody kicked in, she leaned back so far I feared she might topple off the organ bench.

To the right, opposite the organ, stood the pulpit, rising gracefully from a stone floor with a circular staircase leading up to it. Directly over the pulpit hung an acorn-shaped cap of carved stone. Fine stained glass windows lined the sanctuary. I peeked over the tops of my sunglasses at the one nearest me, a colorful depiction of Christ calming the sea. The early-morning sun blazed through the windows, scattering a patchwork of dazzling jewels over the heads, shoulders, and backs of the congregation, shapes that buckled and bent as they moved; distorted triangles that slid along an arm, down a leg, to fall into bright, geometric puddles on the floor. I was thinking of a kaleidoscope Emily had played with as a child when I suddenly became aware that the organ music had stopped. A rustling from the front made me turn my attention again to the altar, where a young African-American girl, her hair an elegant sculptured cap, had stepped out from the choir stalls to stand near the organ. Within seconds the haunting, unaccompanied strains of "Amazing Grace" filled the sanctuary, her sweet soprano voice soaring into the rafters.

Behind us the west doors opened, and through them glided Katie's casket, drenched in flowers, three pallbearers in dark suits on each side, guiding it, towering over it. The shortest of the six pallbearers must have been at least six feet. The only one I recognized was Bill from Ellie's Country Store.

Connie inclined her head toward mine until our temples touched, her voice a husky whisper. "It's the Jonas Green basketball team from the time Katie was in school. That's Chip in the front on the side nearest us. I'm amazed they were able to get them all together."

It was hard to tell from where I was sitting, but

Katie's former boyfriend appeared to be six feet five or six if he was an inch. His hair was straight, the color of strong tea, parted on the left and combed neatly to the side, where a single lock had escaped and hung, quivering, over his eyebrow. I'd never seen anyone who looked less like a murderer. Except maybe Ted Bundy.

Several rows up a too-tall toddler—she was probably standing on the kneeler—peered over the wooden pew, pointed a chubby finger, and shrilled, "Daddy!" None of the pallbearers appeared to notice. A woman who must have been her mother put an arm around the child and whispered something to her, her lips close to the little girl's ear. The child sat down abruptly. Two older children, a boy and a girl, sat in the pew to the woman's left, busily occupied with pencil stubs taken from the pew racks, using them to scribble on their bulletins and, when space on the bulletins gave out, on the backs of offering envelopes. "That's Chip's wife, Sandra, and their kids," Connie explained.

The service continued with a congregational hymn, "All Things Bright and Beautiful," which, according to the program, had been Katie's favorite. In the front pew I could see the back of Mrs. Dunbar's head, bowed while we sang. Next to her Mr. Dunbar stared stoically ahead. When Reverend Lattimore stepped up to deliver the eulogy, Mrs. Dunbar gazed at the rose-colored casket where it rested in the center aisle near the steps leading up to the choir. Bands of colored light streamed in from one of the windows, spilled over the casket, and reflected off the white of Mrs. Dunbar's hair, which had been coaxed into an old-fashioned French twist. She kept reaching up to touch it, perhaps to check for escaping strands or wayward hairpins. Or maybe the hairdo was simply unfamiliar. When we sang "I Sing a Song of the Saints of God," a white gardenia pinned to her left shoulder trembled as she sobbed.

Connie and I waited until almost everyone had left the church before following the crowd outside. We exited through the west door and proceeded around the north transept, weaving through ancient headstones, some dating back to the eighteenth century, where the carving and inscriptions had been etched away by weather and the years. *Ashes to ashes*, I thought. *Dust to dust.*

The sun, high in the sky by now, slanted through elm and maple branches, casting dappled shadows on the tombstones. This was a day to live, not a day to die! Would anybody care as deeply for me when I died? Would Paul? Would Emily? My daughter and I had come a long way toward mending our relationship after she'd more or less gotten herself straightened out in college, but the fact that much as I tried, I could never mask my disapproval of the men in her life kept her at a distance.

Emily was attracted to the wounded birds and lame puppies of this world. I kept waiting for her to bring home a boyfriend who didn't need rehabilitation, but despite our objections, last year she'd moved to Colorado Springs with a Haverford dropout named Daniel

Shemanski, who pierced his body in places I didn't even want to think about and made a living massaging the slope-sore bodies of the almost rich and famous. He was asking everyone to call him Dante these days. Just Dante. One name, like Pavarotti or Cher or Madonna.

During the short interment service I stood at the edge of the crowd with Connie, keeping well back, while my heels sank into the soft, grassy earth. I counted my blessings: I still had a living daughter to worry about. And if I should die, at least it would be the right way around. No parent should every have to go through the anguish of burying a child.

Afterward we followed a long train of mourners as they turned right out of the parking lot and strolled in silent groups up Church Street toward the Dunbars', where the family, the bulletin had announced, would be receiving condolences.

At the Dunbar house rectangular tables covered with white damask tablecloths were placed on the front porch at either side of the door. On one sat a punch bowl surrounded by dozens of crystal cups, neatly stacked. On the other, someone had arranged glass tumblers and a selection of sodas in two-liter bottles around a huge bowl of ice. I was about to ask Connie how on earth the Dunbars had managed the time to put all this together when I noticed the familiar purple of a van from Washington, D.C.'s premier caterer in the driveway. I had amended my question to *How can they afford . . . ?* when it was answered for me. The sister.

"Welcome." Elizabeth Dunbar, prominent attorney, held out a well-manicured hand. "Thank you for coming. My parents appreciate it so." Connie introduced me as her sister-in-law, and Liz favored me with half a smile, but her eyes were already looking ahead to the next guest.

I checked out the sodas and the punch (fruit base, no additives) and found myself hoping they'd have some adult beverages inside. In the living room I snagged a glass of white wine from the tray of a passing waiter and checked out the crowd over the rims of my Foster Grants. I didn't see anybody I knew. Except for Connie, of course, who had wandered away and was busily chatting with Reverend Lattimore. I figured that somebody I'd recognize would walk through the front door eventually, so I leaned against the fireplace and watched it, sipping slowly on what turned out to be a crisp dry chablis.

Liz wasn't at all as I expected. A handsome woman, she stood straight and solid as a pillar, a role model for the good-posture people. Her hair was neatly cut in a stylish wedge and of a color so seriously black that I thought it must be dyed. She wore a long-sleeved black dress that stopped at mid-calf, partially covering sturdy legs firmly planted in proper black Ferragamo shoes. Diamond studs glittered in her ears, and a matching necklace was fastened around her neck. I calculated a total of two carats, one at her neck and a half on each ear.

Liz shook hands. She smiled. I got the feeling she didn't know many of the guests either.

Eventually I wandered into the dining room looking for Connie and got involved in a conversation with Mindy, a former cheerleader. Mindy breathlessly explained, emphasizing every third word, how *privileged* and *lucky* she had been when *they* invited *her* to try out for *Katie's* vacant spot on the *Wildcats'* *cheer*leading squad. Relentlessly cheerful in spite of the occasion, I expected her to pull out the pom-poms at any minute. As Mindy launched into a dissertation on the joys of the 1990 winning basketball season—clearly a defining moment in her life—it was with some relief that I spotted Angie and Ellie occupying chairs in the corner, small plates of food balanced on their chubby knees. I excused myself and joined them.

Angie showed me her plate. "Have a mushroom cap? I'm not very hungry." She looked almost as tired as I felt.

Ordinarily I love mushroom caps, but today, in spite of the elaborate spread, nothing looked good. "Neither am I."

"So, how long are you planning to stay in Pearson's Corner?" Ellie asked.

"A week or two, I should think. While I'm looking for a new job, I'm helping Connie with her bookkeeping."

"What kind of work do you do?" Angie wanted to know.

"My experience is as a librarian and legal records specialist, but at this point I'd probably take anything, short of flipping burgers at McDonald's."

"Flipping burgers isn't so bad." This must have reminded Angie of something because her eyes filled with tears. "Excuse me," she said, handed her plate to her mother, and bolted through the crowd toward the powder room I had noticed earlier, built into a triangle under the stairs leading to the second floor.

"I'm sorry," I said to Ellie. "I didn't mean to be insensitive."

"Oh, it's nothing you said, dear. She goes off like that at the drop of a hat. She'll get over it. Excuse me for a moment while I find a place to put these plates down, will you?"

Ellie wound through the crowd grazing around the dining room table, a plate held high in each hand. She disappeared into the kitchen. Feeling abandoned for the second time, I decided to check out the food. I was picking halfheartedly at what was left of the fruit plate when someone tapped me on the shoulder.

"Well, hello!"

I must have jumped a mile. "Oh, hi, Hal." I brushed droplets of wine from the front of my dress, thinking thank goodness I'd chosen the chablis. "You startled me!"

"Sorry." He offered me his napkin, a small cloth square more suitable for a doll's tea party than for a grown-up do.

"Thanks. No damage done." I nibbled on a chunk of cheese and pineapple skewered together on a toothpick. "I suppose you know nearly everybody here."

"Just about." He pointed with a carrot stick to a bulky man in a dark polyester suit. "That's the high school principal over there. Most of the rest are teachers and former students. You can probably figure out which is which."

"Actually it's one of the students I'm looking for. I'd thought I'd like to meet Katie's old boyfriend."

"I saw Chip earlier out back, talking to Mr. Dunbar."

"Thanks, Hal. Catch you later." I dropped my used toothpick into a silver bowl that I hoped had been put there for that purpose and headed toward the living room.

A familiar figure appeared in the dining room door, then made a beeline for the stuffed ham. Dr. Chase, whom I had first seen at the crime scene, acknowledged me as I passed with a slight nod and a quizzical expression that indicated that he was trying to remember where he knew me from.

I wandered in what I hoped was a nonchalant and casual way toward the back of the house, passing from the living room through a comfortable family room that had apparently been converted from a screened porch. It was decorated in Early American style. A six-lamp chandelier like a stagecoach wheel cast a bit of modest light over furniture which looked to have been bought in a matched set, circa 1975, from the Ethan Allen showroom. Framed certificates and diplomas covered the paneled walls. I studied them curiously. Liz's high school diploma and her college degree from Brown hung on the wall over a table lamp, and occupying a place of honor in an elegant black frame was her Harvard Law School degree. Harvard! Even if Emily had wanted to, how could we afford to send her to Harvard Law or anyplace else if Paul lost his job? I crossed to the opposite wall, where framed and laminated magazine and newspaper articles followed the meteoric rise of Liz's career.

I was finding Liz's presence in this room overwhelming and beginning to wonder what role poor Katie had played in the family when I turned and saw it. On a polished table to the left of the door, someone had arranged dozens of photographs of Katie, lovingly displayed in a variety of frames, their corners draped with swatches of sheer black silk. There was Katie as an infant in a hospital nursery, squinting, one tiny fist jammed into her left cheek. Katie dressed for Halloween as Shirley Temple, an enormous pink ribbon fastened to a halo of golden curls, an oversize lollipop to her lips. Katie as a cheerleader, balancing in top position on the Wildcat pyramid, pom-poms aloft. Katie in a slim electric blue dress and Chip in a charcoal gray suit standing under an arch of haystalks and pumpkins, a picture that I figured must have been taken at the homecoming dance only hours before she disappeared.

I picked up an eight-by-ten of Katie at about four, her blue eyes at the same time both mischievous and direct as if challenging the camera, a ghost of a smile lighting her lips. An angel child. So like my Emily at that age.

Hal found me sitting on the sofa, the photograph pressed to my chest, tears pooling on my cheeks, where they were trapped against them by my sunglasses. "Hey.

Hey." He sat down and circled me with his arm. "I think I'm doomed to offer you napkins all day."

I accepted the napkin that dangled from his extended fingers, lifted my sunglasses, and dabbed at my eyes. I didn't start out to tell him about Emily. I seldom mention that sad chapter in our lives to anyone.

"It's just . . ." I turned the photograph in his direction. Sun glanced off the silver frame and flashed across the ceiling. "Katie looks—looked—so much like our daughter, Emily, at that age." I started to cloud up again. "When I think about how many times we nearly lost her . . ."

Before I knew it, I was telling Hal about the miserable weeks we spent worrying while Emily hitchhiked around the country following Phish, sleeping with God knows who and ingesting God knows what substances. "And just when we'd given up hope of ever seeing her again, she breezed back home, acting as if nothing had happened!"

"I followed the Dead around California once, eating incredibly bad food and sleeping in cars." He smiled as if recalling something amusing. "It really wasn't as dangerous as most parents imagined. Pretty harmless, actually. Fifty years ago she'd have been running away to join the circus."

I did a quick calculation. "But you were an adult then, not a headstrong fifteen-year-old without the good sense God gave a goose."

Hal gave my shoulders a squeeze, then draped his arm casually along the top of the sofa. There was something about the way he sat there, rock solid and steady, that made me want to confide in him. "We didn't ask for much, Hal. Passing grades, calling home if she was going to be late." I massaged my temple, where a dull throb signaled an oncoming headache. "Then she got mixed up with this boy who was into computer games and fantasy role playing, and suddenly her father and I had turned into ogres. How did she put it?" I mustered my best Valley Girl accent: "Like, you're squashing my creativity, Mother. You're interfering with my life concept just when my creative juices are at their most fertile!"

Hal threw back his head and roared with laughter. "I wish you could hear yourself!"

"I suppose it did have its funny moments, but I certainly didn't think so at the time." I set the photograph down on the coffee table, angling it so I could still see Katie's face.

Hal leaned forward, took the photo in his work-worn hands, and studied it in silence. I expected the silence. What was there to say after all? The usual BS: "I know how you feel" or the ultimate in New Age sympathy-speak, "I feel your pain."

Hal turned the frame facedown on the sofa cushion. "I imagine the grieving never stops. A parent never gets over the loss of a child."

I stared at him while dabbing at my nose with his napkin, surprised by his sensitivity. "No, you never do. That's why all this has hit me so hard. As if finding Katie's body obligates me somehow to find out who killed her."

"I suspect they'll discover it was an accident."

"I don't think so, Hal. Lieutenant Rutherford told Connie that Katie had been shot with some sort of small-caliber pistol."

Hal sat silently for a moment, then swiveled his body in my direction. "Sure you're all right?"

I blew my nose and crumpled the napkin in my fist. I offered it to him on an open palm. "I don't suppose you want this back?"

He chuckled, a rich, warm sound. "I don't think so." He stood and offered me his hand. I took it, surprised at the firmness of the grip and the roughness of the skin. He pulled me to my feet. "Better?"

I nodded and tucked the napkin into my sleeve. "Well, if I'm going to play at Jessica Fletcher, Ubiquitous Small-Town Snoop, I think I'd better start outside with the boyfriend."

Hal pushed aside the sliding glass door to the patio, motioned me through ahead of him, then followed me out onto a low wooden deck with three steps leading down to the lawn and to a garden just beyond. Near a wall where espaliered spring roses climbed, heavy with white, honey-scented blossoms, the pallbearers clustered. They drank beer from tall glasses and looked as if they would be much more comfortable had someone given them permission to loosen their ties, unbutton their shirt collars, and drink straight out of the can.

"Hey, fellas!"

The pallbearers turned their heads in our direction. Chip and his friends wore a variety of hairstyles but were uniform in age, height, and present facial expression, which was something akin to annoyance at being interrupted.

"I'd like you to meet Hannah Ives. You might remember her husband, Paul. He grew up on the farm between the old Nichols and Baxter places." Two of the former players rudely wandered away at this point, so I was introduced to someone named Spike, to Bill Taylor, whom I already knew from Ellie's store, and to David Wilson, a handsome man in a Leif Ericson sort of way, sporting the most distracting pair of stark white eyebrows. Hal left to fetch me another glass of wine from a bartender at a table set out under a wistaria arbor while the Wildcats and I stood around, awkwardly staring at one another.

I was trying to think of a clever way to break the ice when Chip stepped forward. "I wanted to thank you. I understand you found Katie's body." Of all the things I'd imagined he'd say, I certainly hadn't expected a thank-you. He set his beer glass, half full, on a small, round table that held a tray with six or seven empty ones. "You can't imagine how relieved I was to know what happened to her after all these years of wondering."

"I'm so sorry," I said, meeting his steady gaze.

"It was a long time ago," he said. "I'm married now, with three kids."

"I think I saw them today at St. Philip's."

"You did. They've gone on home to Baltimore with Sandra. I've been criticized for bringing them so young, but I don't pay much attention to narrow-minded people like that. Funerals are a part of life, a celebration of having lived. I don't believe we should shield our children from life, do you, Mrs. Ives?"

I didn't know what to say to such an earnest declaration, so I changed the subject, picking my words carefully, particularly since the wine was beginning to make significant inroads caused by my sending it down into a stomach empty of all but a large Kalamata olive and a few pitiful bits of fruit and cheese. "I was talking to Angie at her mother's the other day, and she told me that you and Katie used to date."

"That's true. We'd been going out since that summer. I used to stop by the Royal Farms, where she worked, for a cold Coke after practice. I'll tell you the truth, I was sweet on Katie. She was a fun kid, but she was interested in a more serious relationship. I started dating Katie when David here broke up with her." David, an inch or two taller than Chip, looked like an ex-marine with his hair worn in a short, closely cropped crew cut that a midshipman would have described as "high and tight."

David shifted his weight from one foot to the other, fists firmly stuffed into the pockets of his trousers. "Katie dated most of us at one time or another, but the only one she was serious about was Chip."

"Katie was an atheist," Chip said, as if that explained everything. Seeing my look of confusion, he added, "I accepted Jesus Christ as my personal Savior when I turned sixteen, Mrs. Ives. It never would have worked out with Katie and me." He ran long, slim fingers through his hair.

"Chip didn't have anything to do with her death. None of us did." Up until then Bill had been so quiet that I had almost forgotten about him. His mouth opened to elaborate, or so I thought, but nothing came out. I noticed he was looking over my left shoulder, a curious expression on his face. I turned and attempted to follow his gaze but could see only Connie and Dennis and Hal's broad back as he strode over to greet them, a wineglass in each hand. I wondered if it was the unexpected presence of a police officer that had made Bill clam up.

"No, I don't suppose you did." A door had slammed shut. I could see it in the rigid set of his jaw. I tried to come up with a graceful exit line. I glanced at my watch. "Well, I'd better go pay my respects to the Dunbars. Sorry to be meeting you all under such circumstances." As I walked away, I kicked myself for such stunning originality.

"Mrs. Ives?"

I halted in mid-stride and turned to see Chip leaving his friends, hurrying to catch up with me. David Wilson stared after Chip, his face set in a scowl, his eyes almost supernaturally blue in contrast with his white eyebrows. He gave me the creeps. It was a relief when Chip's handsome face blocked my view of David.

Chip hadn't changed much since that homecoming picture was taken. His broad brow, prominent nose, and high cheekbones were a photographer's dream, evidence of German blood somewhere in his family tree. I wanted to trust him but was wary. Emily's boyfriends had never been particularly trustworthy, despite their well-brushed hair and clean-scrubbed faces.

I smiled. "Yes, Chip?"

"I really mean what I said back there. The thank-you, that is."

"You're welcome," I said, although it seemed singularly inappropriate under the circumstances.

"I hope I didn't give you the wrong impression, is all. Katie and I were still going together the night she disappeared. But it was kind of an up-and-down thing with Katie and me. Three weeks before the dance she was barely speaking to me. When I called, Liz said she'd gone away for the weekend. To tell you the truth, I suspected she was seeing somebody else. A college guy, maybe."

I couldn't imagine any girl dumping a hunk like Chip. "So what happened to get you back together?"

"It's a mystery to me. The week before the dance she was all lovey-dovey again." He shrugged. "Women! Begging your pardon, ma'am, but today they'd probably chalk it all up to PMS."

When I finally rejoined the group surrounding Connie, puzzling over Katie's odd behavior in the months before her death, Hal handed me a fresh glass of wine.

Dennis raised his wineglass in my direction, as if offering a toast. "Hello, Hannah." His smile was dazzling, like a light turned on in a dark room. "Even though it's officially my day off, I've got to stick around here for an hour or two, check out the guests, but after that, Connie and Hal have cooked up a sail for us. Connie tells us you've had a rough week and could use a break."

I glared at Connie and didn't care if anyone noticed. "I don't really feel much like sailing, Dennis."

"What else is there to do? Sit around the house? Watch TV? Or"—he smiled at Connie—"I understand you've been helping Connie with her books." Dennis was being exasperatingly reasonable.

I looked down at my open-toed shoes. Before Memorial Day. Mother would have had a fit. "I'm not exactly dressed for sailing, either."

Connie looked at Dennis. "We'll have to go home and change first."

I was half listening, still wondering what was eating Bill and David and their close-mouthed Wildcat pals. "I think those guys know more about Chip and Katie than they're saying, don't you, Dennis?"

Dennis ignored this remark and turned his persuasive moss-green eyes on me. "Meet you at the marina around two?"

I couldn't think of a single good reason to refuse so, with the hope of coaxing more information out of him, I caved in. "Okay, around two."

Connie and I eventually found the Dunbars receiving condolences in the kitchen. I suspect Mrs. Dunbar had wandered in there to escape the crowd, only to become trapped in a corner next to the stove by a chain of sympathizers. When we finally worked our way to the front of the line, Mrs. Dunbar still wore the haunted look I had seen on her face at the Nichols farm, as if nobody were home behind the eyes.

"We thank you so much for coming." Mrs. Dunbar had said exactly the same thing to the last twelve people. Mr. Dunbar simply shook our hands and said nothing. I was relieved that they didn't recognize my name.

We had nearly escaped out the front door when Liz, appearing suddenly from the dining room, chirped, "Don't forget to sign the book!" She scooped up a guest book from where it lay on the table in the hallway and thrust it and a ballpoint pen into Connie's hands. Connie signed for both of us while I stood there tongue-tied, smiling stiffly at Katie's older sister. Liz was acting more like a funeral consultant than a grieving sister, I thought.

As we walked back to Connie's car, I noticed the 1990 championship Wildcats heading off together in the opposite direction, sauntering up High Street toward the high school. Maybe they were planning to shoot a few baskets. As I watched, a car sped by close to the shoulder, and to avoid it, one of the men was forced to step sideways out of the friendly huddle. Suddenly I could see they were not alone. Angie was in front, between Chip and David, almost running in her struggle to keep up with her long-legged companions. I saw Angie grab Chip by the arm, as if to attract his full attention. He shook loose from her grip and kept walking. She followed, clearly angry. I could see her mouth working overtime. Not basketball then. Something very different must be on their agenda, and I couldn't wait to get my hands on Angie and find out what.

IT WAS TWENTY MINUTES PAST TWO AND DENNIS'S Taurus was already parked in the shade next to the icehouse when Connie and I finally made it to the marina. It was my fault we were late. I spent ages looking for my jeans, the ones I had come close to ruining the day I discovered Katie's body, until I remembered they were still in the dryer. Connie had dressed in a bathing suit and had thrown on over it the white shorts and striped top that made her look disgustingly like a twenty-year-old model for a mail-order catalog. Me? I pulled a Dive BVI T-shirt over my jeans. I wasn't ready for swimsuits yet, even if the Chesapeake Bay had been warm enough for swimming in May, which since I was not a polar bear, in my opinion it wasn't. I had nightmares of diving overboard and resurfacing only to discover that the little latex foam pad I used for a breast had come bobbing up to the surface like a discarded shoulder pad.

Sea Song lay in slip number thirty-two at the end of a long wooden pier hinged every five feet or so and floating comfortably on sturdy pontoons. It undulated slightly as we walked, and with or without the wine I'd consumed, I reeled down it like a drunk. We found Dennis waiting in the cockpit, feet propped up on a small ice chest. He was dressed in a navy blue T-shirt tucked into khaki shorts and wore Dock-Siders with no socks. He removed his sunglasses and smiled at us, and I saw once more what Connie might have found so attractive about the man. One could easily be mesmerized by those Mel Gibson eyes! Dennis unlatched a section of the lifeline and helped me aboard while Connie fussed with something on the dock.

Hal's head popped out of the main hatch. "Hello, ladies." He pointed to the cooler. "The drinks are on ice, and I picked up a half dozen submarine sandwiches at Ellie's."

"Sounds good, Hal." I was starving. Despite the elegant catering, I had got hardly anything to eat at the Dunbars'. Hal moved aside in the companionway, so I could step below and stow my jacket. While I wolfed down half a chicken sandwich, I noticed someone had opened up the hatches so that a fresh breeze flowed through the boat, chasing out the musty, mildewed odor of its having been shut up for weeks.

I felt *Sea Song* tip slightly as Connie hopped aboard. "I see you've opened her up. Thanks, Hal."

"No problem." He pointed to his head, where a maroon cap with the Calvert Marina logo embroidered on it in white was mashed down over his wiry hair. "That's what you pay me for."

Connie laughed. "Enough of your BS, Hal! Just hand me the clipboard, will you?"

Although Connie's bookkeeping is a mess, her sea-faring life is governed by checklists. This is the part I hate: when she grabs that damned clipboard of hers with the laminated checklist and a black grease pencil tied to it with a string, looks around at the crew, makes some sort of quick assessment, and assigns everyone a job. I'd much rather be pulling on lines and cranking things, but Connie must have decided it'd be too strenuous in my convalescent condition, so she asked me to turn on the water cocks. "And don't forget that one there, Hannah. It's for the water supply that cools the engine."

I lifted the floorboards near the companionway ladder. "Really, Connie!" I complained, my knuckles scraping on the fiberglass as I reached into the bilge and twisted the various levers until they were parallel with their respective hoses. "I don't know why you bother. Craig never did. It's not like the boat is going to sink or anything if you don't turn them off each time you bring *Sea Song* in."

"Hoses can develop leaks, floors can be ruined, so humor me," she said, then handed me the handle for the bilge pump.

While I sat in the cockpit and worked my arm up and down as I listened to what little water there was in the bilge gurgle out a hole in the back of the boat,

Hal and Dennis removed the lines that secured the stern to the dock and the spring lines at each side that kept the boat from crashing into the pilings when the tide in the Chesapeake rose and fell. The lines attached to the bow were still firmly tied. At a signal from Connie, Dennis untied the two remaining lines and flung them to Hal on the dock, who, in a matter of seconds, draped them neatly over the pilings before leaping nimbly back aboard. Connie flipped a few switches, turned the key, and started the engine, shifting smoothly into reverse. She backed *Sea Song* neatly out of the slip, then pointed her toward the mouth of the Truxton River.

Hal took the opportunity to reach inside the cooler, root around in the frigid water, select and discard several brands of beer until he retrieved a Samuel Adams golden pilsner. He shook the water from his hand, then reached into his pocket for a bottle opener. He popped the cap, flipped it overboard, and took a long drink. "I sure appreciate this chance to get out on the water. My boat's out of commission. Hull delaminations."

Dennis's head swiveled in Hal's direction, and a look I couldn't read passed over his face. Whatever message he meant to convey was lost on Hal as he settled back against the seat cushions, picked absentmindedly at the label on the beer bottle with his thumbnail, and turned his full attention on me. "First noticed it after I got back from Puerto Rico."

Connie spun the steering wheel expertly to the left, straightened it, then eased the lever that controlled the accelerator slightly forward. *Sea Song*'s speedometer inched upward to three knots. "Hal practically lives on that boat, Hannah. You wouldn't believe the places he's sailed on her."

"Paul keeps promising to take me to the Virgin Islands." Tears pricked at the corners of my eyes as I thought about how easily lifelong dreams could be shattered. I turned my head away and looked out over the water.

We were motoring past the point of land where the business end of Calvert Marina lay: Hal's office, the ship's store, a gas dock, a couple of sheds. Connie pointed to a huge, tentlike structure with something like streetcar rails leading into it from the water. "*Pegasus* is in there. He's cut a hole in her to remove a large section of wet fiberglass. They're shining heat lamps on her and letting her dry out for a few days before beginning the real work."

"When do you think she'll be back in the water, Hal?" I asked.

"About a month. Certainly in time for the Memorial Day regatta. Maybe you'd like to crew for me?"

"Not if you've got your heart set on winning."

A smile exaggerated the creases in his suntanned cheeks, shaving years off his age. Something that I hoped was hunger fluttered in my stomach.

At the No. 2 flashing green buoy that marks the entrance into the bay from the Truxton River, Connie nosed *Sea Song* toward Holly Point. "Hoist the main!" she shouted.

Hal grabbed my hand and pulled me to the cabin top after him. We released the sail ties and raised the mainsail. He cranked the winch handle while I held the tail end of the line where it wound off the winch as the big sail rose slowly to the top of the mast. When the mainsail was fully raised, Hal took the line from me, wrapped it in a figure eight around a cleat, made a reverse loop, and pulled it tight. Connie adjusted the main sheet and pointed *Sea Song* into the bay. Meanwhile, Dennis cranked in the line that unfurled the jib sail.

The wind caught both sails with an audible snap that caused *Sea Song* to surge forward. Connie turned the wheel and squinted up toward the billowing mainsail, adjusting her course until the bits of colored string that were attached to the sail, called telltales, began streaming straight back. *Sea Song* cut through the water, a craft perfectly balanced between the natural forces of wind and sea. Smiling in satisfaction, Connie shut off the engine.

As I stepped back into the cockpit, I thought, *This is the part about sailing I like the best. When the only sound you hear is the wind, the snapping of the sails, and the clean sloosh of water as it curls up, foaming and hissing, along the sides of the hull.*

Several hundred yards off Holly Point, Connie tacked toward the Eastern Shore, trimmed the sails in tight, and *Sea Song* heeled to starboard. The cooler slid sideways in the cockpit, reminding me I was thirsty. I reached inside for a Coke. "Connie, Dennis, what's your pleasure?"

While I dug around in the icy water, Dennis drained

the remaining drops of beer from a bottle he had opened not five minutes before. I produced a can of Heineken and waved it in his direction; he eagerly made the trade. I watched him pop the top and made a quick calculation. Three glasses of wine at the reception, two beers already: It should turn out to be a relaxing day on the water for our friendly neighborhood policeman. Earlier he had stonewalled when I asked him, casually, about how it went in his interviews with the Wildcats. I decided to forget the direct approach and keep the beer coming in hopes it would loosen his tongue.

Before long Dennis went below, to use the bathroom, I thought, until I heard him call, "Hey, Con! Where'd you put Craig's old tackle box?"

"It's in the V berth, on the port side. The poles are on the shelf opposite."

In a few minutes two long fishing poles emerged from the main hatch, followed by Dennis's arm, then the rest of his lanky body. The trailing arm held a gray plastic toolbox, which he placed on the floor of the cockpit before returning to his seat next to me. Hal had already relieved Dennis of the fishing poles and had set them into rod holders attached to the chrome-plated stanchions on the stern.

Dennis lifted the tackle box to his lap and opened it, revealing a fascinating assortment of lures. I leaned over and selected an iridescent fish made out of a gooey plastic material that reminded me of the jelly shoes Emily made me buy for her when she was twelve, but it felt so creepy I put it right back. Plastic squids shared a compartment with wiggle jigs like big-eyed minnows in hula skirts, and in the next compartment lay something blue with flecks of gold still clipped to a cardboard card labeled "crippled crab." "Yuck," I said. In spite of all the decorative foliage, the one thing they all had in common was a nasty-looking hook hidden underneath somewhere.

"Craig used to enjoy making these." Dennis lifted out the top tray to reveal rolls of monofilament line, plastic boxes containing metal swivels, packages of wire leaders, feathers and bucktail "teasers," paint, brushes and nylon thread, and miscellaneous hooks and lead sinkers. He held up a particularly large fish-hook. "They call this a number nineteen Tony. There's some smaller sixteen, seventeen, and eighteens in here, too."

I watched while Dennis selected a bright red "eel" fashioned of surgical rubber tubing and a large silver "spoon." Looking not at all like an eating utensil, the spoon consisted of a six-inch fish-shaped piece of bright chrome with yellow tail feathers covering a wicked-looking hook. "Maybe we'll catch some blue-fish today. They say they're running." He attached a lure to the lines at the end of each pole, then swung the lures in turn out over the stern. I figured we could eat for weeks on any bluefish big enough to clamp its mouth around that spoon.

"Anything I can do to help?" Hal asked.

Dennis regarded him coolly. "Thanks. I think it's under control." Slowly he played out the fishing lines until the lures were trailing well behind the boat, held by lead sinkers at a depth of three or four feet under the surface of the water. At the leisurely speed we were sailing, they'd bob and weave, looking like tempting snacks to any hungry blues that might venture into the neighborhood.

"What do you do now?" I asked.

"We troll. We wait. And have another beer. How about it, Hannah?"

I handed him a fresh Heineken. *This was going to be easy.*

Dennis stretched his legs across the cockpit, leaned back against the seat cushions, and sipped his beer in contentment. Every once in a while in a quiet voice Connie would ask Hal, who was seated in the cockpit to her right, to make some adjustment to the sails. I had nearly mustered up enough nerve to ask Dennis a question about Chip when Connie inquired about Dennis's father-in-law's health. I listened to their conversation for a while, hoping to get a word in edgewise, but after a few minutes the topic shifted to his daughter Maggie's current state of mind. I was annoyed at Connie for making me feel like an intruder, but I didn't feel like horning in on their private tête-à-tête, so I excused myself and took a fresh Coke to the bow of the boat, where I lay down on the warm deck with my head resting against the bump of the forward hatch. I was nearly asleep, the sun full on my face, when everything went dark under my eyelids. I opened my eyes to find Hal sitting next to me. I was lying in his shadow.

"I thought you might like a sandwich." He passed me a sub, still wrapped in white paper with "veggie" penciled on the side in black grease pencil.

I elbowed my way into a sitting position. "Thanks, Hal. Looks good." We unwrapped our subs and ate in silence. I donated some limp lettuce and a surfeit of onions to the fish.

"I was wondering, Hal. How do you know those guys on the basketball team so well? Not that you look all that old"—I smiled at him—"but they must be at least fifteen years younger than you."

"Sorry, Hannah. I thought Connie might have told you. Before Dad became too frail to run the day-to-day business of the marina, I was the high school basketball coach."

"Really? For how long?"

"From the time I got out of the army until 1990. About ten years, I guess." Hal took a sip of his beer and looked over my shoulder toward the Eastern Shore, still a blueish smudge on the horizon. "That last year was the best. We won the state championship." He raised his bottle. "Here's to the 1990 Wildcats!"

"You must have hated to give it all up."

"Yes, but it was time to go. Move on. Quit while you're ahead, my papa always said."

That didn't make sense. A coach with a string of losing seasons might see the handwriting on the wall and hang up his Nikes, but with a championship season under his belt, Hal should have been able to name his price. Maybe there was a woman involved?

"Have you ever married?" I asked.

"Came close to it once. After Vietnam." He looked at me and beamed. "Other than that, never met anyone I particularly wanted to marry."

He stared at me so long with that charismatic grin on his face that I began to feel uncomfortable. His hand reached out, touched, and lingered briefly over mine before closing over my empty Coke can. "Want another drink?"

"No, thanks, Hal. Not just yet. But I'll bet Dennis does." Hal disappeared aft but returned almost immediately with another beer, before I, heart racing, had had time to fully recover from whatever it was that had just happened.

As Hal stretched out on the deck close beside me, I searched through my database for some discouraging words. "Paul and I were married just out of college, in '73."

"Lucky guy."

Maybe it was something in the way he said it or maybe it was the casual way he lay next to me, oozing testosterone and hops from every pore, that made me flash back to high school. I suddenly felt like the girl who prayed to God every night for a week that the sore spot on her nose wouldn't erupt into a full-blown zit before Ron Belanger had the chance to ask her to the prom.

I floundered on. "We've been quite happy, but I sometimes think I'm more than he bargained for."

Hal had been lying on his back but now turned on his side and propped himself on one elbow to look at me. "You seem perfect to me."

"Hardly. Hasn't Connie told you? I've recently had cancer. And a mastectomy. Under these clothes and this ridiculous wig, I look like an anorexic Yul Brynner."

His face turned serious. He turned on his back and rested the beer bottle, half full, on his chest. "My mother died of breast cancer, Hannah, when I was seven. But that was a long time ago. Medical science has come a long way since then."

"That's what I've been told, but I've read that the ancient Egyptians treated breast cancer about the same as we do today—slash and burn—although I will give medical science points for Taxol, tamoxifen, and Herceptin."

"You crack me up, Hannah!" He adjusted the bill of his cap to shade his eyes better and was silent for a moment. "You ever worry about dying?"

"Every day. That's why I find myself wanting to spend time with my family and friends, doing things I love. I want to make memories, Hal. Not only for me but for them. Maybe that's what immortality is all about."

"No one could forget you, Hannah. You could be anywhere in the world right now. Instead you've chosen to be here in Podunk, U.S.A."

I decided not to mention that my choice to come to this forgotten little corner of the world was triggered by the possibility that my husband had been unfaithful.

"I know I should be back home in Annapolis right now, but I can't get Katie Dunbar out of my mind."

"She was a likable kid." Hal turned his head and

stared off toward the horizon, where the water met the sky in a seamless wash of blue and gray.

"Did you know Katie well, Hal?"

When he didn't answer right away, I figured he hadn't heard me over the wind. Or maybe he'd nodded off. "Hal?" I poked him with my finger.

"Huh?"

"I was wondering if you knew Katie Dunbar?"

"Not really. Saw her around, is all."

"But you just said she was likable."

"Everybody liked Katie. Most popular girl in the high school."

"It's hard to imagine anybody wanting to murder a sweet girl like that." I recalled her sudden academic problems and fickle behavior. "Maybe she had a dark side that nobody knew about."

Hal struggled to his feet and poured his remaining beer, now warm, overboard. "I wouldn't know anything about that."

I stood up, too, suddenly thirsty for a Coke. "I wonder if Dennis has made any progress on the case?"

Hal grinned at me. "I'm here to report that the good lieutenant has finished off the Heineken and has started on the Bud Light. When last seen, he was rubbing sunblock number eight into your attractive sister-in-law's shoulders. I'd say there's no time like the present to ask."

Hal followed me along the leeward side of the boat, holding on to the lifelines that circled the deck like a double clothesline, then stepped into the cockpit. "Hi, you guys."

Connie raised a lazy arm. "Hi, yourselves. Have some chips." She had removed her shorts and top. Dressed in her bathing suit, she was sprawled on her stomach on one of the seat cushions. Dennis, looking a little looped, stood behind the wheel, piloting the boat. I wondered if it was such a good idea. All we'd need was for the coast guard to pick up a cop on a drunken boating charge.

Hal and I arranged ourselves on the cushion opposite Connie and munched on chips we took from an opened bag that had been rolled down and secured with a clothespin. Connie's work, no doubt.

No one was saying anything at the moment, so I leaped right in. "Dennis, when I talked with Chip at the funeral this morning, he seemed the farthest thing from a murderer than anyone I could imagine. I know you interviewed him. I figured if he were guilty, you would probably have arrested him by now."

For a moment I thought he wasn't going to say anything, but to my thanks, the beer had wrought magic on its journey from stomach to brain to tongue.

Dennis eyed the compass and adjusted his course slightly. "We brought him in yesterday for a couple of hours, and at first he recited, almost word for word, the same story he did in '90. I still think he might be hiding something, but I couldn't trip him up. He never denied leaving with Katie after the dance or tried to cover up the fact that witnesses had seen them in the car arguing. So I asked him what the argument was about, and he said it wasn't important. I told him I'd keep him there, in a cell if I had to, until he told me what they fought about. After about fifteen minutes he gave up. 'Over sex,' he says."

"So what else is new?" Hal chuckled and opened another Bud Light for each of them.

"My first thought," Dennis continued, one hand on the wheel, the other holding the fresh beer. "Then he claims that they drove to the parking lot behind Hamilton's Restaurant and that Katie put the moves on *him*. He goes with the flow for five minutes or so until it gets so hot and heavy that they're steaming up the windows and he pushes her off. Buttons up his shirt and tells her to put her dress back on, he's taking her home. She cries and wails that he must not really love her and he explains that *au contraire*, he loves her too much to violate her chastity. That if he slept with her, she wouldn't be the kind of girl he would want to marry."

Connie squinted at her watch and sat up. "That sounds so wacko it almost has to be true." She pulled on her shirt and took the wheel back from Dennis. "Time to head home, crew. Ready about!"

"Sounds like born-again logic to me!" I shouted above squealing winches and the noise of the sails swinging and flapping to the other side of the boat.

Once *Sea Song* was heading confidently back in a homeward direction, Dennis chose to sit next to Connie behind the wheel, where he calmly reeled in each fishing line. "I'm beginning to believe his story myself. Besides, we've turned up absolutely no physical evidence linking Chip Lambert to the crime. It's been a frustrating week." He handed the rods to Hal, who disappeared below with them. "Can't catch a damn fish, either." He leaned back and breathed in deeply. "But what a fabulous day! Someone gave me a mug that says, 'A bad day fishing is better than a good day at work,' and ain't it the truth!"

Just off Holly Point, with the wind blowing down the Truxton directly on *Sea Song*'s nose, we lowered the main, furled the jib, and cranked up the engine. Dennis talked a little more about his plans to reinterview Angie and the rest of the Wildcats before we sighted the marina and everyone became busy with predocking tasks.

Hal stood on the bow with a boat hook, ready to snag a dock line and hand it to me. Dennis stood aft, waiting to grab a line from a piling to act as a brake. Later I tried to reconstruct it all, to figure out how something so stupid could have happened. One minute I was standing there minding my own business, waiting for Hal to hand me a dock line, and the next I was tripping over an anchor line or a coiled-up dock line, something soft anyway, and flipping overboard, feet over ass. In retrospect, I suppose it would have been best to simply get wet, but natural instincts being what they are, I grabbed for the lifelines, connected, and nearly ripped my arm out of its socket. A pain that can only be described as searing, like a hot knife, spread across my chest as the muscles on my "good" side felt as if they were separating from my chest wall. I remember seeing Hal's hand shoot out a fraction of a second too late, and I recall hanging from the lifelines, screaming.

Four knots per hour might not seem all that fast until you're trying to scrabble up the side of a polished hull with the water licking greedily at the bottom of your shoes every time the boat slices into a wave. While I flailed ineffectually with my feet, Hal caught my hand and held on tight. I heard Connie shouting something to Dennis about the boat hook. Out of the corner of my eye, I saw Dennis drop the line he was holding and stagger forward. He snatched the metal pole that Hal had dropped and thrust it in my direction. After a few unsuccessful attempts I was able to grab on. Shouting contradictory instructions and swearing loudly at each other, the two men gradually pulled me aboard. I lay on the deck in pain, gasping like a beached fish.

I have no memory of the docking of the boat, but somehow she got into the slip, Connie's checklist was completed, and I ended up resting against Hal with a plastic bag of ice wrapped in a towel clamped under my left arm. I refused to cry but kept moaning and apologizing, "How can I have been so clumsy?" I looked up into the face of this man who had the knack of being around when I was at my very worst and felt a strong tug of affection that frightened the bejeezus out of me.

Yet I didn't push him away. Hal accompanied me on the ride home, sitting with me in the backseat of Connie's car, insisting all the while that I let them take me to the emergency room at Chesapeake County Hospital. I was equally adamant that they did not. I had no desire to call more attention to myself. Dennis, shocked sober by adrenaline, followed in his car. When I was comfortably settled on the couch in Connie's living room and they had extracted a promise from me that I would call the doctor if I didn't feel better in the morning, they left, but not before I heard them muttering together just out of earshot.

Around eight-thirty I wandered out to the kitchen to eat the cream of mushroom soup and peanut butter sandwich Connie made me for supper. Later, back on the couch with a heating pad under my arm and Connie comfortably nearby, reading the latest P. D. James in an overstuffed chair near the window, I dozed. I awakened just in time to catch the end of a dreadful made-for-television movie I had seen before and the beginning of the eleven o'clock news. I was about to flip over to the weather channel when the screen filled with a perfectly coiffed reporter standing in front of the honey yellow brick wall outside Gate Three at the Naval Academy. "Connie! Come here, quick!"

By the time she reached my side, the camera had shifted to the Administration Building. I was so involved in watching Paul leave the building with Murray Simon, his lawyer, that I didn't hear what the reporter was saying. As they walked down the sidewalk, the camera followed along, with Paul looking straight ahead, ignoring it and the idiot reporters. He wore his best blue suit and the yellow tie that Emily had given him for Christmas. It was the tie that almost broke my heart. *How could he do this to us?* Someone asked a question, and Paul waved them away, smiling stiffly. The camera then panned up the flagpole to the U.S. flag, flapping and snapping in the breeze. It reminded me of the sails. While Paul was going through this ordeal, I was lying on the deck of a sailboat with another man, joking and trading life histories. I felt so overwhelmed by sadness and guilt that the tears I had fought to suppress since the afternoon finally came.

Connie, bless her heart, must have been listening to the voice-over. "It's okay, Hannah. The academy isn't saying anything. The midshipman hasn't been identified. Channel Two must be hard up for news today, that's all."

I blew my nose. "I should have been there for Paul today, Connie. Guilty or innocent, I should have been there."

I RAIDED CONNIE'S MEDICINE CABINET THAT NIGHT—
slim pickings, I can tell you—rooting through leftover
vials of prescription medication that had been lying
around since the Nixon administration. My hopes
were raised when I discovered a brown plastic container labeled "Percocet" hidden behind a blue jar
that might once have held Noxzema, but with the ex-
ception of some telltale dust at the bottom, the Percocet container was empty. I fought the urge to dip
into it with a wet finger. I had to settle for a nearly
empty bottle of aspirin that had expired in 1995. Praying that vintage aspirin wouldn't kill me, I swallowed
three tablets with a swig of bottled water and two
hours later took three more, which turned down the
fire in my chest until 4:00 A.M., when the tablets ran
out. This allowed me to lie uncomfortably awake,

watching the numerals on the digital clock flip over one by one while I rehearsed what I was going to say when I telephoned Paul in the morning.

How is it, I wondered later, that a plan with such good intentions could go so terribly wrong? In the hour or so before dawn, I had carefully worked out my she-said-he-said scenario, but once on the telephone with my husband, the conversation galloped off in directions I hadn't anticipated.

—I said I was coming home.

—He said I wasn't.

—I said I was, too.

—He said he didn't want me there.

—I said I didn't care whether he wanted me there or not. As his wife I would be standing with him the next time the press showed up.

—He said there wouldn't be a next time. He was going away.

—I said well, thanks very much for telling me and why couldn't he come away to the farm?

—He said it was too close to Annapolis. They'd find him.

—I said well, where then?

—He said he didn't know where just yet, but away.

Things rapidly deteriorated after that. We didn't stoop to hurling insults at one another like "So's your old man!" or "Your mother swims after troopships!" but it was close. I hung up, deeply regretting that I had called and so pissed off that I forgot to tell him about falling overboard.

Connie, who had overheard the last part of this

heated discussion, silently handed me a glass of orange juice.

I sipped it gratefully. "Now he's mad at me. He said he doesn't want me to come home."

"So I gathered."

"I feel so useless, Connie. I want to help, but I don't know how. Everything I suggest, he shoots down."

"Paul knows how stubborn you can be, Hannah, and he wants to protect you. I'm sure he's doing what he thinks is best—for him as well as for you. I think you're just going to have to trust him on this."

I watched Connie crack three eggs into a bowl, using one hand, and tried to imagine what it would be like living under the constant scrutiny of the press. I would be looking for a job soon. I had classifieds to read. Letters to write. Phone calls to make. I decided that appearing on the nightly news wouldn't look good on my résumé. When Connie started beating the eggs furiously with a fork, I said, "I have to confess that it's a relief in a way that Paul doesn't think I'm needed at home. I don't picture myself as the type of woman who gazes adoringly at her man while he's being grilled on *60 Minutes* about his sex life. I guess I just wanted to be given the opportunity to try."

Connie poured the eggs into a cast-iron skillet that had been heating on the stove. "You sound like you don't believe him!"

"You want the truth? At this point I'm so tired and sore that I don't know what to believe."

Connie checked her spatula in mid-stir and turned her cool green eyes on me. "I've known Paul far longer than you have, Hannah, and if there's one thing I would stake my life on, it's his fidelity. He would never cheat on you. Never!"

During this conversation I had been sitting at the kitchen table, busily folding and refolding my napkin. Connie's attempt to pull rank on me stung. While she stirred the eggs, I sulked, trying to think of a good excuse to get out of the house. I didn't want to think about Paul today; the wound was too fresh. I wanted to go into town and talk with Angie about her argument with Chip. But Connie was in one of her bossy, mother hen moods, and she'd probably insist that I stay home and take it easy.

When I had coaxed the napkin into a shape like a duck, I propped it up against my plate. I decided to ignore my bad mood and try the direct approach. "Honestly, Connie, your medicine cabinet is pathetic! You have dried-up Dippity-Do dating back to the Flood, but no decent drugs. After breakfast I'm driving into town to pick up something a little stronger than aspirin. And Ellie will give me a cold beer to take it with and won't even mention that it's not yet lunchtime."

Connie popped some bread into the toaster. "I hate to burst your bubble, Hannah, my love, but Ellie doesn't sell beer."

"Pooh! Iced tea then. And I'd like to talk to Angie. Do you think she'll be there?"

"She almost always is. I doubt the poor creature has any place else to go," Connie said pleasantly. I couldn't believe she wasn't giving me grief about my plan. Maybe I was getting on her nerves, too.

After a plate of Connie's excellent scrambled eggs—not too wet, not too dry—I cranked up the car, told a droop-tailed, disappointed Colonel that he couldn't go with me, and headed into town.

Ellie's Country Store had just opened. Through the screen door I could see Bill Taylor moving a broom around, sweeping dust between the cracks of the old hardwood floor. A bell attached to the top of the door jangled when I entered. Bill looked up.

"Hi, Bill. What do you have in the way of painkillers? I pulled a muscle in my, uh, arm yesterday." I didn't feel much like discussing my medical history with him.

"Gee, Mrs. Ives. Sorry to hear that. How'd it happen?"

"Carelessness, I guess. I fell overboard."

He pointed to a shelf marked "Sundries." "Take a look over there. Heard you'd gone sailing after the funeral."

"Pretty dumb idea, huh?"

"Oh, I don't know. I would have preferred it to cleaning up after the reception." He pushed the broom forward another six inches or so. "Story of my life." He sighed and continued sweeping. "After the University of Maryland I worked for Hal a bit, back when he and his dad still built boats. Old Mr. Calvert taught me everything I know about woodworking." He paused and propped the broom against a nearby shelf. "But nobody builds boats like that anymore. It's all molded fiberglass now."

It seemed to me that a sizable teak tree had been sacrificed to construct the handsome cabin and provide the exterior trim on *Sea Song*, but I didn't mention it. "And after that?"

Bill straightened the canned soup display. "After that I worked as a computer programmer for the army down at Fort Belvoir in Virginia, but I quit about a year ago, so I could write full-time."

"Oh? What are you writing, Bill?"

"A novel."

"That's ambitious."

"I figured I wasn't getting any younger. I'm almost finished with the first draft."

"What's it about?"

"It's a suspense thriller. Like, John Grisham meets Stephen King."

"What happens? A lawyer goes berserk and starts eating his clients?"

Bill didn't laugh and looked so serious that I was almost sorry I teased him. "Oh, no! All this guy's family starts disappearing without a trace, so naturally the police are suspicious, and so he hires this lawyer to defend him. It's called *Vanished*."

How could I tell him that Fletcher Knebel had beaten him to that title twenty-some years ago? "Sounds promising," I lied. I didn't think *Vanished* would find its way onto my towering bedside pile of to-be-reads anytime soon.

"Thanks." He resumed sweeping.

I couldn't resist. "Danny DeVito in the lead and Harrison Ford as the lawyer."

"I wish," Bill mumbled.

I looked over the shelf he had indicated, where a

limited selection of pain relievers was flanked by laundry powders and dish soap on the one side and notebook paper and Magic Markers on the other. I ticked them off: "Bayer, Advil, Tylenol. What I really need, Bill, is some good drugs."

Behind me the sound of sweeping stopped abruptly. I turned to smile at him. "Just kidding. I think!"

I had selected a bottle of Motrin and pulled a bottle of iced tea out of the cooler to take it with when Ellie suddenly appeared from the direction of the kitchen. "Poor you! Hal was in earlier and told me about the accident. How are you feeling?"

"Not too bad. It walks. It talks. I think I'll live." I opened the bottle of Motrin—damn thing was sealed up like Fort Knox—pulled out the cotton wadding, and tipped two tablets into my palm. I swallowed them with the tea. "Ugh!"

"Excuse me for butting in, Hannah, but I think you should see a doctor."

"I'll be fine."

"Look, Dr. Chase's office opens in just ten minutes. It's only a few doors down. He probably won't charge you more than twenty-five dollars or so."

"It's not the money I'm worried about. I just don't want to waste his time." I rotated my shoulder to demonstrate how nearly cured I was, then winced and sucked air in through my teeth as a hot arrow of pain shot down my arm. Ellie gave me an I-told-you-so look.

"Your argument is persuasive." I pushed the tablets toward her on the counter and saluted with my half-empty drink bottle. "I'll just get these, then, and head on over to the good doctor's."

Ellie patted my hand and yelled toward the kitchen. "Angie! I need you out here!" She turned back to me. "Sorry. I've got the UPS guy coming in five minutes. Angie'll take care of you. Gotta run." She disappeared in back.

Almost immediately Angie appeared, wearing a chef's apron over a pink V-neck T-shirt and a faded denim skirt. Tennis socks the same hot pink as her shirt peeked out over the tops of her tennis shoes. "Oh, hi, Mrs. Ives." She raised a hinged section of the counter and squeezed through the narrow opening.

"Please call me Hannah. Between you and Bill here, this Mrs. Ives business is making me feel ancient."

"I'll try to remember that."

While Angie tapped the amount of my purchase into the cash register, I tried to figure out exactly what I was going to say. "Angie, could I talk to you for a minute? In private?"

She had bent over to search for a paper bag. Her head popped halfway up over the counter so I could see only small dark eyes and luxurious eyebrows with a deepening furrow in between. "I guess so. Why?"

"I just wanted to ask you a question." Angie straightened and was staring at me now. "A question about Katie."

She accepted my money, made a long job of counting out my change, then closed the cash drawer with a firm shove with the palm of her hand. From the body language, I expected her to clam up, tell me to mind my own business. Instead, she leaned back against her stool. "You know, after Katie disappeared, a lot of years went by before one day I stopped to realize that I had actually gone through a whole day without thinking about her even once. But now, now I just can't stop thinking about her!"

I was aware of Bill busily sweeping next to the nearby rack of candy bars, practically breathing down my neck. "I know that, Angie, and I'm really sorry." I waited until Bill moved around to the other side of the shelves before asking. "Can we go out on the porch?"

"I guess so. Mom!" Ellie's head appeared from behind the UPS counter. "I'm stepping outside with Hannah. Be back in a minute. Do you mind?"

Ellie, a piece of packing tape clamped firmly between her teeth, simply waved a limp hand.

I followed Angie's broad, swaying hips as she pulled open the screen door and passed through. I caught the door with my hand so that it didn't slam shut behind me. Angie pulled a paper towel from the pocket of her apron and used it to wipe the dust off a slatted wooden chair, then eased her ample bottom into it as the chair loudly complained. I sat on the end of a wooden bench and faced her.

"Angie, when we talked yesterday at the funeral, you claimed you barely knew Chip. But I saw you afterward, walking down High Street with him and the other basketball players."

"Oh, that. That wasn't anything. They were just going my way."

I knew that Angie and her mother lived behind the

store, the opposite direction from where Chip and the Wildcats had been headed, so I tried to remember what else was out on the road toward the high school. The fire station for sure. The Royal Farms store. But nothing had been on fire, and she'd certainly had plenty to eat and drink at the reception. The library then? Angie didn't seem the type to pass her days in the stacks. While I thought, Angie sat fidgeting with the paper towel, twisting it into a corkscrew and weaving the results around the fingers of her left hand. "Angie, I'm not going to beat around the bush here. When I saw you with Chip, it looked very much like you two were having an argument."

Angie shrugged and glanced away. "It wasn't an argument, Hannah."

"You could have fooled me. You were shouting so loudly I could hear your voice all the way from here." Angie stared at the bank across the street where a short queue was waiting to use the ATM. A teardrop materialized in the corner of her eye, and I suddenly felt sorry for her. I touched Angie's hand where it lay, restless on her knee. "Tell me what you and Chip were arguing about, Angie."

She pressed her full lips firmly together and shook her head, like a stubborn and unhappy child. Two big tears coursed down her pale cheeks. "Angie," I said. She turned her head to look at me then, her face a mask of misery.

"I promised Katie I wouldn't tell. Ever."

"But Katie's dead, Angie. Surely the secret can't matter now."

"It matters to me." Her body sagged. "At first I thought she'd just run away and that she'd come back. Even after all these years with no word, I thought she'd come back. I expected her to walk into the store with that funny, lopsided smile of hers and say, 'Hey, Ange. Guess who?' But now she's dead, and it's all Chip's fault." Her shoulders shook as she sobbed.

"But the police talked to Chip, Angie. Don't you think they'd have arrested him by now if they thought he had anything to do with Katie's death?"

"Maybe they would have if they knew what I know."

"Angie, if you have information that would help the police find out who murdered Katie, you shouldn't be keeping it to yourself."

Her face was red now, bloated and unattractive. Between her plump cheeks and swollen eyelids the tiny eyes she turned in my direction had nearly disappeared. "Even if it would hurt Katie?"

"There's nothing anybody can do anymore to hurt Katie."

Angie seemed to have reached a decision. She untwisted the paper towel and used it to wipe her eyes and blow her nose. "You're right, Hannah. I was mad at Chip. I was absolutely furious with him. You see, it's all his fault that Katie's dead."

"What do you mean?"

"A couple of nights before the prom Katie came over to my house all excited. She dragged me into my bedroom and shut the door. Then she told me that she was pregnant. It blew my mind! She said that Chip was the father!" Angie threw both her hands into the air. "How can he deny it, Hannah? Yesterday he looked me straight in the face and denied ever having sex with Katie." She leaned her head back against the chair and blew a slow stream of air out through her lips. "And I certainly know that wasn't true! Katie told me everything!"

"So she was having sex with Chip?"

"Like rabbits. In his car, in the locker room after school. He was crazy about her."

"But wouldn't she have used some sort of birth control?"

"Katie told me that Chip used a condom, but it broke."

I sat in silence, digesting this bit of news. I thought about what Chip had told Dennis. It made me wonder if Katie had made up the story about the baby. Somebody was lying, that was for sure.

"She wanted the baby, you know. You should have seen her at the dance, Hannah. Her feet were so far off the ground . . . she was so happy!" Angie pressed her hands together and giggled. "Katie told me in the rest room that she was sure that when she told Chip about the baby, he would be happy about it, too. She knew he would marry her. But then she disappeared and—"

"And you thought something had gone wrong with her plans?"

"I thought Chip had refused to marry her and that she'd decided to run away and have the baby on her own. Put it up for adoption, maybe. I thought she'd come back after that. I always thought she'd come back."

"And now? What do you think now, Angie?"

"I don't know! I think Chip's lying through his teeth! He claims he didn't have anything to do with any baby. He says Katie never said one word to him about being pregnant, and if she was pregnant, it certainly wasn't with his child!" Angie's balled-up fists pounded on the arms of her chair. "All that religion! All that 'Thou shalt not' crap. What a crock! So I hit him and kept hitting him until David Wilson made me stop. He grabbed my hands . . . oh, they all thought that was *so* funny. They just laughed and laughed. Jerks!"

"Angie, you need to tell Lieutenant Rutherford what you just told me." Angie's head drooped, and she whispered something into her lap. "Angie . . ."

She looked up at me sideways through dark lashes glistening with tears. "But then he'll know that I lied to him when he interviewed me the other day."

"If you don't tell, he's going to find out anyway."

She played with her ring, a star sapphire set in gold, twisting it around and around her finger with her thumb.

"Angie?"

"Okay. I'll call him."

I wasn't entirely convinced. It was like reasoning with a child. "Call him right now, Angie."

"I'll need to tell Mom first. Then I'll tell the police." She stood up and extended a hand. "I promise. And thanks, Hannah. You can't imagine what a relief it is to get this off my chest. You're so much easier to talk to than my mom. I'd give you a hug, but—" She nodded toward my injured arm.

"Oh, that!" I shrugged. "I'm heading over to Dr. Chase's in a few minutes. I'm sure he'll fix me up as good as new." The Motrin had kicked in and was taking the edge off, but I found myself very much looking forward to my visit with the doctor. I could kill two birds with one stone; maybe Dr. Chase could ease the discomfort in my body as well as in my mind. After my conversation with Angie, I had something very important I needed to ask him.

chapter

10

BECAUSE I WASN'T EXACTLY SURE WHERE I WAS GOING, Bill joined me on Ellie's front porch and pointed out the back of the old Chase house on Princess Anne Street. He told me that Frank Chase's office was on the ground floor of the house he had inherited from his parents, but that the doctor actually lived in a luxury condo catering to young professionals on Ferry Point Road, not far from Hal's marina.

"What's on the second floor then?" I asked.

"I haven't the foggiest. Files, I imagine. Boxes of paper gowns."

I thanked Bill, waved good-bye, and backed my trusty Toyota out onto High. At the light at Church Street I turned left. As I prepared to turn left again onto Princess Anne, preoccupied with the questions I planned to ask Dr. Chase, I had to slam on my brakes to avoid an old man who was proceeding through the middle of the intersection, hunched over a walker.

"Damn fool!" I shouted before it came to me. *I know that face.* Old Mr. Schneider.

Oblivious of the traffic that was screeching to a halt all around him, Dennis's father-in-law crept across the road, pushing the walker in front of him. An attendant shot out the back door of the nursing home and caught up with him. Mr. Schneider paused, glanced up, and studied my car as if wondering where he'd seen it before. I tooted my horn, and he lifted a shaky hand from his walker to wave, but he couldn't have had any idea who I was. He probably waved at everyone. The attendant pointed Mr. Schneider in the opposite direction, signaling an apology to me and the three other cars waiting at the intersection. I smiled, and waved back, thinking he looked familiar, too. He might have been the same guy I'd seen on the porch the day of Katie's funeral, but all the attendants looked the same to me in those ugly green uniforms.

Before Princess Anne dead-ends at the water next to Hamilton's Seafood Restaurant, it winds through a handsome residential neighborhood and is lined with trees whose leaves were already beginning to form a canopy that by midsummer would shade the street so completely that you'd need a flash to take a photograph there. As I pulled up to number 37, the fleet of cars parked in front of the office surprised me. Maybe I'd arrived in the middle of a flu epidemic. Not wanting to catch anything from some sneezing, sniveling child, I considered not going in, after all, but was reminded by the pain that shot up my arm when I set the parking brake that that might not be such a good idea.

"Come *on*, Julie Lynn!" I held the door open for a young woman in her twenties dragging a reluctant toddler by the arm. Julie Lynn's face was flushed, and she clutched a bright orange Elmo doll to her chest. Julie Lynn's mother swiped with the back of her hand at a strand of hair that curled damply down over an eyebrow. "Thanks. It's really packed today. We were here for two hours . . . but everything seems like hours when you've got a sick three-year-old on your hands."

Inside, in what must have been the former living room of the house, I saw she was right. The doctor's waiting room was full; at least all ten chairs were occupied. Several patients looked up as I entered, then returning to reading, knitting, or just sitting there listlessly, staring at the walls. In a corner near the reception desk a freckled blond-headed kid sat at a small table on one of two wooden chairs, an assortment of crayons and several coloring books spread out before him. Bits of discarded crayon wrapper littered the floor at his feet. As he colored, he experimented with a variety of humming noises combined with wetly buzzing his lips as if he'd just learned the trick and was trying to impress (or annoy) as many of us as possible. As I watched him work, I remembered, with a pang, that Emily had never liked to color within the lines, either.

The reception desk was waist-high and stretched the width of the room. No one was sitting behind it as

I approached, but a nameplate, Nora Wishart, was propped up on the polished Formica. I stood there for a few minutes listening to the phone ring and looking for a bell to push, waiting for Ms. Wishart to appear. "Hello?" I warbled hopefully.

A voice somewhere behind me said, "He'll be out in a minute. You'll just have to wait. Nora's not here, so things are a little backed up."

The advice came from a very pregnant young woman, sprawled uncomfortably in the molded plastic chair, her feet stretched straight out in front of her.

"I see." I lounged against the counter and watched in fascination as the blond kid colored Mickey Mouse green with an orange face. A red feather gradually took shape over the top of Mickey's head. "That's a nice hat," I said.

He scowled up at me as if I were the stupidest grown-up in three counties. "That's not a hat." Tongue protruding with the effort, he ground the red crayon up and down a few more times over Mickey's ears. "His hair's on fire."

I was imagining how the little monster would look with a violet blue Crayola shoved up his nose when Dr. Chase suddenly appeared, helping an elderly woman into her coat. "Don't forget now. One of the white pills and one of the blue pills with each meal. Here, I've written it down for you." He pressed a piece of paper into the woman's hand, watched with patience as she transferred the paper to her purse, then opened the front door for her. Dr. Chase stood there for a few minutes observing the woman's progress as she tottered down the sidewalk. When she had safely reached her car, he turned and addressed the pregnant woman. "I believe you're next, Mrs. Quigley.

Mrs. Quigley struggled to her feet, but before the doctor could get away, I thought I'd better let him know I was there. I crossed the room, grinding one of the brat's crayons into the carpet with my heel. "Dr. Chase, I'm Hannah Ives. I can see you're very busy, but I just wanted to know if you would be able to see me today. I fell off my sister-in law's boat—"

Dr. Chase ran a hand through hair that was thick and dark, except for a bald spot in the back the size of a pancake. "Of course, but I'll probably be another hour or so." He spoke to Mrs. Quigley. "Excuse me for a minute, will you?" The phone was ringing again, and he reached over the counter to answer it. With the receiver tucked between his ear and shoulder, he retrieved a clipboard with a blank form attached to it along with a ballpoint pen on a string. He made a scribbling motion with his fingers, then nodded in the direction of the waiting room. I gathered from this pantomime that I was to have a seat and fill out the darn thing.

I took the clipboard, mouthed a thank-you, and eased myself into the chair that had been well warmed by the mother-to-be.

Numbers! So many numbers. And boxes to check (both sides). Sometimes I could almost forget that I'd had cancer until something like this cropped up as a grim reminder. I hurriedly filled out the medical questionnaire and turned to more interesting matters, true facts that can only be gleaned by reading old issues of *People* and *Time*. I didn't know that Loretta Young had had a daughter out of wedlock with Clark Gable! Amazing! Doctor's offices can be such educational experiences, like standing in long checkout lines at the grocery, catching up with the tabloids. I was in the middle of an article about Fergie, Duchess of York, when the phone rang. Nobody picked up. It rang and rang and rang, insistent and shrill. I couldn't stand it. I crossed to the counter, reached out, snatched the receiver off the hook, and said, "Doctor's office." Someone wanted to cancel an appointment. I wrote the information down on a slip of paper torn off a prescription pad, then returned to my magazine.

The blond kid was eventually dragged away from his artwork by a father with nerves of steel and the patience of Job, and the room gradually emptied until it was just me and the old fellow sitting next to me. By now his chin had dropped to his chest, and he was snoring loudly.

Dr. Chase appeared and waved a man dressed in overalls, like a farmer, out the door. "Sir?" I jiggled the old guy's arm. "Sir. I believe you're next."

He awoke with a snort. "Hunh?" When he finally remembered where he was, he stood, patted both breast pockets of his tweed jacket and produced a brown plastic prescription vial. "Just need a refill." He thrust the empty container in the doctor's direction. "For this."

Dr. Chase smiled. "I am sorry you had to wait so long, Mr. Finch, particularly when it wasn't necessary. It says here on the label 'two refills.' Just take this bottle directly to the pharmacy next time. No need to wait here."

"Oh." Finch turned the bottle in his hands and stared at the label, looking forlorn. "Lucy would have known that."

"I'm sure she would have. I'll call the pharmacy for you, shall I? Then it'll be ready when you get there." Dr. Chase escorted Finch to the door with one arm encircling his shoulders. When the old man was safely away, Dr. Chase flipped a sign on the door from Open to Closed, pushed it shut, and leaned back against it with a sigh. "Whew! What a madhouse! My nurse is down with the flu, and my office manager was called out of town early yesterday on a family emergency. Phone's been ringing off the hook."

"Yes, I know. I took a call for you. A Mrs. Allen apologizes profusely and says she won't be able to keep her appointment at ten tomorrow." I handed him the scrap of paper along with the clipboard and the questionnaire I had filled out.

He studied the note first, then tucked it into the pocket of his lab coat. "Well, thank heaven for small favors." He scanned my questionnaire. "Oh, right. You're Paul Ives's wife." He appraised me over the top of his glasses, and I hoped he'd been too busy to watch the local news this week.

I shifted my weight uncomfortably from one foot to

the other and waited to be embarrassed, but he didn't say anything. Instead, his eyes moved rapidly down the page. I could tell by the raised eyebrow when he got to the mastectomy part.

"You've had a rough week, haven't you?" he said at last. "First finding the body. Now, what's this about falling off a boat?"

"Well, I didn't fall off . . . not exactly. I just sort of hung off. Pulled the muscles here." I touched my left side. "It's awfully painful." I rotated my shoulder.

"Can you raise your arm?" He demonstrated by extending his arms to his sides like a football referee calling off sides.

I held my arms out from my body at a ninety-degree angle. "That's as far as I can stretch without screaming."

Dr. Chase grinned. "If you can do that, I shouldn't worry. There's probably nothing that a day or two of taking it easy won't cure. Wait here just a minute."

He disappeared down the hall and through a swinging door. He appeared again a few minutes later with a handful of colorful packets. "Here are a few painkillers. Should be enough to get you through the next couple of days."

I cupped my hands as a few dozen packets cascaded into them. "Cute," I said.

"They're samples. Pharmaceutical companies inundate me with the stuff. Thought I'd save you a few bucks."

I crammed the tablets into my purse. "Thanks, Doctor. What do I owe you?"

"Not a thing. You answered the phone. Remember?"

I shrugged. "No problem. It was self-defense. Ringing phones make me crazy."

Dr. Chase began pulling down the window shades, preparing to close the office for the day. I didn't want to leave until I had asked him about Katie, but in spite of all the time I'd just spent sitting in his waiting room thinking, I still hadn't come up with a subtle way to phrase it.

"Connie tells me you inherited this practice from your father," I blathered.

"That's right." He flipped a switch on the wall, and the Muzak went quiet in the middle of an orchestral version of "My Way." "Dad and I began working together in the early nineties."

"When did your father pass away?"

"Almost three years ago. He just seemed to give up after Mom died. You know, some days it's hard for me to believe that they're both gone."

Dr. Chase continued turning out lights while I tried to think how I could ask my questions without betraying Angie's confidence. "Was the body I found— was Katie Dunbar ever a patient of your father's?"

Dr. Chase looked thoughtful. "Could have been, I guess. Almost everyone in town was at one time or another. I don't exactly know. I was still in medical school when she disappeared."

"I was just wondering if there might have been anything in Katie's medical file that could have shed some light on her death."

"I doubt it. But even if there were, it's probably long gone. I had my father's inactive files shredded last year."

"Shredded? Don't you have to keep medical files forever, or have them microfilmed, or something?"

"We're only required to keep inactive files for seven years, thank God, otherwise . . ." He gestured toward the back of the office. "Here, let me show you something."

Dr. Chase passed ahead of me through a swinging door that led into a dark hall. Within a few feet the hallway widened into a rectangular room that might originally have been an elegant dining room. Now, however, the room was filled with row upon row of lateral file cabinets, four drawers high and crammed with folders, enough, I thought, for every man, woman, and child in Chesapeake County, maybe even the state of Maryland.

Dr. Chase pointed to the desk, where a stack of charts teetered precariously in a standard wooden in box. Other files were fanned out over the desktop. "That's just the patients I've seen since yesterday." He tapped my questionnaire. "Don't know when I'll get your chart made up and filed if my office manager doesn't return soon. I'm still waiting to hear back from the temporary agency. The woman they sent yesterday was a disaster."

I had a brainstorm. "How much were you paying for the temp?"

"I beg your pardon?"

"Sorry. I suppose that sounded a bit nosy, but I didn't intend it to be. I'm in between jobs at the moment. I'd be happy to fill in, but just until Nora gets back."

"I couldn't ask you to do that."

"Don't think I'm volunteering to do it for free! Just pay me whatever you were paying the temp agency."

Dr. Chase stared at me, disbelief written all over his face.

"Don't worry," I added. "I'm experienced. Ask Connie. Until recently I managed a large office in Washington, D.C."

He brightened perceptibly. "That's not what was worrying me. How about your injury?"

"Will I have to lift heavy boxes?"

"No."

"How about three-hundred-pound patients?"

"Hardly!"

"So, just as long as I'm lifting nothing heavier than a file or a telephone, and I don't run out of these"—I patted my purse—"I should be all right."

"Can't deny that I need the help." He waved his arm in the general direction of the reception area. "I don't even know how to forward the darn phones to the answering service."

"I can do that, too."

Dr. Chase removed his lab coat and hung it on a nearby coat-tree. Looking vastly relieved, he pulled a linen sports jacket off a hanger and shrugged into it. "Then we have a deal. Tomorrow at seven-thirty? Your first assignment is to call the temp agency and tell them thanks but no thanks. And the phones?"

But I had lifted the receiver and was already punching buttons. "My pleasure."

We left the office together a few minutes later, the pain in my arm all but forgotten. Tomorrow, I thought, there'd be no need to bother the good doctor. I would help Dr. Chase with his overdue filing and look for Katie's file, if it still existed, myself.

CONNIE STOOD BEHIND HER WORKBENCH AND scowled at me. "You're out of your tree, Hannah! You're in no shape to go back to work. You should be resting."

I nibbled on an Oreo. "If the doctor thinks I'm okay, who am I to argue?"

"I think his need for a temporary receptionist is clouding his medical judgment." Connie agitated her paintbrush in a mason jar of turpentine, then wiped it on a rag she had tucked into the waistband of her jeans.

"It's only a few days, Connie," I said, polishing off the cookie and helping myself to another from a cellophane package that lay open on the counter. I thought I'd use the money to pay down my VISA, which was out of control. Paul worries that I treat my credit card limit like a goal. I'd been trying to watch my spending recently, but the way I felt about my husband just then, it would serve him right if I decided to indulge in a little retail therapy and max out all my credit cards.

I watched Connie paint a brown-gold streak on a gourd that was going to be a rooster and decided not to tell her what I had learned from Angie about Katie's pregnancy. At least not until I had discovered whether it was true or not. In her present mood I knew Connie would accuse me of meddling, and I didn't want her snitching to Dennis. Not just yet anyway.

We had tuna casserole for dinner, made just the way I like it with cream of mushroom soup and green pimento olives, followed by rum raisin Häagen Dazs eaten right out of the carton, with two spoons. Between decadent mouthfuls I tried to call Paul but kept getting the blasted answering machine. Hoping he'd be better about returning my call, I left Dr. Chase's office telephone number as well.

The next morning I wiggled stiffly into my little black dress. Connie appeared at breakfast in a more tolerant mood, so I was able to borrow a green blazer and a Monet "water lilies" scarf from her closet. "Take care of that scarf," she warned.

"Is it special?" I wondered if it had been a gift from Dennis, but Connie wasn't saying.

"Just take care of it, that's all."

Dr. Chase was already at the office when I pulled into the driveway and parked my Toyota next to his blue Crown Victoria. In the darkened reception area I could see he had left the shade raising and light turning on to me. That done, I stuck my head into the medical records room. "I'm here."

The doctor was bent over at the waist, flush-faced, elbow deep in a lateral file. "Thank goodness!" He straightened and poked at his glasses where they had slid halfway down his nose. He showed me where to hang my jacket and find the coffee, then gave me the twenty-five-cent tour of the office, ending up in the file room where we had started, in front of a large desk set into an alcove that used to be a fireplace. Over the mantel were mounted lighted panels where the doctor could read X rays. Farther along the wall stood a Xerox machine.

I ran my fingertips along a row of folders, each one distinguished by a set of multicolored tabs. "What do these colors mean?"

"We assign a color to each letter of the alphabet. Each medical chart gets marked with the colors representing the first three letters of the patient's last name. Makes them easier to file."

I must have appeared more competent than I felt because the doctor abandoned me almost at once with the appointment book and a suggestion that I pull the charts for today's patients.

Holy cow! Searching for Katie's chart was going to be easy. I consulted the appointment book and made a small production of pulling charts for an Abbott and a Morris before inching my way in the direction of the lateral files where I knew the *D*'s began: Danville,

Dickson, Donner. I thumbed past chart after chart until I arrived in the vicinity of the green, yellow, and orange tabs that told me I'd reached DUN territory. I found what I was looking for between Dubonnet and Duncan. Frieda and Carl had charts, and there was one for Elizabeth Marie. I looked inside. There appeared to have been no entries in the record since 1988, when Liz left for college. As I shoved the charts back into place, I puzzled over this; if the inactive files had been shredded as Dr. Chase had told me, why had Katie's file gone missing while Liz's was still there?

Dr. Chase's first appointment was not until eight o'clock, but already the waiting room had begun to fill up and three people had autographed the sign-in sheet. He asked me to stay near the reception desk unless he called for me, so I busied myself answering the phone and making appointments for equally packed days in the future. When the phone wasn't ringing off the hook, I filed patient charts away.

By nine I had booked the doctor solid for the next three weeks. Five people sat in the waiting room, and he had patients in both examining rooms. Eventually Dr. Chase took a bathroom break. I used the opportunity to revisit the Dunbar files, pawing meticulously through Katie's parents' charts, riffling through each page just to make sure her chart wasn't misfiled. No luck.

At eleven, two miracles occurred: Emeline Potter didn't show up for her vitamin B_{12} shot, and Scott Waldron broke his arm playing softball. At first I didn't see the potential of these two seemingly unrelated events because I was busy hustling the whimpering ten-year-old and his father into an examining room. As I helped the little guy onto the examining table, my heart ached for him. He sat on the end of the table, back rigid, legs dangling, bravely holding his injured arm to his chest and trying desperately not to cry, but the pain must have been terrible. Tears streaked his dirt-stained face, and his lower lip trembled.

I soaked a disposable cloth in warm water, wrung it out, and gently wiped Scott's cheeks clean while Dr. Chase bent over the boy. He carefully cut the child's uniform away from his damaged arm and examined the injury. Without looking at me, he said, "Hannah, grab that tray over there, will you, please?" I stood by as the doctor worked, nodding and listening to Scott's father natter on, wishing I could stuff the roll of gauze from the tray I held down the big windbag's throat.

"That was some home run, wasn't it Scotty?" He turned to me. "You should have seen the little bugger! Hit it clean over the fence." His son, tears still glistening on his pale eyelashes, managed a weak smile.

"How did he break the arm, Mr. Waldron?"

"Sliding into home, Mrs. Ives. Collided with the catcher right over home plate. Damn, the kid's good!" Scott squirmed in embarrassment.

Mr. Waldron had launched into a play-by-play description of the ninth incredible inning and Scotty's starring role therein when I thought I heard the phone at the reception desk ring. I looked at Dr. Chase for guidance. "Go ahead, Hannah. We can manage fine here. I'll need to take a few X rays anyway." I thrust

the tray into the hands of the startled father in mid
two-out-and-two-on-with-Boogie-at-the plate and hurried to answer the telephone.

A pharmaceutical salesman was spending time
stuck in traffic by checking in with his customers via
cell phone. I thanked him for his thoughtfulness, then
stared, unbelieving, at an empty waiting room. I'd already searched the file room and all the cabinets in
the reception area for Katie's chart; perhaps it was
time to check out the second floor. Bill had suggested
that Dr. Chase used the upstairs for storage. I knew
one way to find out.

With a furtive glance over my shoulder, I eased
through the swinging doors and into the entrance
hall. To my right, a single flight of stairs led straight
up to the second floor. Paneled in walnut, it stood in
dark contrast with the unrelieved off-white of the
first-floor suite. I stood with my hand on the banister,
squinting up at a door barely visible in the dim light.
I took the carpeted stairs two at a time and tried the
door. It was locked. *Damn!* On the off chance that it
might work, I pulled the front door key out of my
pocket and slipped it into the lock. It fitted easily but
wouldn't turn. *Double damn!*

I sat down on the top step to consider my options,
feeling a bit like Bluebeard's last wife. I knew the doctor kept the narcotics in a locked cabinet in his combination kitchen/laboratory, so what could be on the
other side of this door that was worth so much protection? I pushed on the door in frustration, then
studied the lock.

Back in college I used to be good at picking locks. I'm not as proud of that as I am of my degree in French, but I have to admit that it's a skill that has come in a lot handier than being able to recite the whole of *Las de l'Amer Repos*. At Oberlin, I'd used hairpins, but hairpins weren't something I had sitting around in the bottom of my purse these days. I hurried downstairs to my desk and rummaged through its drawers. Maybe I could use paper clips. I pawed through an assortment of items in the pencil tray until I located what I needed. Nora Wishart's metal nail file would also come in handy. I tucked it into my pocket.

Amazingly, the waiting room was still empty. If people came in while I was upstairs, I knew they'd just sign in, sit and wait, but what would I do about the phones?

Dr. Chase's phone was one of those old-fashioned beige models with a row of clear plastic buttons across the bottom labeled "01," "02," "03," and "04." A fifth button was red and labeled "hold." I picked up the receiver, got a dial tone on line one, and put the dial tone on hold. Then I punched down the remaining buttons and put them on hold, too. Until I returned, anybody calling Dr. Chase's office would get a busy signal.

Back in the hallway I stopped to listen; Mr. Waldron droned on and on. His voice behind the door of the examining room rose and fell, punctuated by laughter. I couldn't for the life of me figure out what was so funny, but as long as he kept it up, the coast would be clear.

I hurried up the stairs, bending one paper clip at a ninety-degree angle as I climbed. At the locked door I knelt and inserted the short end of the bent paper clip into the bottom of the lock and held it there while maintaining a steady sideways pressure. With the straightened end of the second paper clip, I jiggled the tumblers inside the lock up and down, gently coaxing them into position. After a few tense minutes I feared I had lost my touch. My mind wandered, plotting a late-night return engagement wearing gloves and dressed in black clothes when the tumblers fell suddenly into place and the lock turned. *Ta-dah!* I fell back against the wall, dizzy with relief. Using Nora's nail file, I eased the lock all the way around, heard a satisfying click, and slowly opened the door.

Before me a corridor ran the entire length of the house. An uncurtained window at the far end filtered pale light into the hallway. On my right was a large bedroom, dominated by a double bed with cannonball posts centered on a richly colored oriental carpet. A white chenille spread covered the mattress and plump pillows were propped up against the headboard. A hand sink stood in the corner, like a European B&B. What on earth did Dr. Chase need a bedroom up here for? I wandered down the hall to check out the bathroom and poked my nose into the medicine cabinet. If he'd entertained any ladies recently, I observed, they'd taken all their personal effects with them. I stood for a moment at the bathroom sink and stared at my face in the mirror. Why would he bring female guests here anyway? He was a bachelor, after all, and had his own apartment. Unless—unless it was a relationship he wanted to hide! Maybe the good doctor was in the habit of having extracurricular affairs. I pulled aside the lace curtain at the bathroom window and peered out toward the water. Frank Chase had been in medical school at the time of Katie's death, I remembered. Could he have been the college guy Chip suspected of souring his relationship with Katie?

From downstairs came a piercing wail. Dr. Chase must have reset the bone. He'd be putting a cast on Scott's arm any minute now. I crossed the hallway above them on tiptoe, hoping the floors wouldn't creak and give me away.

The room at the front of the house was uncarpeted, its hardwood floors spotless. A long wooden table ran the length of the far wall, and bookshelves framed both windows. Clean jars with ground glass stoppers were grouped together on the shelves, their labels missing or peeling. I picked one up and examined it closely. If anything had ever been written on the label, it had long ago faded into illegibility. Everything in the room was neatly arranged and impeccably clean, like a museum. I wondered if this had been old Dr. Chase's laboratory, where he prepared his herbal and homeopathic cures. But whatever it was, there was no place to store even so small a thing as a medical folder in this austere environment.

The back bedroom also promised to be a major

disappointment. Oversize warehouse-style shelves of tubular steel held boxes of paper towels, toilet paper, disinfectant soap, plastic garbage bags, and, as Bill had predicted, paper robes, all purchased in bulk sizes like the kind I brought home from Sam's Club. Smaller boxes and cartons contained medical supplies. Near the window that overlooked the parking lot, four plastic chairs in the same style as those in the waiting room below were stacked, seat on seat.

I had turned to leave when I thought I'd hit the mother lode. After all those years in Washington, D.C., if there's one thing I know, it's archival boxes. And there they were, box after cardboard box of them, labeled "A-B" and "C-D" et glorious cetera, neatly piled in an alcove. I prayed these were the old doctor's files. Maybe they hadn't been shredded after all but were just on their way to the shredder. I lifted the lid from the box nearest me. It was empty. So was the box next to it. I pulled the lids of nearly a dozen boxes, but every damn one of them was empty.

My heart sank. Until that moment I'd never really understood that expression. But my heart sank, right down to the floor, and lay there. I chided myself for spinning my wheels on what was turning out to be a wild-goose chase. Yet I had discovered many theoretically inactive folders, like Liz's, among the files downstairs. Futile or not, I knew I wouldn't be satisfied until I had searched every last inch of Dr. Chase's office, and maybe his condominium, too.

As I stood in the alcove, woolgathering, I was startled by the thunk of a car door closing. I rushed to the window just in time to see Mr. Waldron get into his car. Scott was already installed in the passenger seat, a clean white cast on his arm, cradled in a blue sling. *Holy shit!* I needed to get back downstairs, pronto!

But then I heard the footsteps behind me and knew it was too late.

"Hannah? What are you doing up here?"

I pasted a smile on my face and turned. "I noticed we were low on paper towels, Doctor. I couldn't find any downstairs, so I thought I'd take a look up here."

Chase's eyes were wary slits. "I'm surprised you could get in. I usually keep the door locked."

I shrugged. "I just turned the knob." That wasn't a lie, not exactly.

I crossed the room to a shelf and selected a four-pack of toilet paper and several rolls of paper towels. "Here, could you help me?" I handed a roll of towels to the doctor. He opened his mouth as if to object but apparently changed his mind. His lips clamped shut, and he sucked them in between his teeth, giving him an odd, lipless look. I prayed he didn't suspect me of snooping. My spur-of-the-moment explanation had been brilliantly plausible, after all, but I noticed as I preceded him down the steps that he locked the door securely behind him.

As we reached the entrance hall, an elderly woman was just hobbling up the walk, saving me the trouble of making idle conversation with the doctor when my mind was racing off in all directions. Dr. Chase greeted the woman like a long-lost relative, then escorted her back to his private office.

I put the spare toilet paper in the bathroom, then dumped the paper towels on the counter in the kitchen, where I stood for a few moments at the sink and tried to control my shaking hands. I splashed some cold water on my face, dried it with a paper towel from a roll that was, I noticed, nearly new, then hurried to take the telephone lines off hold. But before I went back to work, I returned to the kitchen and spun yards of paper towel off the roll and stuffed them in the bottom of the wastepaper can, underneath the soiled paper robes.

Two patients arrived at noon, but by one o'clock there was a brief hiatus, and Dr. Chase suggested he could handle things on his own while I picked up sandwiches. I called Ellie's Country Store and ordered a chicken salad for me and a tuna on rye for the doctor.

After my narrow escape I welcomed the lunch break and took my time getting to Ellie's by walking around the block the long way, turning left down Princess Anne and left again at the old library. I strolled along Ferry Point Road and paused at the old pier across from the Tidewater Pub. I watched the khaki-colored water of the Truxton gently lick the pilings and tried to think of a way to get Dr. Chase out of his private office long enough to search it, too. So far, he'd kept me so busy I'd hardly had time to go to the bathroom, let alone give the place a thorough going-over. That business this morning was just a fluke; I couldn't count on another broken arm materializing out of the blue. Didn't the man have rounds to make at the local hospital? Medical meetings to attend? By the time I reached Ellie's store, I was wishing emergency appendectomies on total strangers and pining for the good old days when doctors made house calls.

Angie already had the order made up and ready for me at the counter. "I put in two iced teas. Hope you don't mind. That's what the doctor always orders." She looked cheerful and well rested and smiled at me in a conspiratorial way because, I supposed, we shared a secret. She must have read my mind. "You won't tell anybody about Katie's baby, will you, Hannah?" she whispered.

"No," I promised again. "No one will find out about it from me."

"I went to see Lieutenant Rutherford, just like you told me to."

"I'm glad to hear that, Angie."

"He was really nice. Brought me a Coke. Thanked me for coming in."

"He's only interested in the truth." I added two Milky Way Darks to the bag feeling just a wee bit guilty about it, paying for it all, including my sweet tooth, out of money the doctor had given me from the petty cash.

"Did Lieutenant Rutherford say anything to you about reopening the case?"

Angie dropped the change into my outstretched hand and shook her head. "Not to me. But they'll have to now, won't they? Now that they know Katie was murdered?"

I said good-bye and left her busily wiping the countertop with a damp rag. On Ellie's front porch, I fished one of the Milky Ways out of the bag, tore off the wrapper, and took what I reasoned was a well-deserved bite. I chewed thoughtfully and watched while an armored truck made a pickup at the bank across the street. Next door S&N Antiques was just opening for business; its door stood open, and the proprietor had dragged a Victorian high chair, a wagon, and two end tables onto the porch. I sucked the caramel off my teeth and studied the back of the Chase house. A huge magnolia tree dominated the backyard, shading what remained of the old doctor's garden. I remembered what Connie had told me about it and decided to cut through the parking lot and take a closer look.

The garden was a tangle of overgrown shrubs, wayward vines, desultory weeds, and dried, drooping stalks still tied to redwood stakes, but I could tell that the plot had once been extensive and well planned. My experience with herb gardens was limited to what I had read in the Brother Cadfael mystery series. The good twelfth-century monk grew things in his garden at St. Giles with interesting-sounding names like betony, coltsfoot, hyssop, and dock that were used to treat wounds, skin irritations, and stomach ailments. Except for unruly clumps of dill, mustard, fennel, and mint, however, and a scrawny lemon thyme bush, there wasn't much in Dr. Chase's garden that I recognized.

I stripped some thyme from a spindly stalk and rolled the leaves between my fingers until the sweet, sharp aroma reached my nose. It would have taken days of major-league weeding, hoeing, and pruning to get that garden looking even halfway presentable. A breeze rippled through a clump of pampas grass, suddenly reminding me of the weeds growing wild about the cistern where I had found poor Katie's body. Where had she spent the last hours of her young life, I wondered, and, more important, with whom?

I shuddered and reminded myself that the answer might very well lie somewhere inside this house. Using my key, I let myself in through the back door.

When I returned to reception, only one patient remained in the waiting room, an overlarge woman in a loose cotton dress whose broad bottom encroached on the nearby chairs. "Have you signed in?" I asked. She nodded. I pushed through the swinging doors into the medical records room and stood there for a few seconds wondering what to do with lunch when Dr. Chase emerged from Examining Room A. He stripped off his latex gloves with a snap like a rubber band and tossed them into an oversize trash can next to the door.

I cradled the bag in my hand. "If I don't do something with this soon, Doctor, the bag's going to break." I showed him where the condensation from the iced tea bottles was beginning to soak through the bottom of the paper bag. I nodded toward his private office down the hall. "Should I take it in there?"

"Oh, thanks, Hannah." He nodded. "Just put it on my desk, will you?" He lifted the chart I had placed in the wall pocket outside Examining Room B, consulted it briefly, then tucked it under his arm. "And put Mrs. Logan in A. As soon as I finish with her, I'll be able to take a break for lunch."

Dr. Chase disappeared into the examining room and shut the door.

Patting myself on the back for how neatly I'd just engineered an excuse to spend a little legitimate time in Dr. Chase's office, I hurried in. It wasn't any neater than the first time I had seen it yesterday. Bookcases, full to overflowing with books, medical journals, framed photographs, and carved duck decoys covered the chocolate brown walls. A large wooden desk stood in the center of the room, the two legs nearest me planted firmly on the fringe of an antique oriental carpet.

I set the bag down on the desk, first clearing a space by shoving a few charts aside. I withdrew the plastic-wrapped plate holding his tuna on rye and one of the bottles of iced tea. Out of habit, I set the damp bottle down on a folded napkin to keep it from ringing the desk, although a new blemish would hardly have been noticed among the many others that marred the once highly polished walnut. Intersecting circles decorated the surface, like those on the Olympic flag. A nice ring was forming now around the perimeter of a coffee mug, half full of a viscous brown liquid that even a good nuking in the microwave couldn't have made drinkable. I picked up the mug and used another napkin to wipe up the spill and, to be thorough, followed the liquid trail to where it disappeared under a corner of the desk blotter.

I was straightening the blotter when I realized that there was something stuck underneath it. Since I had recently spent long minutes nosing around in the good doctor's records without a second thought, it surprised me that I now felt like a cat burglar. I glanced over my shoulder toward the door, lifted the corner of the blotter, stooped, cocked my head, and peered under it. Green, yellow, and orange tabs. *Ohmagawd!* I had my finger on the chart and was just beginning to slide it toward me when I heard Dr. Chase's voice behind me in the hall.

By the time the doctor appeared in his office doorway, I had dropped the corner of the blotter, twisted the cap off a bottle of iced tea, and was busily stripping the paper wrapper from a straw. My heart was pounding so loudly in my ears that I thought he'd hear it from where he stood—without a stethoscope.

"Lunch is served." I popped the straw into the bottle and tapped it down where it sat for a moment as if thinking about something, then floated up lazily. "Would Monsieur like the see the dessert menu?"

Dr. Chase chuckled and rubbed his hands together briskly. "Tira misu? Crême brulée?"

I pulled the remaining Milky Way out of the bag. "Will this do?"

He settled comfortably into his desk chair. "Thanks, Hannah, but I'm afraid I don't eat chocolate."

"Doctor, I am shocked. Deeply shocked." I pocketed the candy. "All the more for the rest of us, as my mother used to say." With a show of nonchalance that

I didn't feel, I backed toward the door, certain that the letters G-U-I-L-T must be emblazoned across my forehead. I couldn't keep my eyes off the blotter. As I waited for it to rise up, point, and accuse me of snooping, I noticed that Dr. Chase probably hadn't been in his office all morning. The Post-It messages I had taken for him were stuck all over his telephone and lampshade. He picked up one of the messages now, took a bite of his sandwich, and began to dial.

"Anything else you need?" I asked.

"No, thanks, Hannah. Eat your lunch, but stay by the phone. After lunch you'll probably have time to pull charts for the afternoon."

I negotiated the hallway in a daze, then sat down at the reception desk. I unwrapped my sandwich and stared at it, but my stomach was tied in such nervous knots that I didn't feel very hungry. *Please don't move that chart! Not until after I've had a chance to check it out.*

I drank some tea and found myself wondering why Katie's chart had been hidden. Maybe it had been in the file room all along and Dr. Chase hadn't given it a thought until I mentioned it yesterday. Maybe he'd found it in the files and put it under his blotter for safekeeping so it wouldn't get lost in all the clutter. But then again, maybe he was involved in Katie's murder right up to his scrawny little neck. I nibbled my sandwich in silence, watching as the buttons on the telephone blinked on and off as the doctor returned his calls.

Maybe it isn't Katie's chart at all. Lots of names start with DUN, I reasoned. Duncan, for example, or Dunnet or Dunstable. Angie had put an extra pickle on my plate, and I ate it slowly. I'd have to make my opportunity. I checked the appointment book. Beginning at two o'clock, there were six appointments plus two folks who had called in: eight patients in all. I polished off the last potato chip, washed the salt off my hands at the kitchen sink, and pulled the charts. Eight patients would certainly be sufficient to keep the doctor busy long enough for me to get back into his office and take a second look under his blotter.

As I stood behind the reception desk, lost in thought, the intercom on the telephone buzzed so loudly that I nearly jumped out of my pantyhose. "Hannah," Dr. Chase said when I picked up, "if you're finished with lunch, I've got a few prescriptions for you to call in."

I tossed the remains of my lunch in the trash and hurried back to his office. As I reached for the prescriptions, I noticed that the blotter had been moved a few inches closer to the lamp. *Blast!* I flashed what I hoped was a disarming smile, told him I'd take care of the prescriptions right away, and turned to go.

"Hannah?"

Oh-oh. I held my breath.

"How are you feeling? I've been so busy I forgot to ask."

I had to think for a minute before I realized what on earth he was talking about. I'd nearly forgotten about my tumble off the sailboat. "Much better, thanks. The medication really helped."

The doctor balled up his sandwich wrapper and, with a flip of his wrist, made a perfect rim shot to the trash can. "Good. Just make sure you don't overdo it, okay?"

I promised I wouldn't, all the time thinking, *Fat chance!* I called prescriptions in to the local Giant and Safeway pharmacies and waited, with butterflies in my stomach, for the waiting room to fill up. At two-thirty I got a break. With a Pap smear in A and an EKG in B, I calculated that Dr. Chase would be busy for a while.

I felt guilty about hustling the poor woman in A into a paper gown and assisting her up onto the examining table without so much as a magazine to pass the time. How many countless hours had I spent lying about on upholstered tables covered with paper, feeling forgotten, with the air-conditioning whistling through gaps between the ties in my robe, freezing my back, boobs, or buns? How many doctors had kept me waiting with nothing to do but count the holes in the acoustical ceiling tiles? So I used up precious minutes making sure she had everything she needed.

"Comfy?" I asked.

She held the inadequate gown together at her chest with a heavily ringed hand. "You've got to be kidding."

"I am," I said, and handed her a copy of the *New Yorker* magazine that was, amazingly, only two weeks old. She looked like the *New Yorker* type.

"Do me a favor," she said.

I raised my eyebrows.

"Ask him to warm up the speculum."

I laughed and patted her chubby knee. "Will do!"

I closed the door behind me and tiptoed down the hall feeling like the thief I was about to become. Just outside the door of Examining Room B I paused. Inside, I could hear the doctor's low voice speaking in soothing tones to a patient who was a nervous mountain of a man in his late seventies. As cover—I figured I needed it—I grabbed two charts from the pile waiting to be filed and scurried back to Dr. Chase's inner sanctum, trying to appear as if I knew what I was doing. Even so, when I finally stood in his office doorway, my face burned and I found myself acutely aware of everything in the room. The framed diploma hanging crookedly on the wall next to the window, the faded floral drapes parted to reveal the untidy garden with the Crestar Bank sign in the near distance behind it, a VCR blinking red at 12:00, even the damned decoys all seemed to have eyes and were staring at me.

I crossed to the desk, held my breath, and raised a corner of the blotter. The chart was still there. I pulled it out, hardly daring to believe what I read on the label: Dunbar, Katherine Louise.

I stood there wasting valuable time, my heart thudding in my ears, flipping through the pages, trying to interpret old Dr. Chase's scrawls, symbols, and abbreviations. I don't know what I expected, notes in a neat, round hand maybe like "This girl's pregnant" or "The rabbit died," so I was disappointed when at first I couldn't make heads or tails out of anything I saw. Katie's chart might just as well have been written in code. I found a date: 10/2/90. That was a good sign.

BP125/70 must have been her blood pressure and I certainly knew what Pap and menses were, but the meaning of the rest of it, including a funny little diagram with lines and numbers, completely escaped me. I had the feeling that even if I had worked for Dr. Chase's father for a hundred years, I'd still have needed an interpreter to decipher those Martian runes. It wasn't until I turned to the next page that I saw it: "A/P:① 8 wk pregnancy." I didn't need a translator for that!

It had been my intention to slip a few pages out of the chart and photocopy them, but I forgot about the fasteners. Katie's chart consisted of approximately twenty pages held together by a metal bar that passed through two holes that had been punched through the top of each sheet with the ends folded over and secured with another thin strip of metal. *Nuts!* I'd have to borrow the whole chart. I stuck Katie's chart among those still in my hand. Clutching the booty to my chest, I ventured out into the hallway and was halfway to the photocopier when the door to Examining Room B opened and Dr. Chase emerged with the old gentleman, who looked so fat and flushed that I expected him to stroke out at any minute. I stood in the hallway grinning stupidly as the two men passed and the doctor began what I now recognized as his customary farewell ritual. I knew he'd spend time standing at the front door waving the old guy down the sidewalk, so I made a mad dash for the photocopier.

The machine was ominously quiet.

Damn and double damn! Dr. Chase must have

turned the photocopier off while I was fetching lunch. Now I would have an infuriating wait while the blasted thing warmed up. I folded a few pages back and slammed Katie's chart against the glass. I mashed the photocopier cover over the chart and held it down while I waited for the ready light to come on. *Shit!* I heard a familiar thud as the front door closed, followed by the sound of Dr. Chase's footsteps returning down the hall. Through the glass panels of the swinging doors I could see the approaching expanse of his white lab coat and flashes of light reflecting off his little, round glasses.

At that moment the copier's ready light blinked on. I punched the green copy button, deathly afraid that he'd figure out what I was doing. A brilliant bar of light swept over the page from right to left and back again. A single copy dropped into the paper tray. I could see Dr. Chase's arm extended toward the door, pushing it open ahead of him.

I snatched the chart from the photocopier and held it behind my back like a naughty child, but Dr. Chase entered the room and passed me with merely a nod before vanishing into Examining Room A. I flipped to the next page of Katie's chart, slapped the chart down on the photocopier and had another go with the print button. Just as the copy emerged into the tray, I heard him call, "Hannah, I'll need you to assist."

Damn! I'd forgotten a doctor couldn't be alone with a female patient during a gynecological exam. I stalled for time. "She says she'd like you to warm up the speculum, Doctor." I folded the photocopies I had made into quarters and stuffed them into the pocket of Connie's blazer.

"I always do."

Although Dr. Chase was in the examining room, the door stood wide open. I couldn't get back to his office without his seeing me. What would I do with Katie's chart? I shoved it into the nearest file cabinet. I would sneak it back under his blotter later.

But I never got the chance. Dr. Chase kept me busy the rest of the day. Even after the last patient left at four-thirty, he remained in his office. I was determined not to leave until I had replaced the chart, so I dawdled at the reception desk, straightening up a desk that was already impossibly neat. I washed dirty coffee mugs. I cleaned the coffeepot. I watered the potted plants. I telephoned folks to remind them of tomorrow's appointments, mostly talking to answering machines.

The next time the telephone warbled, it was for me.

"Hi, hon."

"Paul!"

"Just got off the horn with Connie. Glad to be back on the employment rolls?"

"If you called me more often, you wouldn't have to ask." There was a long silence, and I could hear the antique clock in our entrance hall strike five.

Paul cleared his throat. "I just turned in my final grades and wanted to let you know that I'm off. For a few weeks at least."

"Where to, may I ask?"

"Cape Cod. Do you remember Steve Zelko? He's renting a summer house in North Truro."

"The strange little English prof with the black glasses and the fifties crew cut?"

Paul laughed. He sounded like the old Paul, warm and comforting. "You remember! Look, honey, I just wanted you to know that I'd really like you to join us up there. It's a big house, and Steve's offered us a room of our own overlooking the water. With adjoining bath. I'll drive down to Pearson's Corner and pick you up."

"Sorry, Paul, but I promised Dr. Chase I'd see this through." I couldn't bring myself to admit to my husband that I'd been snooping around my employer's office like an amateur sleuth in a bad paperback novel. He'd think the chemo had gone to my brain.

"Sounds like just an excuse to me. Connie tells me you've gotten yourself all wrapped up in that cheerleader's murder."

"Your sister should stick to her painting," I said. In the moment before I spoke again, I imagined I heard our clock ticking. "Look, Paul. Let me think about it. I'll call you when I'm free."

Paul must have expected excuses because he already had the flight schedules handy. "You can fly from BWI to Logan and take the shuttle to Provincetown. Just call me and I'll meet you at the airport."

"I said I'd think about it, Paul!"

I had pushed him too far. When he spoke again, his voice bristled with anger. "What's so fascinating about this dead girl anyway? You didn't even know her, for Christ's sake!"

"It's hard to explain. I feel like I owe it to her, having found her body and all. In some convoluted way I'm thinking that if I can figure out who murdered Katie, it will make up for all the times I failed with Emily."

"That's bullshit, Hannah. You bent over backward for Emily. We both did."

"Well, bullshit or not, that's the way I feel." I waited for Paul to say something, and when he didn't, I added, "A few more days, Paul. That's all I'll need. Where can I reach you?"

Paul read me the telephone number of Steve's rental house, and I wrote it down on the prescription pad in front of me.

"Hannah?"

"Yes?"

"I'm sorry I snapped at you. I'm just trying to understand." He paused and then chuckled, his good humor returning. "Sometimes you are a colossal pain in the ass."

"I know."

"And, Hannah?"

"What?"

"I love you."

He probably expected to hear me say, "I love you, too." A few days ago it would have been easy. Practically automatic. I twisted the telephone cord around my finger in silence.

"I *love* you," Paul repeated.

"I know." We listened to each other breathe for a few seconds, then hung up without actually saying good-bye.

When I replaced the receiver after talking to Paul, the light indicating my extension went dead, but the 02 extension remained brightly lit. The doctor was still on the phone. While I watched, 03 came on, too.

I wandered into the waiting room, turned off the Muzak, and pulled down the shades. I decided to join Paul in Cape Cod, eventually, if I didn't get myself arrested first. I worried that it was way after closing time and Dr. Chase was still in his office, keeping all the telephone lines lit up like a department store Christmas tree.

At five-thirty all the lights on the telephone went out, and he emerged, looking perfectly normal. "Thanks, Hannah, that's all for the day."

"Do you want me to lock up?"

"No, no. I'll do it. You've worked hard. Please go on home." He surprised me by heading for the staircase that led to the second floor.

"Aren't you going home?"

"Afraid not. I'm sleeping here tonight. My condo's being painted."

Screwed! So much for sneaking back later to replace Katie's chart. I must have looked puzzled because he explained that he'd kept his old bedroom upstairs, "for emergencies."

"Handy," I said.

"It certainly is."

I thought I detected a hint of suspicion in his voice

but reasoned that if he'd discovered that the chart was missing, he'd surely have been all over me by now. Dr. Chase didn't seem too organized to me, so maybe he hadn't even noticed that his blotter was flatter than it had been several hours before, or if he had, perhaps he'd think he'd merely misplaced Katie's chart.

Nevertheless, I pulled the door shut behind me with my lunch sitting in my stomach like a softball, and just about as indigestible. *Please God,* I prayed in the parking lot, *please don't let Dr. Chase discover that Katie's chart isn't where he left it.* As I unlocked my car, I looked back at the house and thought I saw the doctor standing at a window on the second floor, watching me, the light of the early evening sun glinting off his glasses.

chapter

12

MY TOYOTA HAD SAT IN THE SUN ALL DAY WITH THE windows closed, allowing the heat inside to build up high enough to broil meat. While I waited for the steering wheel and plastic upholstery to cool down enough to touch, I imagined Dr. Chase's eyes boring into my back, but when I turned around to check, whatever I had taken to be Dr. Franklin C. Chase, Jr., had disappeared from the window.

I tested the temperature of the upholstery with the palm of my hand, then threw my purse behind the driver's seat and climbed in. I slotted the key into the ignition, turned it, and as the engine started, both the air conditioner and *All Things Considered* blasted into life, right in the middle of the news.

Keeping the air conditioner set to high, I headed for the farm. Just after I passed through the intersection at Church and High with the light in my favor, a black Lexus sped through on yellow, going in the opposite direction. I was wondering where I had seen the car before and then I remembered: Katie's sister. Opposite St. Philip's, I checked the rearview mirror and watched Liz's Lexus squeal around the corner on Princess Anne. Where on earth was she going at such speed? Dr. Chase's? My paranoid imagination had clearly shifted into overdrive. *She doesn't have to be going to see the doctor,* I reasoned. *There's a lot of stuff down that road. Ten to twelve houses. A beauty parlor. Harrison's Restaurant*—I checked my watch—*and it's almost dinnertime.* Maybe I was adding two and two and coming up with five. Then again, maybe not. I had always been good in math.

I turned into the parking lot at Harmony Baptist, reversed, and headed back to the doctor's office. As I drove past, I saw that I hadn't been paranoid after all. Liz's Lexus was parked in the lot next to Dr. Chase's Ford. I tried to recall an earlier conversation with the doctor. Hadn't he told me he hardly knew Liz? It could be true, I supposed. Maybe she was sick. Or perhaps Dr. Chase had called her in because he had discovered something in Katie's file that he wanted to share with the family.

I was reminded of the photocopy, which now rested safely in my purse along with the slip of paper on which I had jotted down Paul's telephone number. I thought about Paul, trying in his sweetly clumsy way to make up to me after our stupid fight yesterday morning.

To reassure myself that the documents were safe, I slipped my hand into the side pouch of my purse. The photocopy felt warm to the touch, as if it had just rolled out of the machine, but I couldn't find the scrap of paper anywhere. I scrabbled around in my purse and checked the pockets of my jacket with no luck. *Shit!* I must have left it on my desk. Dr. Chase had warned me about his cleaning lady: anything that wasn't tied down would be out with the trash by morning. Now I'd have to go back for it.

Erring on the side of caution, I parked in front of an old Victorian house several doors down. From there it took only a minute to reach the office and climb the steps to the porch. I peered through the glass in the front door. Everything inside was dark. My key grated noisily in the lock and I held my breath as I twisted the doorknob and let myself into the deserted waiting room. I stood still and listened. Nothing. Maybe they were in the back.

I crept to the reception area and peered over the counter. The slip of paper on which I had written Paul's phone number was right where I had left it, half under the telephone, printed in neat capital letters. 508 something. I thought that if I could just reach over the counter, I might avoid going through the double doors where there'd be a risk of running into Dr. Chase or his visitor. If Liz and Dr. Chase were in cahoots, being caught here after hours could prove injurious to my health.

I stood on tiptoe and leaned as far over the counter as I could, but the slip of paper remained just out of reach. In that awkward position, the edge of the Formica counter cut uncomfortably into my stomach and I thought it would be all I'd need to be caught here like this, balancing on my stomach, good arm outstretched, reaching over the counter like a common shoplifter. I squirmed backward until my feet touched the floor, then pushed cautiously through the swinging doors and turned right into the reception area. From there I could hear the low murmur of voices on the other side of the wall.

I snatched Paul's number off the desk, then pressed my back against the cabinets that lined the wall, not even breathing, straining to catch something of what they were saying. Unexpectedly Dr. Chase's voice reached me, distinctly louder. Someone must have opened his office door.

"How was I to know that she was one of Dad's patients?"

"You should have checked it out, Frankie. You should have thought of it."

Frankie? So much for his feeble story about hardly knowing the woman.

"You were a damn fool to leave it lying about." Liz was shouting now.

"It wasn't just lying about, Liz. I stuck it under my blotter, for Christ's sake."

"Are you sure she saw it?"

"Almost positive. I never would have misfiled a chart like that. The colored tabs stood out like a sore thumb when she stuffed it in the U's."

I shrank back into the shadows near the coatrack,

sandwiched between a soft wool coat and a down jacket left over from winter, feeling like a complete idiot. It would have been so easy to file Katie's chart back in the *D*'s, and he might never have noticed. Now that I was clearly persona non grata, in addition to being *muy stupida*, I prayed for an opportunity to escape. I hoped that with the lights turned off in the waiting room, they couldn't see me, although I could see them plainly enough through the glass panels in the swinging door as they bickered in the brightly lit hallway.

Liz stood with her back against the door of Examining Room B, flipping briskly through the pages in Katie's chart. She must have been a speed reader. "What *is* all this shit?"

"As I told you, even if she'd looked at it, I doubt that she'd have understood my father's shorthand."

"But what if she did, Frankie? What then?"

"She'll know for sure that you sister was pregnant. That's all. We should have reported that to the police in the first place, Liz. You know that."

"Well, we didn't. And I can't afford to have the fact that we didn't come out now." She waved Katie's chart under his nose. "Get rid of this, Frankie."

Dr. Chase stood with both hands in the pockets of his slacks.

"*Now,* Frank!" She slapped his right arm with the back side of the chart. "Take charge of something for once in your life, for Christ's sake! I'm damn tired of cleaning up after you."

Dr. Chase snatched Katie's chart from Liz's hand and tucked it under his arm. For a second I thought Liz was heading for the front door. My stomach lurched, and I was suddenly reminded of the sandwich I had eaten for lunch. But Liz had merely turned my way to pick up her purse, an expensive leather Coach bag, from where it hung on the doorknob of Room B. She hitched the strap over her left shoulder, then headed toward the back door. I was beginning to relax a little against the overcoat when she turned. "And I'll take care of the other thing, too."

Dr. Chase shook his head silently at the back of Liz's departing hot pink Evan-Picone suit. He waited until the door had latched behind her, then walked over to it and engaged the dead bolt. I saw him return to his office and shut the door.

I sat back on my heels, heart racing, to mull this over, waiting to leave until I heard the sound of Liz's engine and the crunch of gravel under her tires. Surely Liz was overreacting? How could a deceased eighteen-year-old's pregnancy make any difference now? This was the 1990s, for heaven's sake; Queen Victoria had been dead for years.

Liz was going to extraordinary lengths to protect her dead sister's reputation, I thought. Or perhaps it was her family's reputation that concerned her now? *Fat chance!* I nearly laughed out loud. This was much more than the congenital fear of a lawyer finding herself implicated in a cover-up. I was convinced that Liz knew much more than she was saying about Katie's death.

I was turning scenarios over in my mind as I quietly let myself out the front door into the waning sunshine of an otherwise perfect spring day, fresh with the smell of new-mown grass.

I drove back to the farm in a preoccupied haze. Fortunately I was familiar with every turn of the road by now. My car seemed to drive itself, hugging the curves and gliding gently up and down the hills. It's probably just as well I didn't own a car phone or I would have telephoned Dennis Rutherford and started babbling like a blithering fool. I didn't know what significance to place on the fact that Katie had almost certainly been pregnant when she died, and I wondered if that could have been determined at the autopsy had the medical examiner been looking for it. Would there be any trace of such a tiny fetus? Or was Katie's body too badly decomposed to tell?

Something distracted me from these morbid thoughts of death and decay. I noticed it first in my side view mirror, a dark shape loitering behind me, highlighting that nutty notice on the mirror about objects being closer than they appear. When I glanced to the rearview, the dark shape turned into a van that filled the mirror from rim to rim.

At this point the road became narrow and twisty, and I had this guy right on my tail. Or guys, rather. I could see ball caps and dark glasses on a pair of otherwise generic faces.

Stop tailgating, you jerks! I accelerated to 50 mph and careened around a curve, hoping to widen the gap between us, but the driver of the van stayed with me, so close I couldn't even see his front bumper.

Okay. *Pass me then, dammit!* I slowed to thirty-five. We had come to a straight stretch in the road, and there were no cars approaching from the opposite direction, yet they stuck with me like lint on a cheap black suit. I honked my horn and slowed to twenty-five, but still the bozos refused to pass.

Who were these people and why were they following me? I remembered what Dennis had told me about local hooligans and prayed that I would make it to Connie's before somebody got hurt. Like me. I checked the rearview again, and this time I caught the expression on the driver's face, mouth set in a determined line, arms straight and elbows locked. Where his hands grasped the steering wheel, I imagined the knuckles were white. I remembered Liz's parting words to Dr. Chase, that she'd take care of something. Could that something have been me?

But how did she have time to arrange this ambush? I'd left Liz only five minutes ago. Then I remembered Dr. Chase's telephone, the extension lights flashing on and off like the control panel on the starship *Enterprise*. I had assumed he was calling patients, but he could have been talking with Liz. *Oh, shit!* Maybe they were both involved.

I eased around the next curve, still going twenty-five, keeping well to the right. On the next straightaway my head suddenly whiplashed against the headrest with considerable force, sending explosions of light swimming behind my eyelids. The SOB had rammed me

from the rear! I shook my head to clear away the cob-
webs and jammed my foot down, hard, on the accelerator. Speed limit or no speed limit, I had to get away
from these thugs before they killed me! In seconds I
was driving a good 10 mph over the 55 mph limit, yet
not only did I fail to lose them, but they seemed to be
overtaking me.

I was aware of the blast before I heard it. The back
of my neck stung as if it had been hit by a thousand
tiny pins, followed by a whoosh! as my rear window
exploded into the backseat. The right wheels of my
Toyota hit the soft shoulder, and the steering wheel
spun wildly, catching my right thumb and jerking it
painfully as I tried to regain control of the vehicle.
Somehow I wrestled the car back onto the road, but
something wasn't right, and it took all my strength to
keep from plunging into the ditch. The way the car
pulled toward the shoulder, I suspected my right front
tire was flat.

Even in that crippled condition, I was still going
fifty-five when I reached the pond and I realized with
absolute certainty that barring a miracle, I wouldn't
make it around the curve. I pressed both feet on the
brake pedal, sending the car fishtailing across the
centerline. As I pulled back into my lane, I was vaguely
aware that the dark van was still with me, but I was
too busy to think about much more than slowing the
car down. *Hold on, Hannah! Here we go!*

My car sailed over the ditch, shot through a hedge,
ripped through a barbed-wire fence, and plunged, nose

first, into the murky water of the Baxters' pond. The last thought I had before everything went dark was not of Paul or Emily or the fear of dying but: *Oh, damn, I'm going to ruin Connie's scarf.*

ANGELS. I HADN'T EXPECTED ANGELS.

In the silence following the crash, two of them swam before my face. My eyes gradually focused, and I realized that my angels were air bags that had deployed, saving my life.

The car had nose-dived into the pond at a forty-five-degree angle, and I found myself sitting in water up to my hips, trapped in the driver's seat by my seat belt. By the time I'd figured out that I wasn't actually dead and that I'd need to do something, the water had risen to my waist.

I pushed the red release button with my thumb, and as the seat belt recoiled, I floated up a few inches. *Get out, Hannah!* I felt frantically along the door and finally located the door handle a few inches underwater. I wrapped grateful fingers around it and pulled. But when I pushed at the door with my shoulder, it wouldn't budge. *Oh, God! What had I seen on TV? Wait for the pressure to equalize, something like that. Easy enough for actors to say.* With rising panic I waited, watching the water creep up to my chest. When it was even with the window, I tried again to open the driver's side door. It still wouldn't move.

A dead animal floated by. I was trying to put as much distance between me and the poor creature as I could, when I realized it was only my wig. I reached for it and noticed splotches of red on the blazer I'd borrowed from Connie. *Blood? Where was it coming from?* I touched my cheeks, my forehead, my nose. *Oh, Lord!* Blood was pouring from my nose and dripping all over Connie's precious scarf! I felt with all five fingers along the bridge of my nose and was relieved to discover that nothing appeared to be broken.

By then the water had filled the glove compartment, which hung open with the owner's manual floating about inside, still in its plastic cover. *This car,* I thought, *is a goner.* But not me! I'd worked too hard to live—through the triple ordeal of surgery, recovery, and months of chemotherapy. I wasn't about to let a couple of demented juvenile delinquents take my life. Not without a fight anyway!

Open the window! I pushed on the button, but nothing happened. *The engine's dead, you dope! The electric windows aren't going to work.*

I pushed fruitlessly against the driver's side window

and began to get hysterical. *Take deep breaths, Hannah. Breathe! You can do this.* I floated over to the passenger side of the front seat, fumbled for the door handle, pulled it toward me, and then pushed outward. Much to my relief, the door opened as the car was, by now, nearly full of water. A sizable pocket of air remained between the dome light and what was left of my rear window. With my face hovering near the ceiling I gulped in some precious air, held my breath and, kicking hard, swam out of the car and bobbed to the surface. Still clutching my wig, I swam a few yards and turned to tread water as I watched my car tilt and teeter, list and slide on its inexorable way to Toyota heaven, that happy scrap yard in the sky.

I splashed about, feeling for the bottom of the pond with my feet. *Where's my damn purse?* I remembered throwing it into the backseat and thought briefly about diving down to retrieve it until visions of Chappaquidick rose unbidden to my brain, and reason prevailed. Instead, I swam the short distance to shore, waded onto the muddy bank, pulled myself out, and lay back, panting, on a patch of tall grass. When I dared to look, my trusty Toyota, barely two years old, disappeared into the pond with a final blub-blub-blub as water poured over the bumper and my Save the Bay vanity plate.

I don't know how long I lay on the bank of the pond, trying to regain control of my breathing. *In. Out. Calm down, Hannah.* The utter silence surprised me. Baxter's ducks and chickens must be laying low. No frogs ribbiting. No crickets chirping. In this tiny town where the populace seemed to communicate by some form of rural telepathy, I expected help to materialize at any moment. Police cars, an ambulance, the volunteer fire brigade. But if it hadn't been for the bubbles rising from the center of the pond and the concentric rings spreading across its surface, lapping in tiny waves at my feet, I might have dreamed the whole episode. Except for the blood.

Lying there in my sodden, borrowed clothes, I began to shake as the adrenaline rush subsided and a light breeze began to cool my skin. I wrapped my arms around my chest, hugged myself for warmth, and waited. And waited. No mounted cavalry cresting the hill. Prince Charming was busy, hiding out from the wicked press in Cape Cod. And there wasn't a sign of Hal or Dennis, so no knight in shining armor to the rescue either.

Regretting that real life wasn't much like the movies, I started to walk.

"My God, Hannah, you're bleeding!" Connie screamed this into an ear that was still ringing with the echo of an already deafening shotgun blast.

"It's just a bloody nose." I ripped a paper towel from the roll and used it to wipe my face. I looked down at the mud and blood that dotted the blazer and scarf I had borrowed from Connie. "But I'm afraid I've ruined your scarf."

"Never mind about that." She pushed me in the direction of a kitchen chair. "What on earth happened?"

"Some maniacs ran me off the road and into the

Baxters' pond." I began to shiver. "This just isn't my week, Connie."

Connie disappeared into her studio, came back with the familiar afghan, and wrapped it around my shoulders. "I'm calling the doctor."

That was the last thing I needed, but I didn't say so. "No, Connie, don't do that. I'm fine. Really. I just need a hot bath. A good, long soak."

"Dennis, then." I didn't argue with that.

While she went to the phone, I peeled off my ruined clothes and settled into a lovely tub of vanilla-scented bubble bath. I was gingerly feeling around my scalp for cuts when Connie rapped twice and poked her head around the door. "Dennis will be here in fifteen minutes." The door closed, then opened again almost immediately, as if she'd forgotten to tell me something. Connie entered, lowered the toilet seat lid, and sat on it. "And I'm not leaving you until he gets here."

Ordinarily I would have asked Connie to go; since my disfiguring surgery it made me uncomfortable to be seen naked by anyone other than Paul. But my heart was still pounding, and I had to admit I was simply afraid to be alone. What if those lunatics had intended to kill me and decided to come back later to finish the job? I turned my body toward the wall slightly and asked Connie to hand me the shampoo so I could wash my wig.

Ten minutes later Dennis rang the doorbell. I decided to let them have a little quality time in the studio while I finished washing and drying my portable hair. Later, sitting in the kitchen wearing Connie's fluffy terry-cloth bathrobe, I described the van and its two occupants. When I got to the part about the ball caps, I thought hard, trying to remember their color and if there had been a logo or anything written on them. Something about the driver of the van was bothering me, too, but I couldn't think what. By the time I finished telling Dennis everything I could remember, I was absolutely certain of one thing, though. No matter what Dennis thought, my assailants hadn't been juveniles.

"Sorry. That's it. That's all I can remember, Dennis." Connie had set a cup of hot tea in front of me, and I wrapped my hands around it gratefully.

"Not much to go on." Dennis closed his notebook and tucked it into the inside breast pocket of his jacket.

"Maybe there'll be paint chips where they rammed me."

"We'll have a look when we pull your car up."

"My purse is still in it, Dennis."

"We'll get that, too."

"And in my purse—"

"Is this some sort of parlor game? 'And in my purse there is a dollar and on that dollar there is an eagle?' " Dennis smiled to let me know that he was pulling my leg.

"I was going to say, Mr. Smarty Pants, that in my purse is positive proof that Katie Dunbar was pregnant. I found the file in Dr. Chase's office and made a photocopy for you."

"Holy cow," said Connie.

"So Angie was right." Dennis studied the ceiling. "Yet Chip insists he didn't sleep with her—"

"And you believe him?" I was incredulous. I described the scrap of conversation I had overheard between Liz and Frank Chase. "Clearly her sister knew about the baby."

"I wonder why she never said anything?" Connie added hot water to my teacup.

"She probably thought it didn't matter now that her sister has been found dead. Or maybe she didn't want to embarrass the family," Dennis said reasonably.

"Liz doesn't have an unselfish bone in her body," Connie remarked. "She would have covered up anything she thought might screw up her chances of getting into law school."

I plunged my used tea bag up and down, hoping to coax a decent second cup of Earl Grey out of it. "The more I think about that conversation and about those creeps who ran me off the road, the more I'm convinced that Liz has to be involved in Katie's death." I sipped my tea and studied Dennis over the rim of my cup. "Liz must believe I know something, but what? I could just kick myself for losing that copy of Katie's chart."

Dennis stood up. "I can see I'll need to talk to those two in the morning."

"Please, Dennis, don't bring my name into it."

"I'll avoid it if I can." He lay a gentle hand on my shoulder. "You take it easy, now, Hannah. You know, this used to be a quiet little town until you came to visit."

The next day at nine I watched as the Pearson's Corner volunteer firemen dredged my poor car, festooned with brown and gray grass, its rear window a mass of cobwebbed glass, out of the pond. I recognized a couple of the volunteers: Bill Taylor, of course, the would-be novelist, and David Wilson, the guy who had given me the willies at Katie's funeral. It was Bill, in fact, who waded into the water holding a great iron hook attached to a chain that reeled out behind him. The other end was connected to a tow truck that had been driven into the field and parked on a patch of hard-packed clay near an old chicken coop. I could see the hook, clamped to my rear bumper, just visible under six inches of water.

Bill raised his hand and waved it in a tight circle. The tow truck's engine began a methodical grind. The chain grew taut, then wound itself around and around a drum as my car emerged from the muck, slowly, inch by battered inch.

As it dangled nose down from the winch, water poured from the windows and from the open passenger side door and finally from the wheel wells and engine compartment. While they waited for my car to drain, the workers clustered around Mrs. Baxter, who had just arrived carrying a thermos, a large jar of lemonade, and a dozen paper cups. She set the cups down on the hood of one of the parked cars and poured out refreshments for the volunteers. She offered me some, but I said I wasn't thirsty. I felt bad enough about ruining everyone's Saturday without horning in on the refreshments, too.

I was thinking how nice it might be to live in a town like this where people go all out for folks they barely know when David approached me with a plastic garbage bag of items retrieved from my car.

I picked out a sodden box of Kleenex with two fingers. *Gee, thanks.* The bag also contained a single tennis shoe and an old pair of gym shorts that had probably begun moldering long before this most recent dousing. "How embarrassing," I muttered aloud. I upended the bag and dumped its pathetic contents out onto the grass: a thermos (unbroken), a coffee mug (minus handle), three waterlogged CDs (Placido Domingo), an umbrella, two pens, a snow scraper, and the car's owner's manual.

"Where's my purse?" I could dry out the money, I thought, and my credit card should be okay. I turned the bag upside down and shook it.

"Sorry, Mrs. Ives. It wasn't in the vehicle."

I was short on patience. "It has to be! Look again!"

David regarded me with steady, unblinking eyes and shook his head.

I covered my eyes with my hands. I was certain that the only copy of Katie's medical record lay somewhere—along with my checkbook, credit cards, and pictures of Paul and Emily—at the bottom of the Baxter's pond. If Dr. Chase had destroyed Katie's file, as Liz had ordered, without that photocopy, it was just my word and Angie's against everyone else's.

IN THE WEE HOURS, WHEN DREAMS ARE HARD TO come by and good sense sometimes prevails, I made my decision. If the good citizens of Pearson's Corner wanted me gone badly enough to kill me, I would leave. My narrow escape from the pond had left me weak and shaking. As mad as I was with Paul, I didn't want to spend another day in Pearson's Corner if it meant sleeping with one eye open or flinching every time another car tried to pass me on the road. In the morning I would call Paul and ask him to meet me at the Provincetown Airport, if only I could remember where I had put the scrap of paper on which I'd written his phone number.

In the soft glow from the bathroom night light I could see Connie's green linen jacket, a tragic canvas of stains and wrinkles, draped over a hanger in the doorway, dripping dry. I thought I had put Paul's number inside Connie's jacket, but a frantic middle-of-the-night search of the pockets had yielded nothing.

"You don't suppose Paul's phone number was inside my purse?" I said to Connie as we were having breakfast the next morning.

"If it was, you can always look the number up in the phone book. How many Zelcos can there be in North Truro?"

"It's a rental place, Con. Lord knows whose name the phone is actually listed in." I sat at the table opposite her and pinched pieces off a slice of dry toast.

"Call the Zelcos in Annapolis," she suggested. "Maybe someone's at home who will know."

"Already did. Got the answering machine."

"I wouldn't worry about it then, Hannah. Paul will get the message eventually, and even if he doesn't, surely he'll call when he hasn't heard from you."

I wasn't so sure. After our recent telephone conversation he'd know I was still furious with him over that disgusting Jennifer Goodall business.

Connie leaned across the table to fill my empty glass with orange juice from a carton, pausing in mid-pour to examine my face. "Except for that red spot on the bridge of your nose, I'd never guess you'd been in an accident." She handed me the raisin bran. "So what are you going to do today, now that you've more or less snooped yourself out of a job?"

"Go to work, of course. Dr. Chase doesn't know that I know he knows about my finding Katie's chart.

It'd be suspicious if I *didn't* show up at the office today, don't you think?"

"Brilliant, Hannah. Now I'm convinced you've lost your so-called mind."

"I'm not sure how Dr. Chase got involved in this cover-up, but he seems to be a decent sort of guy. I'm going to 'fess up. Admit I saw the chart. Reason with him about it. I should be able to persuade him to share whatever he knows with Dennis. Dr. Chase works with the police department, don't forget." I poured some cereal into my bowl. "If he had anything at all to do with those people who ran me off the road, I figure the best way to protect myself is to let him know that I told Dennis all about it."

Connie stared at me without speaking, a frown of disapproval clouding her usually cheerful face. Suddenly I remembered that I was without wheels, completely at this woman's mercy. She read my mind. "And I suppose you'll be wanting to borrow my car?" I nodded. "Jeez, Hannah. With your track record, how can I be sure it'll be safe with you?"

"Trust me."

"Oh, I trust *you*. It's the maniacs you seem to attract that I worry about."

I had to agree. I'd been mulling it over all morning. I must have stepped on someone's toes. Big time.

I finished my raisin bran, then spread some toast with grape jelly. I had eaten my toast and was licking the crumbs off my fingers before Connie relented. "Okay, you can have the car, but this is absolutely the last time I loan you any clothes. I don't need to be shopping for a car *and* a new wardrobe. And, Hannah?"

"Yes?"

"Be careful. I don't need to be shopping for a new sister-in-law either."

Dr. Chase stood on the porch watering geraniums when I pulled into his parking lot twenty minutes before Saturday afternoon office hours were scheduled to begin. I was dressed in comfortable black slacks and a pink, short-sleeve knit top, accessorized with a frayed tapestry vest. Instead of black patent leather pumps, I wore a sensible pair of Easy Spirit sandals. On my head was my wig, washed, brushed, and looking ratty. Following yesterday's dunking, it was barely presentable, but I wore it anyway. I didn't have a hat that matched my vest.

As I climbed the steps to the front door, the doctor rested his watering can on the porch rail and smiled as if nothing had happened, completely disarming me. Finding Katie's chart must not have been that big a deal; otherwise he would have been much cooler toward me. Dr. Chase wore his emotions on his face. He didn't strike me as that good an actor.

"Hey, Hannah. Thought you were Connie for a minute." Then he noticed I didn't have my car. "Your car in the shop?"

"So to speak. A tow truck pulled it out of Baxter's pond this morning."

His eyes grew wide. "No kidding? How'd it get in there?"

"Haven't you heard? I thought the news would be all over town by now."

"Nope. I've been holed up here since last night."

Without going into detail, I told him about the black van that had run me off the road. I watched his face transform from a mask of amusement into one of deep concern. "I was going to make some smart-ass remark about your being accident prone, but this is serious!"

"Dennis is treating it as a hit-and-run, but he's not optimistic he'll find the driver."

"I'm surprised you've come to work today. Sure you're okay? Come inside. Let's have a look at you." The way he fussed over me made me miss my mother.

"I'm fine, Doctor. Really. But I would like to talk."

"Well, of course. Come in, come in." He set the watering can down on the porch next to a fuchsia plant in full bloom and held the door open for me. I headed directly down the long hallway and turned into his office. Dr. Chase followed and tossed his key ring on the desk. While he got settled, I pulled up a blue upholstered armchair, tried to collect my thoughts, and began to sweat. My anxiety must have showed.

"Sure you're okay?" He appeared genuinely concerned.

"Quite sure." I leaned forward and took a deep breath, knowing when I did so that the charade would be over. I'd be putting an end to my part-time employment. "Dr. Chase, I have a confession. I know you told me Katie Dunbar's chart had been shredded, but yesterday, when I came to work, my curiosity got the better of me. I'm sorry, but I went rummaging through the file room, looking for it."

Dr. Chase stared at me, eyes enormous behind his glasses, his tented fingers just touching his lips.

"As you know, I didn't find it there. But I did happen to notice a chart on your desk when I was cleaning up some spilled coffee." I pointed. "It was stuck under your blotter."

The doctor still didn't comment, so I floundered on. "I meant to put it back, of course, but things were so hectic yesterday, I just stuck it in the nearest file cabinet." I thought it would be wise not to mention the photocopy. "I'm sorry. I feel just awful about this. I know I've betrayed the confidence you placed in me. But what's done is done."

I straightened my back and took another deep, steadying breath. The next part was going to be harder. It would have been easier if the doctor had reacted to anything I'd told him so far but no, he sat there like the great Sphinx, drawing the point of a pencil mindlessly forward and back along a seam on the arm of his chair. "Dr. Chase, I need to tell you that I *did* read the chart. I know that when your father examined Katie in 1990, she was two months pregnant."

Dr. Chase rested his elbows on the arms of his chair and adjusted his position slightly, as if trying to get comfortable. "Sometimes charts that would normally be declared inactive get missed when they're part of a family unit that includes current patients. In Ms. Dunbar's case, though, the chart was shredded."

"But, Doctor, I saw it!"

It was weird. Dr. Chase was staring at the book-shelf near the window, but I had the feeling he was aware of every move I made. "You're mistaken." The doctor removed his glasses by the nosepiece and, still holding them, rubbed his eyes with the back of his hand. Maybe it was easier for him to lie to someone whose face appeared before him as an impressionis-tic blur.

"Katie Dunbar is dead, Dr. Chase. What can her pregnancy matter to anyone now?"

Dr. Chase sprawled in his chair and stared at the ceiling, his mouth a thin, tight line. His eyes traveled from the ceiling to the window where sunlight dap-pled the sill. "It's too complicated to explain." He was addressing the magnolia tree in his garden, not me.

"Explain about Elizabeth Dunbar, you mean?"

His head snapped in my direction, his dark eyes wide. "What do you know about Liz?" *At last! My questions had triggered a reaction.*

"Only what I overheard of your conversation with her last night." I thought I'd keep him guessing about the point at which I'd stumbled upon their argument.

Dr. Chase closed his eyes and wagged his head silently from side to side. When he finally spoke, his words lay flat and frosty in the space between us. "You seem to be everywhere, Mrs. Ives."

"I admit I had ulterior motives when I volunteered to help out here. I thought it'd be an opportunity to check out the information in Katie's file without both-ering anyone. But discovering you and Liz together was purely accidental. I'd left the phone number to the vacation house my husband is renting at the reception desk, and I had to come back for it."

"Humph." The doctor scowled in my direction.

"And while we're on the topic of Liz Dunbar"—I blundered on—"what did she mean by 'I'll take care of the other'? Maybe I'm being a bit paranoid here, Doctor, but there's something I've neglected to tell you about my so-called accident. I lost control of the car because two jerks in a dark van tried to force me off the road." I saw, rather than heard, Dr. Chase's intake of breath. "And when I didn't drift off the shoulder obediently, like a good little girl, someone in the van decided to shoot at me."

Five seconds passed with no sound in the room but the tick-tick of his pencil as it slipped through his fingers and dropped, point down, on his desk. And again. How could I get him to talk? I decided to change tactics. "*I* know she was pregnant, Dr. Chase, because I saw it on her chart. But I'm not the only one who knows it. She told a girlfriend, you see."

Dr. Chase, who seemed at that moment a bunch of loosely connected parts, gathered himself together at last and responded directly to what I'd said. "Let me deal with this." He mumbled something I couldn't catch.

"What?" I leaned forward.

"I said . . ." He paused. "Never mind."

"Do you know who shot Katie?" He shook his head. All of a sudden I thought I knew what he feared. "Are you covering up for your father?"

"No!" The word exploded from his lips.

"Who then? You must be protecting somebody. Why else would you destroy that chart?"

Dr. Chase rose from his chair and walked around the desk, wearing his kindly physician face, once again in control. Standing over me like that, he looked taller than his five feet ten, but his face was so calm that it didn't occur to me to be frightened. "This is more complicated than it looks, Hannah, and I know this is going to sound melodramatic, but for your own protection, I'd suggest you mind your own business."

"But—"

"Lay off it, Hannah."

I considered reminding him of his duties as a coroner, threatening to go to Dennis with what I knew, but thought better of it. "You're a good doctor," I said instead, grasping his free arm and squeezing it gently. "I've seen the way you care about people, and I know you couldn't have done anything to hurt Katie."

"I have no idea who killed that young woman." He stepped to his desk and fidgeted with a glass paperweight that had a dandelion in full white-headed bloom encapsulated inside like a moth in amber.

"Then tell the police what you know," I insisted. "We're talking about 1990 here! An out-of-wedlock pregnancy wasn't the end of the world like it was in the forties and fifties. It may not have had anything to do with Katie's death, but it may help the police."

"I'll consider what you've said, but I won't make any promises." Dr. Chase returned to his chair and flung himself into it so hard that it rolled backward and the wheels slipped off the edge of the carpet. I decided to leave him there, scowling, with his feet stretched out straight in front of him and his arms dangling limply over the upholstered leather arms of his chair. From my position in the hall he looked small and defeated.

"Hannah? I'm sorry about your car."

I massaged a sore spot on my shoulder. "Me, too, Doctor. Me, too."

"But under the circumstances, I don't think we can work together anymore."

I couldn't argue with that. "I'll call Redi-Temp and get someone to fill in for me on Monday."

"That will be fine." His voice seemed lifeless.

As I left the office, I was sure of only one thing: Until I sprang it on him, he didn't know about my accident. But by the frightened look on his face, I was certain he suspected who was behind it. And, although I couldn't work out exactly how she managed it or why, that somebody was probably Liz.

I ACCELERATED AWAY FROM THE DOCTOR'S OFFICE, feeling relieved, even though I had just lost my second job in less than four months. On my left, halfway down High, I could see the low brick and cinder-block building of the Volunteer Fire Department, its over-size garage doors rolled open. A single fire truck had been pulled into the drive, and someone had bathed and polished the vehicle until its yellow paint and chrome grill gleamed in the sun. A volunteer dressed in blue jeans and a Grateful Dead T-shirt was washing down the drive with a hose. At the end of the drive stood a sign on wheels with removable letters: WEDNESDAY NIGHT SPAGHETTI SUPPER—ALL YOU CAN EAT. My stomach rumbled.

I wasn't in the mood for one of Connie's PB and Js. My mouth was all set for a thick, flavorful tuna fish sandwich on whole wheat (with fries) from Ellie's when I remembered I had no money or credit cards to pay for it. I'd last seen my purse as the pond gulped down my car. I checked my watch. Bill Taylor was usually working the afternoon shift at Ellie's. The last time I'd seen him he'd been standing in water up to his waist, rescuing my car. As a volunteer fireman I knew he would be tuned in to what was going on at the fire hall. Maybe they'd found my purse. He also might sell me a sandwich and an iced tea on a smile and a promise. I wanted to ask him about Katie and his former teammates anyway.

I pulled into the parking strip in front of Ellie's and breezed into the store. Neither Angie nor her mother was about. Somewhere a radio played softly, but otherwise, the place was deserted.

I stuck my head into the kitchen. "Hello?" Nobody was there, either.

I was about to leave, when I smelled cigarette smoke. Curious, I ambled through the kitchen and stuck my head out the back door. Bill was sitting on the back porch, smoking.

"There you are!"

"Just taking a break, Mrs. Ives. Been kinda slow today."

I didn't want to hit him up for a sandwich right off the bat, so I asked, "Any news about my car?"

Bill took a drag from his cigarette and held the smoke in his mouth for an extraordinarily long time. "We towed it to the Exxon station," he said as he exhaled. "Rutherford doesn't want anyone to touch it until his forensic team's been over it with their tweezers and magnifying glasses."

"That's good. How about my purse, though? Any word about that?"

He shook his head. "Probably sitting in the muck at the bottom of that old pond, Mrs. Ives. If I were you, I'd just buy a new one, claim the expense on your insurance. That's what insurance companies are for."

I slapped myself in the forehead. "I was here to pick up a sandwich for lunch, but I don't have any way to pay for it. How can I have been so stupid?"

"You've had a lot on your mind lately." The way he looked at me, one bushy eyebrow raised, made me wonder if he had heard about Paul's predicament. "I think I could rustle you up a sandwich." He crushed out his cigarette, and I followed him into the store, my mouth already beginning to water.

"How are you feeling today?" he asked from the kitchen as I nosed around the empty store.

"A little stiff." In point of fact, I was a mass of scars, scrapes, cuts, and bruises, old and new, and my right arm was aching again. "But I'll do."

"You need to be careful, Mrs. Ives. First you fall off that boat; then you wreck your car. Makes me wonder."

Is that how he saw me? Ms. Klutz? I wasn't sure I liked this guy, even if he was making me lunch. "Makes you wonder what, Bill?"

"Wonder if they might not have been accidents. You come into town and all, pretty much a stranger, and the next thing you know, all these bad things start happening to you. Don't you wonder why?"

I had wondered about that, but I didn't feel like sharing my suspicions with Bill. No telling what he'd do with them. They might even end up in his book. "I can be just as careless or unlucky as the next person, Bill," I said, peering into the kitchen as he scooped tuna fish salad onto thickly sliced bread.

"I'd just watch who you're being friendly with." He squinted back at me. "That's my advice."

"Bill, I hardly know anybody in Pearson's Corner."

"Sometimes it's the people closest to you that you least suspect."

"I think you've been staring at your computer screen too long. You can't mean Connie." Bill shook his head.

"Dennis?" Bill met my gaze with steady, unblinking eyes. "You think Dennis had something to do with my falling overboard? Or the accident? That's impossible. He's a cop, for Christ's sake. Besides, I saw the guys who ran me off the road. I didn't recognize either one of them."

"You don't have to be driving to be responsible for something."

I felt a sudden chill, as if a shadow had passed over the sun and the wind had picked up. My intuition had been telling me the same thing, but I couldn't make it fit. "Bill, I think you're wrong. What possible reason could anybody have for bumping me off?"

"I don't think they're trying to bump you off. I think they want you to go home. Mind your own business."

"Who's 'they'?"

"Don't know. Just a gut feeling I have."

Don't know or won't tell? I checked off the people I knew: Connie and Dennis. Angie and her mother. Frank Chase and Liz. Bill here . . . and, Lord help me, Hal.

"Surely you can't mean Hal? I hardly know the man."

"That's not what I hear." He was folding waxed paper around the sandwich, making surprisingly crisp and neat edges.

"Well, you heard wrong. What is it with this place? Go sailing with a fellow once and every busybody in town has you heading off to Las Vegas for a quickie wedding."

"There's a lot you don't know about him." He slid the sandwich over in my direction and wiped his hands on a dish towel.

"I'm sure there is, and it will probably stay that way." I couldn't protest too strongly without sounding sweet on the guy.

"Let me tell you something about that boyfriend of yours."

"For the last time . . . he's not my boyfriend!"

"Did you know that he used to be the coach of the high school basketball team?"

This was his big secret? A wave of relief washed over me. "Yes. Hal told me all about that. He was very proud of winning the state championship."

"And did he tell you why he left?" I didn't say anything. Bill wore a self-satisfied smirk. "I didn't think so. He was forced to resign."

"Forced? Why on earth?"

"Oh, it was all very hush-hush. Didn't want to upset the parents, create a scandal." Bill seemed to be enjoying himself, dragging out the telling of it.

"A scandal about what, for heaven's sake?"

"It was never proven, of course, but he was suspected of providing some of the team with amphetamines and anabolic steroids." The corners of his mouth twisted up in a hint of a smile. I wanted to smack it off his face.

"But you were on the team, Bill. Surely you'd have known if the allegations were true or not."

"Not me. I was second string, one step up from water boy. Nobody told me anything."

"I can't believe Hal would do such a thing."

"I believe the rumors, Mrs. Ives, because there's more to it."

"There's more?" I hadn't even begun to recover from the first revelation before he zapped me with another.

"I'm fairly certain that Hal was pushing other drugs, too."

"You can't be serious!"

"Marijuana. Cocaine. Even heroin. That's what I heard, anyway. Katie had to be getting them from somewhere. She was high as a kite at her sweet sixteen party, and she was high at the homecoming dance, too, if you ask me."

My God! Maybe that's what Angie was getting at when she told me that Katie was totally spaced out at the dance. "Amphetamines and steroids aren't in the same league with hard drugs," I reasoned. "Why do you think it was Hal who supplied Katie with the hard stuff? Couldn't she have gotten them from someone else? Her sister perhaps?"

"Naw, Liz was a straight arrow. Had to be, didn't she, to get into Harvard Law?" I thought that Bill's confidence in the selection criteria of the admissions board at Harvard was a bit naive, but I didn't say so.

"If you know all this, why don't you take it to the police?"

"It's just rumor. There's no hard evidence."

"Why are you telling me about it then?"

"I like you, Mrs. Ives. You've been real nice to Angie. I'd really hate to see anything happen to you."

I picked up my sandwich and prepared to go. "If you ask me"—I jerked my head in the direction of the doctor's office—"young Dr. Chase over there would have been in a much better position to supply Katie with drugs than Hal Calvert ever was!"

"You don't have to take my word for it." I watched while he took a deep breath and held it while he decided what to say next. "Check out the boat."

"What boat? *Pegasus?*" Bill didn't answer but started to walk across the kitchen. "You have some sort of grudge against Hal?" I aimed my remark at his departing back. The screen door slammed behind him, leaving me standing there alone in the store, except for a calico cat curled up, napping, on the front counter.

*   *   *

Connie was fixing dinner when I arrived, assembling lasagna in an oversize pan. "Thank goodness you're back! And still in one piece." She wiped her hands on a paper towel and studied me. "So, how'd it go with Frank Chase at the office today?"

"I was fired."

"Imagine my surprise."

"There wouldn't have been any point in staying on. The man could never trust me again." I told Connie about my conversation with Dr. Chase and about what I'd learned from Bill.

She ran the back of her hand over her forehead, damp from the steam rising from a pot where the lasagna noodles were boiling. "Do you think I'd have left you alone with Hal if I'd heard even a peep about him dealing drugs?"

"My thoughts exactly."

"But I sure didn't know that Liz and Frank were so tight." She handed me a can of fruit cocktail and a hand-crank can opener. "Drain it in the sink."

"I need you to come with me, Connie," I said as I opened the can.

"Where?"

"Bill's suggesting there's something not quite kosher about *Pegasus*."

"You're kidding."

"I'm not. And he looked so smug."

"What could be wrong? Last time I saw *Pegasus* she was up on jack stands being repaired." Connie had slipped into sailing jargon again.

"What's a jack stand?" I asked.

"Sorry." She dumped a container of sour cream into a bowl and folded the fruit cocktail and a cup of miniature marshmallows into it. "They're metal braces that prop a boat up when it's out of the water."

My stomach growled, despite the sandwich I'd gulped down in the car. When I thought Connie wasn't looking, I snitched a marshmallow from the bowl and popped it into my mouth. "I don't know anywhere near as much about boats as you do," I said, "so if I'm going to check out Bill's ridiculous theory, you'll need to come with me."

Connie looked as if she wanted to rap my knuckles. "Hannah, you are trouble on wheels. Leave it be. I want to live to fifty, dah-link. Hanging around with you could be dangerous."

"But Bill was so insistent, so . . . triumphant! It made me wonder what kind of ax he has to grind with Hal."

"Can't imagine, unless . . . Bill used to work for the Calverts as a ship's carpenter until Hal laid him off and started doing the repair work himself."

"I thought Bill had gone to work for the army."

"He did, but not until after he'd been laid off. There was a six-month period in there when he had to take a succession of odd jobs just to eat while he waited for the government paperwork to go through."

I could sympathize with that, but as much as I despised Coop for laying me off, I doubt I'd have turned him over to the cops. Then I remembered the way he didn't even look at me when he ushered me out of that conference room in Washington, D.C., all those months ago. On second thought, maybe Leavenworth was too good for the miserable worm.

"C'mon, Con. Dinner can wait."

"No, Hannah. It's a complete waste of time. Hal and I go way back. Bill is totally off base." She ripped a piece of plastic wrap off a roll, stretched it over the bowl, turned it, and smoothed the edges down all around before putting it in the refrigerator.

I picked Connie's car keys up from the kitchen table where I had laid them not five minutes before.

Connie opened a jar of spaghetti sauce, threw the lid into the trash, and turned to scowl at me. "And you can forget about taking my car."

I tossed her keys back on the table and scowled back.

"Grow up, Hannah. You should see yourself. Pouting like a three-year-old."

I didn't feel like a three-year-old. I felt like a teenager who'd just been told she couldn't go to a party because her mother knew there would be boys and booze there.

Connie stood at the sink, arms folded, the cleft in her chin deepening and becoming more prominent by the second. Emily had inherited that chin from her father. How many times had she glared at me the way Connie was glaring at me now? Hundreds probably. When I'd grounded her for lying about attending a mixed-sex slumber party, I got the full sulk treatment;

we didn't speak for days. But we Alexanders can be stubborn, too. I was now doubly determined to check out Hal's boat.

I stomped over to the kitchen door and grabbed a key ring off its hook. "If you don't go with me, I'm going to take that old truck out of the barn and drive over there myself."

Connie snatched the truck keys out of my hand. "What the *hell* are you doing? You should be doing everything you can to get out of here and go home to Paul. He needs you, Hannah!"

"I told you. I don't have his number."

"Well, it doesn't seem to me that you're trying very hard to find it. You seem less interested in patching up your marriage than you do in running around Pearson's Corner trying to clear the name of some potential lover!"

"Lover! And how about you and Dennis? Don't think I haven't noticed what's going on between the two of you."

"I don't want to talk about it."

"Why not? It's not as if either of you are married."

Connie stared at me with wide eyes, looking as surprised as if I'd slapped her. She opened her mouth to say something, then apparently thought better of it. "If you're that determined," she said at last, "then let's go. Let's get it over with."

Connie stooped to pick up Colonel's water dish, then thrust it in my direction. "Here. Fill this up while I lock up the house."

I stood there for a moment, feeling foolish, holding

Colonel's dish in both hands. As I ran water into the bowl with Colonel frisking about my legs, I was determined that it would take more than a few dead bolt locks and an unreasonable sister-in-law to keep me away from the truth.

I slouched in the passenger seat of Connie's car, uncomfortably strapped in, with the seat belt webbing chafing my neck. As we passed Ellie's Country Store, I checked the porch, but there was no sign of Bill. I was glad. He'd have recognized the car at once and would have known exactly where we were going. I didn't want him to think I'd paid the least bit of attention to all that garbage he'd told me about Hal.

Where High Street dead-ends at Ferry Point Road, Connie turned left. She pointed out the condo where Frank Chase lived, an attractively landscaped end unit, but his car wasn't in the drive. I assumed he was still at his office, struggling to manage the workload alone. In spite of the lies he had told me, I felt a little bit sorry for the guy.

Five hundred yards ahead I could see the entrance to the marina which was marked by a sign, CALVERT MARINA AND BOATYARD, painted in bold blue letters on a white background. A pair of stout brick pillars flanked the entrance, from which a well-established boxwood hedge fanned out to form a fence, separating the marina grounds from the village of Pearson's Corner. An anchor the size of a wheelbarrow, painted white, rested against one of the pillars.

Skirting the marina to our right, the road followed the water, snaking past the boat slips off docks A, B, and C and ending at a small parking lot. A large grassy area extended well beyond the edge of the parking lot, where boats of all types and sizes were stored, propped up by triangular wooden braces and paint-spattered metal tripods. To my surprise, Connie steered straight through the lot and onto the grass and began to weave cautiously between the boats.

"Where on earth are you going, Connie?"

"To park."

"Excuse me, but wasn't the parking lot back there?"

"When your boat's out of the water and you're working on it, it's much more convenient to drive up and park right next to it."

As we snaked through the land-locked fleet, I gazed out my window at a confusion of masts and rigging; some boats had been placed so close together that the bow pulpit of one vessel extended practically into the rigging of another. Beyond the boats, nearer the water, I thought I recognized the shed that Hal had pointed out to us when we went sailing, where he said *Pegasus* had been hauled.

Connie parked between a small blue cabin cruiser from Wilmington, Delaware, named *My Mink* and a large, nameless wooden vessel being painted dark green. When we climbed out of the car, seagulls were circling the area. One of them settled near an empty paint can and pecked halfheartedly at a discarded sandwich wrapper. I thought Connie'd feel right at home here among the boats and the birds, the fresh, sharp odor of paint and new varnish. From somewhere nearby the familiar whine of a power sander momentarily drowned out the cries of two angry gulls fighting over the remains of a hamburger bun.

"Hal mentioned he'd been experiencing chronic blistering problems on *Pegasus*," Connie said as we wound our way on foot through the maze of boats toward the shed. "He's had to repair her several times." The shed loomed before us, an enormous white Conestoga wagon top, open at both ends.

Inside, the heat intensified. I expected the air to be heavy with moisture, like a greenhouse, but way overhead plantation-style fans nudged any stagnant air gently downward, to be swept away by the cool breezes that passed through the open ends of the shed.

Pegasus was a large boat, longer than *Sea Song*, I suspected, and it nearly filled the space, although there was room to work around her on all sides. I stood with my back resting against the vinyl-coated canvas wall of the shed and admired Hal's boat. From the varnished teakwood trim to the six-inch-wide blue stripe that circled her bright white hull, she was a perfectly proportioned beauty.

"Nice racing stripe," I commented.

"It's called a boot top," she snapped. Connie was still mad at me.

"Why?"

Connie stood at the stern, considering the rudder. "I don't have the foggiest."

"What kind of boat is it, Connie?"

"A Cal 40. Lovely old thing. They don't make them anymore." She took the rudder in both hands and wiggled it from side to side. "They're great cruising and racing boats. Hal loves to race."

I strolled around *Pegasus*, examining the hull. Like the other boats I'd seen, *Pegasus* stood upright, cradled between metal jack stands, curious V-shaped contraptions padded with carpet remnants. Below the white hull, the keel, painted brick red, extended down like an inverted shark fin, touching the ground.

Connie circled the boat twice, hands clasped behind her back, while I stood to one side, wondering what she was looking for. She started tapping on the hull with her knuckles.

"Why are you doing that?" I asked.

"Remember when Hal said his hull was delaminated? I'm checking for that. You know how you tap the wall to find a stud when you're going to hang a picture? Same thing, except I'm listening for the hollow sound you get when the layers of wood that form the hull separate and get all mooshy." Connie tapped her way all around the boat with one of her car keys, too, making sharp, bright cracking sounds. Nothing sounded hollow to me.

Then the tapping stopped. "Hmm, that's odd."

"What?"

"Come here, Hannah. Walk around the boat and tell me what you see."

I circled *Pegasus*, looking at the hull and the keel, feeling like a total dummy. "What the hell am I looking for?"

"Did you notice that one side of the keel has barnacles on it? On the other side the bottom paint is fresh." I could see what she was talking about. The side of the keel nearest me was pockmarked by circular shells the size of my thumbnail. The other side was smooth as a baby's cheek.

"But Hal said it needed repair."

"I know, but you'd expect to see blistering on both sides of the keel, not just one. And another strange thing . . . see that scum line?" She pointed to a brownish green ring that circled the boat several inches below the boot top, like the ring around the inside of a bathtub.

"What's so odd about that?"

"Cal '40s are heavy cruising boats. She ought to be riding lower in the water. This boat's riding high."

"Does that mean she's lighter than she should be?"

"Exactly! Hand me that rag, will you?" Connie indicated a tattered, paint-stained undershirt that had been draped over a nearby sawhorse. I snatched it

up with two fingers and tossed it to her. Connie began to rub vigorously on the freshly painted keel
until the rag was red with paint particles. After a bit
she stopped rubbing and bent over, her face close
to the surface of the keel, then stepped back and
surveyed the spot from several angles. "Well, I'll be
damned."

"What?"

"There's fresh fiberglass here, right in the middle of
what should be a solid lead keel." I looked where she
pointed and saw the hint of a rectangle, just a shadow
about the size of a suitcase beneath the brick red bottom paint. "See, it's duller than the rest of the keel. I
suspect someone was in a hurry, and it wasn't primed
first."

Connie looked at me with wide, startled eyes. "Shit,
Hannah. Bill was right. Somebody's taken a chunk out
of the keel and then tried to cover it over. Someone
could be stashing drugs in there."

Somebody. Someone. Why were we pussyfooting
around the issue? Who else could it be but Hal? I
didn't want to believe it. "But why go to all that trouble, Connie? Couldn't you just hide drugs somewhere
inside the boat? You could build a false bottom in one
of the hatches. Hell, you could hide tons of illegal
substances in the bilge."

Connie shook her head. "The coast guard is trained
to look for things like that. Lockers shorter than they
should be. Fake water tanks. But this compartment
would be under the water and almost impossible to
detect."

"Maybe Hal doesn't know about it." I recalled his gentle manner, his smile, the touch of his hand.

"Not a chance. He does all the work on *Pegasus* himself."

Perhaps it was a reaction to breathing the chemicals in the bottom paint, but I doubted it. I hadn't felt so sick to my stomach since my last chemotherapy session. It nauseated me that I'd actually entertained the idea, however briefly, of cheating on my husband with a man who could well turn out to be a drug lord.

Leaving Connie on her own with *Pegasus*, I ran from the shed, my stomach churning. Gulping air, I located a grassy spot under a tree and knelt down, resting my forehead against the smooth bark. When I judged that the danger of throwing up was past, I raised my head and looked around. Dozens of masts cast long shadows across the boatyard, and I watched a whole row of shadows disappear, one by one, as the sun dipped behind a patch of woods that bordered the boat yard.

A few minutes later Connie joined me. "C'mon, Hannah." She wrapped her arm around my shoulder and gave me a sympathetic squeeze. "Let's go find a telephone."

I climbed wearily into the car, and as Connie backed around *My Mink* and headed toward the parking lot, I slumped in my seat, repeating, "I don't believe it."

She shifted into drive and the car lurched forward. "*You* can't believe it! How about me? I've been working with Hal for years. If what we suspect is true, he's been dealing drugs for at least eight of those years, with no one the wiser."

Connie nosed into one of three parking spaces directly in front of the Ships Store, a neat wooden structure painted gray with white trim to match its neighbors. A sign in the window was flipped from Open to Closed. I was almost relieved.

"Never mind," Connie told me. "The phones are outside anyway, around back, on the side facing the river."

I was inclined to wait in the car, but Connie insisted I come with her. We circled the store to the spot where a wooden pier began, extended across the length of the building, and stretched off in the direction of the gas dock about one hundred feet away. Dock D, where *Sea Song* floated quietly in her slip, was just beyond.

Bell Atlantic had installed the public telephone on a wall directly between the rest rooms, one labeled "Buoys" and the other "Gulls." I thought Connie was perfectly capable of handling the call on her own, so I headed for the "Gulls."

Minutes later, in the privacy of the bathroom, I sat on a wooden bench in a shower stall, closed my eyes, and rested my head against the cool tiles. I hated to admit it, but it looked as if Bill were right. Hal must be dealing drugs. Is that what Liz and Frank Chase were so intent on covering up? Maybe there was something other than a pregnancy recorded in all that mumbo jumbo on Katie's chart, something about her habit. I cursed my bad luck. Unless Dr. Chase still had Katie's chart or was willing to talk about it, we'd never know for sure. I concentrated, trying to recall what else Dr. Chase's father had written down about Katie, wishing I had one of those photographic memories, but it was no good. The important thing, I decided, was to pass on what I did remember to Dennis before I ended up having another inconvenient accident.

I rotated my shoulders, trying to relieve myself of the stiffness along my spine, then spider-walked my arm up the tiles until I felt the familiar tug of damaged muscles still recovering from surgery. I chastised myself for forgetting to do my daily exercises, yet in spite of my neglect, I was pleased to note that progress had been made: I could almost raise my arm overhead. Perhaps taking headers over lifelines and swimming out of ponds counted as physical therapy these days. For a few minutes I stood in front of the mirror and massaged my temples, which had begun to throb. Gawd, I needed a bath, my usual therapy, but figured I would have to settle for running a damp paper towel over my face and neck. I combed through my wig with my fingers but succeeded only in tipping it sideways over one ear.

When I emerged from the bathroom, I found Connie rummaging through her purse. "Dennis isn't at the station. They say he's gone home."

A quarter fell out of her wallet, and I caught up with it before it rolled away between the wooden planks and dropped into the water below. "Here." I handed it to her. "What do we do now?"

"Call him at home, I guess." She picked up the receiver. "Damn! It's thirty-five cents. Do you have a dime?"

I patted my empty pockets and shrugged. Connie let the receiver dangle from its short cord while she rooted through her purse, found a dime, and slotted it into the telephone after the quarter. She punched in a number without looking it up. Abruptly she passed the receiver to me. "Ask for Dennis."

I frowned and listened to the phone ring three times. *I was going to get even with Connie for this.* On the fourth ring a female voice chirped, "Rutherford's."

"Ms. Rutherford?" *Coward*, I mouthed in Connie's direction. She began pacing up and down the dock. "Ms. Rutherford, this is Hannah Ives. I wonder if your father is at home?"

"Sorry, he's not, Mrs. Ives. He went off duty at six. He may have dropped in at the nursing home to visit my grandfather, though. He often does that in the evening."

"Thanks. I'll try to catch him there. If he comes home in the next few minutes, please tell him I called. It's important. Let me give you the number."

"Oh, I know the number, Mrs. Ives." She hung up without saying good-bye, adding fuel to the fire of my suspicion that something intriguing was going on between Connie and Dennis.

I held the receiver to my ear until the dial tone

kicked in, then handed it over to Connie. "Do you think she'll deliver the message?"

"I don't know," Connie said. "Fifty-fifty." In the light from the overhead lightbulb, her face looked flushed.

"She said he might be at the nursing home. Let's go. We can catch up with him there."

Connie didn't move. She was staring out into the Truxton, where the sky had gathered up the blues and grays from the water and lights were just beginning to twinkle on in the waterfront homes on the other side of the river. "I feel numb," she said. "I would have trusted Hal with my life."

I thought about Frank Chase and Liz Dunbar, an odd couple if there ever was one, and wondered what dark secrets they shared. I thought about the glances that passed between Connie and Dennis when they thought I wasn't looking. "I'm finding that nothing in Pearson's Corner is what it seems," I told her.

We headed back to the car, not speaking. Connie had already climbed into the driver's seat and I had a hand on the door handle on the passenger side when I noticed a familiar car in the parking lot, Liz's black Lexus. I wrenched open my door and leaned in. "Connie! Liz Dunbar is here. I didn't know she sailed."

"She doesn't." Connie turned her head and peered through the rear window.

"What's she doing here then?"

"I don't know." Connie slid out of her seat and joined me. She leaned back against the trunk of her car and surveyed the parking lot. "And Frank's here, too."

I had missed it. Frank Chase's blue Ford was

parked farther away, next to the icehouse adjacent to the marina office. "This could not be a coincidence," I said. "If Hal is running drugs, as we suspect, do you suppose those two are involved in the business, too?" Pieces of the puzzle were beginning to fall into place. Katie's habit. Liz's source of money for college. The volatile relationship between Liz and Frank. But I still couldn't figure out what Katie's pregnancy had to do with any of it.

My attention turned from Frank's car to the marina office. From where we stood, it looked deserted. The side facing us was a blank wall of board and batten siding, painted gray like the store. The only opening, a single door, was closed and dark. "Doesn't look like anybody's home."

"You can't tell from here," Connie said. "The main entrance is on the water side."

I had an idea. "Connie, you're a boat owner. We have legitimate business here. Hal doesn't know about . . ." I jerked my head in the direction of the shed where a *Pegasus* lighter than manufacturer's specifications lay. "Let's pay them a call. You can say you're looking for . . ." I cast around in my mind for the name of some nautical part, some little marine gizmo that would probably cost five cents at Ace Hardware or $10.95 if you bought it at the Ships Store. "Say you're desperate for a cotter pin and the store is closed."

"Why do I get this feeling you're about to drag me into more trouble?"

"I just want to see what they're up to in there.

Maybe it'll turn out to be nothing. Maybe they're just eating pizza or something."

"I don't like it."

Nevertheless, Connie went along with my plan, claiming that Paul would never forgive her if something happened to me on her watch.

We skirted the Dumpster that occupied two parking spaces at the far end of the parking lot. Beyond the Dumpster a squat hedge shielded several recycling cans from view. It was my intention to march into the office, bold as a brass band on a Sunday afternoon, but as we drew even with the hedge, we could hear voices raised in anger.

"That's it, I tell you. I'm out of it." Frank Chase's voice carried even over the noise of an air conditioner running in the Ships Store behind us. I put a hand on Connie's back and pushed, forcing her closer to the edge of the hedgerow, where we made ourselves small behind a flowering shrub. From there we had a nearly unobstructed view inside the marina office through the uncurtained window.

"I don't think it's about pizza," I whispered to Connie.

Liz responded to something, waving her arms, but I couldn't hear what she said.

"You can't lay that responsibility on me, Liz. You're the one who wouldn't let me take her to the hospital." Dr. Chase had been sitting in a chair but rose to face her. Mercifully the air conditioner chose that moment to cycle off.

"Fat lot of good that would have done after you shot her, Frankie."

"*I* shot her? That's a crock. You were the one holding the gun, Liz, not me. Ranting on about Harvard and how would you ever live down the scandal!"

I grabbed Connie's hand and squeezed. "Holy shit!" she said.

"Where's Hal?" I whispered back.

I was feeling smug and somewhat relieved that he wasn't there, so when he appeared, my heart sank to my toes. At first I thought he was going to intervene, like a referee, throw a bucket of cold water on the dueling cats, maybe, but he merely observed the escalating argument, standing quietly near his desk where a green-shaded lamp cast a circle of light over stacks of papers and catalogs piled there.

My knees began to ache from being locked in a crouch for so long, but I wouldn't have moved from that spot for a million dollars. Hal finally spoke. "Come off it, you two. You're both responsible."

Liz's head swivelled around. "You're a good one to talk about responsibility. You gave her the money for the abortion, don't forget."

"At least she trusted me, Liz," Hal said.

"And what was that worth? If you'd cared about her at all, you'd have seen to it that she didn't fall into the hands of a quack."

"A quack? How the hell was I supposed to know how she spent the money or where she went? She made it abundantly clear that she didn't want me involved." As he talked, Hal had been pacing in front of his desk, but suddenly he moved away, out of my view.

I stood up and moved to my left to get a better look.

Connie grabbed my pants leg and jerked me down so hard that I thought my wig would fly off. "They'll see you, you idiot!" Her voice was a husky whisper.

"No, they won't," I whispered back. "It's nearly dark out here. That office is lit up brighter than Camden Yards when the Orioles are in town. But if it will make you happy . . ." I scrunched down next to Connie again.

"I can't go on like this!" Dr. Chase sounded miserable.

"Do you think you'll ever practice medicine again if this comes out? Besides, it's not your decision, Frank. There are other people involved."

"It'll come out anyway. Hannah Ives has been asking a lot of questions. It's only a matter of time before she goes to Rutherford and he puts two and two together. If I can't convince you to tell the truth, I'll just have to do it myself."

Good gawd. What a fool. Didn't he ever go to the movies? Watch television? Rule No. 3b. Never threaten to go to the cops, particularly if you're planning to.

But Liz seemed not to have heard. "I thought you'd help her, you jerk. Instead, you said you'd take her to the hospital. Anybody could have taken her to the hospital, for Christ's sake. You're totally useless. You could have stopped the bleeding, but you didn't even turn a hand."

"I didn't have the right equipment, Liz. Katie was hemorrhaging. She was in shock. She needed an ambulance and IVs, probably surgery, not aspirin and a Band-Aid from an inexperienced medical student. I did what I could to help her until you started waving that gun around."

"Gun?" She said it dreamily, as if it were a new word and she had just heard it for the first time. In a deceptively quick move Liz was behind Hal's desk. She wrenched open the top left-hand drawer and pulled out a small handgun, holding it as if she knew what she was doing. "A gun like this, Frankie?" She aimed the barrel at him and held the gun steady, a malicious smile spreading across her face. Hal hurried forward but once again did not intervene.

Liz patted the open drawer with her free hand. "Hal, Hal. What a creature of habit you are!"

"Don't do it, Liz. This time there's no way it can be passed off as an accident. This time it'll be cold-blooded murder."

"And it wasn't murder before? I was just pointing the gun at this witless wonder here. I didn't intend to shoot anybody. If he hadn't jumped me, the gun would never have gone off. Katie would still be alive." The gun under discussion was now pointed squarely at the doctor's chest.

Dr. Chase began desperate bargaining. "It's simple. We do what we should have done in the first place. Explain to the police that Katie's death was accidental."

"Ha!" Liz snorted. "You wish." Her derisive laugh was too big for the room. It rolled through the open window and drifted over the water. She held the gun on both men now, swinging it back and forth in the space between them.

Suddenly Connie was no longer beside me. "I'm calling nine-one-one," she whispered, and disappeared into the darkness behind the Dumpster. I willed her to hurry. I willed Liz to come to her senses. For several long minutes it seemed as if nobody moved inside the marina office. I prayed they would stay that way, but it was inevitable. Somebody would blink.

"This is bullshit!" Dr. Chase did an about-face and headed in my direction, toward the door. He wore the same clothes I had seen him wearing earlier that day, although he appeared to have shrunk within them so that his jacket hung loosely from his shoulders.

I was noticing how much the man had aged in the past twenty-four hours when his eyes suddenly widened in surprise and his glasses flew off. I heard a pop! Liz's hand jerked upward, and I couldn't see Frank Chase anymore.

"Shit!" I sprang up and dashed after Connie but bumbled into the recycling cans, knocking one sideways. The lid slid off, and I dived for it but missed. I watched helplessly as it clattered to the ground, shattering the night air like the cymbals at the end of the *1812 Overture*. There was no chance Liz hadn't heard. A rectangle of light blazed across the dock as someone threw open the office door. I struggled to my feet and scampered into the dark.

I found Connie on the other side of the Ships Store, just reaching for the phone. "They've shot Frank!"

Connie took a step toward the dock, then reversed direction. "The car!" she shouted. We raced for the parking lot, but as we rounded the corner of the building, I saw Liz thundering in our direction, waving the gun.

"The boat, Hannah. Head for the boat!" We turned around and ran like frightened rabbits toward the safety of *Sea Song*, with the dock bucking and heaving beneath our feet.

CONNIE FLEW DOWN THE DOCK AHEAD OF ME, HER shirt a strobe in the darkness, reflecting white from each dock light as she raced by. I sprinted after her thinking, thank God I'd worn sensible shoes. I had no clue what Connie had in mind. Was she planning to call for help on the ship's radio? Was she hoping to make a getaway on the boat? Was she trying to reach the flare gun or another weapon so we could even up the odds? In a minute I would know.

Gasping for breath and still running flat out, I sneaked a glance over my shoulder. Liz had reached the dock and was clattering toward me in her high heels with Hal just a few feet behind. I couldn't tell whether Hal was chasing us or trying to catch up with Liz, who was charging down the dock, still dressed for success, bellowing like an enraged bull. I decided not to hang around and find out. If Hal turned out to be a friend, rather than a foe, maybe we could all have a good laugh about it later.

About halfway down the dock I clipped my thigh on something solid, a wheeled cart left there by a thoughtless boater after he'd schlepped his supplies out to his vessel. Silently blessing the guy, whoever he was, I paused just long enough to drag it into the center of the dock, hoping it wouldn't be visible there in the dark between dock lights. Three slips farther down I did the same with a coil of hose.

I didn't have to turn around to know I'd hit the mark. Liz shrieked in pain as she collided heavily with the cart. I heard a thud and felt the vibration under my feet as her body hit the floating dock, followed by, mercifully, the skitter of her gun along the wooden planks. "Shit, shit, shit!" Her voice pierced the night air, whiny and shrill.

"What'd you do with the damn gun?" Hal seemed utterly calm as if he were asking what she'd done with the car keys. Something big splashed into the water. I hoped it was Liz. But when I heard her voice again, complaining to Hal about his inability to maintain a decently lit marina, I figured one of them must have shoved the push cart into the drink.

"It's here somewhere, you moron. It didn't fall in the water. I would have heard it."

"Which direction did it go? I can't see a damn thing with your big butt in the way."

"Never mind. I've got it," Liz crowed.

I would have known this in any case because the dock resumed its pitching and rolling.

The minute I reached *Sea Song*, I stooped to untie the line holding her to the dock. Connie crouched in *Sea Song*'s cockpit, trying to start the engine. "Never mind that, Hannah! Get up on the bow. Untie the lines from there!" The engine roared to life, drowning her next words, so when I didn't move right away, Connie screamed, "Get the bow lines!"

I scrambled aboard and gained valuable seconds when pained howls told me Hal had rendezvoused with the coiled hose. The port line came easily undone, and I had turned to work, thumb-handed, on the starboard line when Hal leaped aboard. The line was jammed under the anchor chain, and as I struggled to free it, he grabbed me around the waist from behind, yanked me close, and with his mouth touching my ear growled, "You can forget about it, Hannah!"

This instantly erased all doubt about whose side he was on.

We scuffled and I kicked backward, but when Hal stood to his full height, carrying me with him, my feet lost contact with the deck and flailed ineffectually in the air. "Put me down!"

Connie leaped to my rescue, brandishing a propane gas canister, and was preparing to make a sizable dent in Hal's skull. But Liz, panting and near exhaustion, had reached the boat. "Hold it right there." Caught in the circle of light from the dock, I could see Liz had found the gun. The business end was aimed directly at Connie.

Connie froze with one foot in the cockpit and the other raised as she prepared to step up on the seat. "Get back behind the wheel and stay there," Liz ordered.

With Connie's threat defused, Hal eased me to the deck, released his hold on my waist, then twisted my right arm cruelly behind me. A wrenching pain radiated from my chest around my back, and I cried out, tears in my eyes. "Hal, please don't! You're hurting me."

"Is that your bad side? Sorry." The pressure relaxed as he released my arm but was replaced almost immediately by an equally firm grip on my left as he bent it behind my back and marched me ahead of him toward the stern.

Hal instructed Liz to remain in the cockpit. There she could keep on eye on Connie, standing behind the wheel, and on me, tossed, like so much dirty laundry, on the cockpit floor.

He spun the dial on the combination lock that secured the main hatch, yanked the padlock open with a single jerk, removed it, and slid the hatch cover forward. I observed this performance with growing dread, thinking, *We're screwed. There isn't a thing Hal doesn't know about this boat.* I watched as he slid the slatted boards one by one from the hatch opening and thought briefly about pushing him into the cabin below, but Liz and the occasional flashes of light I saw glinting off her gun made me reconsider.

"Stand up." Hal was speaking to me.

I staggered to my feet on legs limp as overcooked spaghetti. "What are you going to do?"

He pointed. "Get down below."

"Hal, please! Think about it. We know you didn't shoot anybody. Let us go."

He studied my face in the semidarkness and seemed to be considering what I'd said, until Liz's unpleasant laugh shattered the silence. "He's the one who'll go away, and for a long, long time, too. How has our Hal broken the law? Let me count the ways."

"I certainly wasn't involved in Katie's death," Hal said.

"Not involved? You've got a selective memory, old boy. Who was it who stuffed my sister's body into an old sail bag and got rid of it? The tooth fairy?"

"Shut up, Liz!" He reached into his back pocket and pulled out a pair of cotton working gloves. "Don't touch anything." He handed the gloves to Liz. "Here, put these on."

"What about you?"

"I work on this boat. My prints are supposed to be all over it."

Connie shot a glance in my direction. If they were already worried about fingerprints, we both knew that our proverbial goose had been cooked.

Hal relieved Liz of the pistol and held it on us while Liz slipped into his gloves. "They're too big for me." She held her hands out for inspection.

Hal returned the gun. "Can you fit your finger through the trigger?"

Liz demonstrated that she could, pointing the gun at him for emphasis.

Hal had pulled me up next to him again. "Then I wouldn't worry about it. Keep an eye on her"—he jerked his head at Connie—"while I take care of Hannah."

As I stood there, pressed up against him, feeling the heat of his body, smelling his soap and nervous perspiration, I was petrified. What did he intend to do with me? Take me below? Shoot me? Strangle me? Throw me overboard? I closed my eyes and prayed as he pulled the remaining slat out of the hatchway with one hand and gripped me securely with the other. "There's not room for both of us on the ladder, Hannah, so I want you to go down first. Don't make me push you."

I didn't have a choice. I grabbed the handrail and obediently climbed down the steep wooden steps— one, two, three, four—into the cavelike darkness of the main cabin, with Hal behind me. In the few seconds it took him to reach my side, I tried to visualize the cabin, tried to remember where everything was. I thought Connie kept the flare gun in the cabinets over the settee on the port side, but I couldn't see the settee, let alone the cabinets, in the dark. I had a mad vision of shooting Liz with this gun, the flare hitting her chest, lighting up her surprised face like a Roman candle on the Fourth of July. Behind me, there was a rustling and clicking as Hal fumbled with something. I wanted to run and hide, but there was no place to go. Besides the main cabin where we stood, *Sea Song* boasted only a small cabin in the bow containing a

V-berth the size of a double bed, and the head, a bathroom no bigger than a telephone booth. It was hopeless.

Hal flipped the master battery switch and toggled on the cabin lights. A light came on over the U-shaped galley to my right. Connie's stainless steel sink gleamed; the Formica counters shone. Everything would be put away, of course, including the knives in their neat little compartmentalized drawer over the sink. I frantically surveyed the cabin, looking for possible weapons while Hal rummaged about in the navigation station. He opened a bottom drawer, stuck his hand in, and came out with a fistful of sail ties.

"Forward." His voice was calm, but seeing the sail ties heartened me. He was only going to tie me up, not kill me. At least not right away. *Where there's life, there's hope.* Well-meaning visitors used to comfort me with such drivel when I was struggling with my recovery in the hospital. What a twist of fate this was.

"Let's get this show on the road!" Liz yelled from above. "Drive this thing out of here." We had been idling in the slip, untied, for only minutes, but it seemed like hours to me. I heard the pitch of the engine change as Connie shifted into reverse and began backing *Sea Song* out of her slip.

I was uncooperative, twisting my body away from him, while Hal secured my hands behind my back. His frustrated grunts gave me satisfaction.

He ordered me to sit on the floor of the forward cabin, a space about three feet square. He tried to secure the cabin door, but space was so limited, he couldn't close it with me sitting there. He could have ordered me to stand up, of course, but then he'd have to contend with the faulty catch. Connie had knotted string around it to hold the door open so it wouldn't bang about while we were under way. Hal must have decided it was too much trouble. "Stay here. Don't move and you won't get hurt."

"Sure, Hal. Like I believe that. I'd be curious to know what you plan to do with us. I think you owe me that much."

He was standing, towering over me, filling the door of the tiny cabin as snugly as a cork. I was aware of everything about him from the Dock-Siders on his feet to his bare knees and khaki shorts, from his leather belt to his plaid cotton shirt. Our eyes met, and even in the dim light from the forty-watt bulb behind me, I thought I saw something there. A flicker. Hesitancy?

Hal knelt in front of me. I squirmed as far from him as I could against the bottom of the V-berth, where I could feel the gentle vibration of the engine against my back. Hal smiled and touched my cheek with his fingertips, dragged his fingers down slowly to touch my chin, then my lips. I turned my face aside, wishing I could move away from him. His face loomed large in front of me, and suddenly his hand tightened on my chin, turned my face to him, and his mouth was on mine, pressing my head back against the berth. I couldn't breathe. When the kiss was over, I wanted to wipe my mouth, but I couldn't do it.

"I've been wanting to do that ever since I met you, Hannah."

I wasn't aware that I was crying until I felt the wetness on my cheeks. Hal brushed my tears away with the gentleness of a lover. "I was hoping I'd have a chance with you. I really was."

I briefly considered playing along with him but figured he would see through my act in a minute. "Cut out the crap, Hal. If you cared for me at all, you'd get yourself out of this mess. Talk to Dennis. Tell the truth. Take your lumps." I remembered when I said it that Hal didn't know we had discovered *Pegasus*'s secret compartment. If we could just get word to Dennis, Hal would pay for that stolen kiss with many, many years behind bars. Right now, though, neither possibility seemed very likely.

Hal rocked back on his heels. "I worried when you started asking questions all over town. Particularly when you started talking with Chip. I just wanted to discourage you, is all. Thought a little swim in the bay might convince you to go home."

"So you tripped me? Why would falling overboard make me want to go home?"

He shrugged.

"And were you responsible for running me off the road, too?"

"No. That was Liz's bright idea. I never thought your life would be in jeopardy. Liz said they'd just frighten you a little, but I should have known." He searched my face, as if looking for understanding. "I really cared about you."

I noticed Hal's use of the past tense and shivered.

"I'm only sorry I didn't meet you earlier. There's

chemistry between us, Hannah. You feel it, I can tell. This kind of chemistry doesn't come along very often."

With difficulty, I kept my face impassive, thinking, *The only chemistry between you and me right now, buster, is saltpeter, charcoal, and sulfur, and the last time I looked, that spelled gunpowder.* I remembered Hal had said he'd had only one serious relationship since Vietnam. Could it have been with Katie?

Hal had stood and turned to go.

"Hal, tell me something." He looked back at me over his shoulder. "Why did you pay for Katie's abortion?"

In the dim light he looked confused, like a little lost boy. "She didn't want the baby."

"*You* were the father of that child!"

He squatted down in front of me again, tracing a finger almost absentmindedly along my slack-clad knee. "Yes, but she wasn't really interested in me, Hannah, an old, broken-down Vietnam vet. She wanted to marry that young Bible thumper. She didn't even tell me about the baby until after Chip turned her down." His voice was almost a whisper.

"Turned her down? You mean he wouldn't marry her?"

"No. He wouldn't sleep with her." Hal knelt before me, head down, staring at his hands.

So that had been her plan! Katie thought she could trick Chip into marrying her, but when he refused to sleep with her, she would never have been able to pass the child off as his.

"I'd have married her. Been a good father, too. But she was only interested in me for—"

I thought I could fill in the blank. "For drugs?"

Hal's eyebrows shot up. "How'd you know?"

"Bill Taylor told me."

"Bill! It figures. He was sweet on Katie, too." Hal's knees popped as he stood up. "Well, it doesn't matter now. None of it matters. When she called me an old man and made it clear that she'd never really loved me, there didn't seem to be any point in pretending anymore." He shrugged. "So I gave her the money."

"Hal, it's not too late. Tell Connie to turn the boat around. Let's go home." I toyed again with the idea of coming on to him, of making him think there might be a chance of something between us, but something had died in his eyes.

"I don't think so, Hannah. It's too late now. Too late for everything."

As he left the cabin, he flipped off the lights, plunging the V-berth into darkness, leaving me alone, struggling to free my hands. Knowing I had to come up with a plan.

I HADN'T THOUGHT ABOUT JAMIE DEMELLA FOR
years. That's why it was all the more surprising that I'd
think about him now while trussed up in the dark, all
alone in the forward cabin of a pirated sailboat. When
my father was stationed in San Diego, Jamie had lived
next door. We played together after school. One summer I'd organized a neighborhood circus to raise
money for the Red Cross. Jamie was supposed to be
ringmaster but decided at the last minute that he'd
rather be a magician. He'd bought a junior magician
kit at the PX, one that came with a top hat, a wand, a
deck of trick cards, some brass rings, and a string of
silk scarves. He practiced for hours in his backyard
until his bratty little sister refused to cooperate anymore. Then he asked me to be his assistant. For the

event I agreed to dress in my ballet tutu and hold his
equipment, but I drew the line when he wanted to
saw me in half. We were both ten. I didn't think he
had the experience.

But Jamie had taught me how to position my
wrists—sideways, not flat—so that no matter how
tightly they were tied, I could eventually wriggle out.
Thanking Jamie, wherever he was, I rotated my wrists
toward each other, stretching and pulling the fabric of
the sail ties, tucking my thumbs under my palms, eas-
ing the loops down over my hands. *So what if my
wrists grow raw?* I thought. *At least when my body
washes up, they'll know it wasn't an accident.*

It wasn't easy, but after about five minutes my
hands were free. I massaged my wrists and made a
silent promise that if I ever got off this boat alive, I'd
locate Jamie on the Internet and thank him myself.
But the only thing free were my hands. I sat quietly in
my cramped quarters, turning over half-baked plans
in my mind.

Liz was a dangerous maniac with a gun, but Hal
was smart, an expert sailor who would be hard to fool.
From my spot in the dark, facing the stern, I could see
into the cockpit, where Connie stood behind the
wheel, her face illuminated by the red light reflecting
off the compass. One of Hal's bare legs was just visible to the right of the hatch, but I couldn't see Liz.

"Where are we?" Hal must have been talking to
Connie, because she answered.

"At green flasher number four. Does it matter?"

"Where are we going?" Liz sounded exasperated. From the direction of her voice, I figured she must be perched on the cabin top.

"Just keep your hand on the gun and your mouth shut." Hal's voice was edged with apprehension. For one thing, Connie was smiling. That was unnerving. I wondered what on earth she had to smile about, and then I smelled it, about a minute before Hal did: burning rubber.

In the next second the engine's emergency alarm began to scream. With a roar of rage Hal launched himself across the cockpit and twisted the ignition key, shutting down the engine.

Liz must have thought he'd taken complete leave of his senses. "Shit, Hal. What the hell's wrong?"

"The engine's overheated. Can't you smell it? Damn water pump must be burned out."

"How'd that happen?"

"No one opened the water intake valve that supplies water to cool the engine."

"That was smart." Her tone made it clear that this turn of events was entirely his fault.

"Well, there's nothing we can do about it now."

Although I knew she couldn't see me, I gave Connie a big thumbs-up.

Sea Song drifted to a dead stop.

"Hal, we aren't moving! Do something!" Liz whined.

"You mind your business and I'll mind mine. Just keep that gun on Connie. I'm going to raise the sails." I could see the back of both legs now, as he faced my sister-in-law. "And you, keep us on course, or I swear to God, I'll tell her to shoot you. Don't think she won't."

There was no doubt in my mind that Liz would gladly take care of anybody who got in her way. I wondered if she'd lost any cases to lawyers who had turned up floating in the Potomac River. She'd killed once, twice probably, and I was convinced she was about to do it again. But not with a gun. That was just to keep us in line. If they wanted to make our deaths appear as accidental drownings, bullet holes in our bodies couldn't be part of the picture.

Hal surprised me by popping into the cabin again. I whipped my hands behind my back, my pulse pounding in my ears like heavy footsteps. At first I thought maybe he'd had a change of heart, but he stopped at the navigation station, pulled open a drawer, and rummaged through it, completely ignoring me. He pulled out something that flashed brightly in the gloom, a winch handle. He'd need this special tool to crank up the sails, particularly as he would be working alone. Halfway up the ladder he stopped and turned back to the navigation station to pull out something else. I heard a click-click. A powerful beam of light swept around the cabin until it caught me, frozen in fear like a possum in headlights. It took all my willpower not to throw up my untied hands to shield my eyes. I sat on them instead.

"You okay?"

"That's a dumb question." I held my eyes open until they watered, staring at the spot where I guessed his eyes would be in the blackness behind the powerful flashlight that Connie used for spotting navigational markers after dark.

"Hal! What the hell's keeping you?" Liz yelled. "Get your ass up here!"

The beam switched off, leaving spots swimming before my eyes, spoiling my night vision.

Hal disappeared through the hatch and almost immediately, I heard the grinding of the portside winch that controlled the unfurling of the jib sail. Behind me up on deck, the jib flapped and slapped its way across the bow.

Sea Song surged forward. "Finally!" I heard Liz exclaim.

"Shut up, Liz." Over my head the fiberglass groaned under Hal's weight as he climbed to the cabin top to deal with the mainsail. I remembered how we'd accomplished that task together, only three, no, was it four days ago? Now completely free, with the element of surprise on my side, I wanted to storm the deck while Hal was distracted, wrestle the gun from Liz, and get the drop on Hal, but I could see that was a lousy plan. Someone would surely get shot in the process, and with my luck lately, it would probably be me.

I needed a weapon. I tried to remember where Connie kept the box containing the flare gun. Was it on my right, in the compartment with the hats? Or was it in the navigation station? I'd never be able to find the stupid thing in the dark. Maybe I could ease a knife out of the utensil drawer? No, that was in the galley, too near the main hatch. I'd be seen. Something big and heavy, then. What?

I looked at Connie for inspiration. I could see her standing tall and straight behind the wheel, the light from the compass reflecting red off her face. I willed her to look at me but knew it would be fruitless. She'd never see me down here in the dark.

The squeal and grind had stopped. The mainsail must be fully raised. When I saw the corners of Connie's mouth turn up slightly, as if she had just remembered a joke, I thought she might be looking at me after all. Hal hadn't left the cabin top. I supposed he'd be tying off the main halyard about now, wrapping it in a neat figure eight around the cleat. I couldn't see Liz, but I figured she was nearby, perched on the cabin top, because I could hear her complaining. "Hurry up, Hal. I don't know a goddamn thing about boats, and this bitch is making me nervous."

It was a subtle thing, and Hal would have noticed it at once if he hadn't been so occupied with the sails. Connie turned the wheel slightly to the right. Sailors are always doing that, I've noticed, moving the wheel back and forth from one side to the other even when the boat is sailing in a straight line, but this was different. *Sea Song*'s course shifted slightly, and suddenly I knew what was going to happen.

Connie had altered course just enough so that the wind crossed the stern, filling the sails from the other side. Any second now the boom would swing to the other side of the boat. The boat jibed, sending the heavy boom slashing across the deck. Hal yelled a warning, but it was too late. With a thud and clanking of metal cables and fittings, the swinging boom connected solidly with something, sending shock waves undulating down the mast, vibrations even I could feel as I sat below. "Liz!" There was the squeak of Hal's rubber-soled shoes scrambling across the deck, followed by a splash. Then something heavy fell into the cockpit, spinning like a pewter plate, and I saw Connie desert the wheel and dive for it. Hal got there a second later, and the two of them struggled, grunting and swearing, for possession of the gun. I sprang toward the hatch and had almost reached the ladder when Hal shoved Connie away and pointed the gun at her triumphantly.

"Get back behind the wheel!"

I melted back into the shadows.

In the scuffle Connie's shirt had ridden up, exposing her bra. Without embarrassment she tugged it down over her slacks and did as she was told. From behind the wheel, she glared at Hal with undisguised hatred.

Hal's voice was controlled and edged with menace. "You've killed her, you realize. Even if she survived the blow, we'll never find her out here in the dark." Since Hal clearly had no intention of going back to look for his partner in crime, I found his sentiment a little cheap.

Connie at least was honest. "Frankly, Hal, I don't give a shit."

Connie couldn't know it, but she'd nearly killed me,

too, with her well-timed jibe. As I crouched in the V-berth entertaining fantasies of rising to the rescue like Superwoman, Craig's tackle box had come sliding across the cushion and fallen to the floor, narrowly missing my head. With all the crashing going on up on the deck, Hal hadn't noticed the racket it made as it landed at my feet.

Back in the forward cabin after my aborted plan to tackle Hal, I lifted the tackle box to my knees. I remembered that lovely sail on the bay, and I remembered the lures. My mind fastened on the bright, shiny spoon Dennis had demonstrated only days before, and I wondered what kind of weapon it would make. I eased the latches open, praying they wouldn't creak. Where was the spoon? Working in the dark, I felt around the upper tray, pricking my fingers on hooks, stifling the urge to cry out, silently sucking blood from a tiny puncture in my thumb. It wasn't on top. Carefully I lifted the top tray and began feeling around in the compartment underneath. I encountered the soft plastic of a surgical eel, the wiggly jelly of something squidlike, and then my fingers closed around it, the silver spoon with the big, ugly hook.

I withdrew the lure from the box and cradled it in my palm, feeling the cool metal, the ornamental feathers, and the hook, now safely capped. I admired the balance and the way it fitted snugly in my hand; thoughts of Peter Pan and Captain Hook rose, unbidden, to my mind. Quietly I reassembled the trays, fastened the lid and pushed the box into the head, where I wouldn't trip over it in the dark.

Now what would I do? I knew that if I appeared on deck, brandishing my lure, one or both of us might be shot. But we'd be floating in the bay anyway if I couldn't come up with an idea soon. Okay, if I couldn't get to Hal, how could I get him to come to me?

I crept into the head and sat on the toilet seat, turning ideas over in my mind, wishing I had paid more attention in sailing school. I couldn't sabotage the electrical system; we were sailing without power. Maybe I could set the boat on fire! But I had no matches; I could think of nothing combustible nearby that I could lay my hands on. I cursed Connie for being so damn fastidious. Tie it down. Turn it off. Put it away. That damn checklist!

My prior experience with operating systems aboard *Sea Song* was limited primarily to the bilge. *What if . . . ?* I knelt and ran my hand over the floorboards near the V-berth, feeling for the opening I knew would be there. The varnished teak felt smooth and clean underneath my fingers, but the boards fitted together so snugly, each butting against the next piece so smoothly, that I couldn't feel the seam. My fingers eventually found the hole, about the size of a quarter. I inserted my index finger and carefully pried the floor panel upward, holding my breath, afraid that it would groan or scrape, alerting Hal to the fact that I was up to something down below. I eased the panel out of position, leaving a rectangular hole.

Even in the daytime, when I could see what I was doing, I felt uncomfortable rooting around in the dark places under the floor. Gingerly I eased my hand into the bilge and felt around until I located the narrow, cylindrical apparatus that controlled *Sea Song's* speedometer. A dangerous little gizmo, Connie had said, which needed to be installed in a hole drilled clear through the hull. I'd assisted one time as she'd pulled it out and cleaned it of algae. But this time I wouldn't be standing by to cram a temporary plug into the hole while she brushed green gunk off the wheel. Holding my breath, I wrenched the fitting out of its hole.

Water fountained into the boat like Old Faithful, wetting me completely. In less than a minute the rising water covered my shoes, and I swallowed hard, fighting back my panic, knowing that I'd need to stay quiet down below for my plan to work.

Perched back on the toilet seat again, I wondered how far into the bay we'd have to sail before Hal decided we'd gone far enough to dump us overboard. I wondered how long I could tread water, how far I could swim with my sore chest and bum arm. Hal would have to make it appear like an unfortunate accident with him as the only survivor. I'd drowned trying to save poor Liz, that would be his story, and Connie had gone in after me. Such a tragedy! We'd make the front page of the *Chesapeake Times* for sure.

Sea Song began to slow. "What's wrong?" Hal sounded unhappy.

"I don't know. I haven't changed course. The sails are full. Suddenly it's like sailing a bathtub."

From the cockpit I heard the click-click of the flashlight, and its beam sliced through the dark into the cabin below. I sat quietly, hardly breathing, trying to merge with the darkness in the head.

"The goddamned boat's sinking! She must have pulled one of the through-hulls!"

From above, I heard Connie laugh.

Hal scrambled into the cabin, flipped on the cabin lights, and began wading in my direction. "Which one was it, damm it?"

I waited where I was, with the door ajar. Soon he would notice that I wasn't where he had left me.

"Hannah?"

I extracted the lure from my pocket and gripped it in my right hand. With my left, I removed the red plastic plug that protected the hook and dropped it into the water. I didn't think I'd be needing it again.

"Hannah?"

Naturally, Hal expected to find me in the forward cabin. As his profile appeared in the doorway, I lashed out, sinking the lure deep into his neck.

Hal screamed, a hideous sound that will haunt me forever, and dropped the gun. It sank to the floor, but neither one of us dived for it. Hal was too busy bellowing and clutching his neck, and I was staring in horror, appalled by what I had done. At first there was surprisingly little blood. Then Hal tried to remove the hook, but the barb held fast and began to tear his flesh. "Hannah!" he cried. The man was in agony. He fell back against the cushions of the V-berth. I couldn't bear to look into his eyes.

I turned and floundered away, moving as quickly as

I could in my waterlogged shoes. I headed for the pilot berth where Connie kept the life preservers.

Connie's head appeared in the hatch. "Connie!" I yelled. "Is it too late to cork it?"

"Oh, God, yes." She jumped onto the seat by the navigation station.

Connie flipped on the ship's radio, punched the button that activated Channel 16, and spoke more calmly than I could believe into the microphone. "May Day, May Day, May Day. This is the sailing vessel *Sea Song*. We're about two miles off Holly Point near the shipping channel, taking on water fast. Three . . . uh . . . four adults. One overboard. We're abandoning ship now." The radio crackled, hissed, then went silent. "Damn!"

"What's wrong with the radio?" I was looking around for the flashlight, but who knew where Hal had dropped it?

"I don't know," Connie moaned. "It's gone dead. Water probably shorted out the wires."

Standing in water nearly up to my knees, I held out the life jackets. Connie threw them into the cockpit and pushed me up the ladder. She slipped her life jacket over her head, snapped the buckles together across her chest and waist, and helped me do the same. I held up the third life jacket. Connie sucked in her bottom lip and shook her head, but I couldn't do it. Just before the rising water shorted out the electrical system and all the lights went out, I tossed it at Hal. "You don't deserve this, you son of a bitch!"

Hal caught the life jacket in his bloody hands. The hook in his neck flashed and sparkled. Blood dripped from the yellow feathers at its tail, drenching his shirt. He looked so pale and weak that I wondered if I had severed his carotid artery.

Connie grabbed a couple of small floating cushions, handed one to me, and we stood together on the seats in the cockpit, waiting. When Connie judged the time was right, we jumped. Hal was on his own.

Connie and I swam a good one hundred yards from the boat, then turned around, treading water. Silhouetted against the gray night sky, we could see *Sea Song*'s regal mast and her sails flapping like wet sheets on a clothesline. Then she tilted, nose down, and sank beneath the water. Connie moaned. "It's like losing Craig all over again," she sobbed.

I felt rotten. I was a curse. A jinx. "Oh, Connie, I'm so sorry. But I couldn't think what else to do. He was going to leave us out here to drown!" I gasped. My lungs burned, as if they would never get enough oxygen.

"It was the right thing." She took a deep breath and let it out slowly. "Absolutely the right thing."

As I bawled and made well-intentioned promises to God if He'd just help me out of this mess, a cloud bank slid across the sky and the moon, nearly full, laid a silver path on the water. I had my answer. I couldn't wish anybody dead. I expected to see Hal's head bobbing nearby, but although I scanned the water for several minutes, I didn't spot him.

"Where's Hal? I thought sure he'd get out."

"Maybe he's on the other side, treading water like we are."

"Hal! Hal!" I called, but the only answer was the sound of my own labored breathing and the clang of the bell on a nearby buoy. I gasped, choking back tears. "I didn't want him to die, Connie. I never wanted him to die!"

Connie grabbed my life vest by the straps and pulled me toward her until we were so close that our foreheads nearly touched. "Of course you didn't, sweetheart." Waves licked at my chin as I sobbed. "C'mon. We're only in about twenty feet of water."

"I'm not that tall," I wailed.

"What I mean, silly, is that if we're lucky, *Sea Song's* mast will still be visible."

I looked all around me. Miles away I could see lights glimmering onshore. A pair moving in tandem must be a car, its driver heading home after a late day at the office. One thing I knew for sure: It was too far to swim.

"Do you think the coast guard heard your call before the radio died?"

"I hope so." She tugged on my vest. "There she is!" I looked where she pointed and saw the top twenty feet of *Sea Song's* mast, jutting out at a sharp angle from the moon-spangled waves.

We swam, arm over arm, and grabbed on, exhausted. My arm and side ached as if I'd spent twenty minutes on the inside of an industrial clothes dryer. I wondered what had happened to Hal. I wondered if he'd focused on those beckoning lights and tried to swim for shore. In spite of all that had happened, I found myself praying that he'd make it.

LIGHTS CAN BE DECEPTIVE ON THE WATER AT NIGHT. While I clung to the mast, I scanned the horizon for approaching lights that might signal a rescue was at hand. Behind me green and red flashing buoys marked the shipping lanes. I thanked my lucky stars we hadn't sunk out there where we could easily have been run over by a freighter on its way up to Baltimore with a cargo hold full of new Toyotas. To my right I stared long and hard at a bright white light. Connie and I argued about it, thinking it might be the mast light of a sailboat under power, one near enough to rescue us, but when it hadn't moved for a while, we decided it must be Venus, always the brightest star in the early-evening sky. Ahead and to my left, scattered lights flashed green or white at two- or four-second intervals, marking the channel into the Truxton, or so Connie said.

The drone of a high-speed motorboat raised our hopes. "Hey! Hey! Hey!" We gripped our flotation cushions by their straps and waved them in the air as the boat passed, unseeing, within two hundred feet of us, swamping us in its wake as it went rooster-tailing by. I inhaled water and coughed, wiping water out of my eyes with a free hand. "See why I hate power-boats?" Connie delivered a rude gesture toward the back of the disappearing boater.

I shivered. "I'm getting cold. How warm is the water?"

"About seventy degrees."

"That's okay, then. It's room temperature. We should be okay."

"We'll be fine for a couple of hours, but I don't want to stay out here too long, if we have a choice. I wish we had something to stand on. Water pulls heat from your body very quickly."

I hugged myself, tucking one hand under my armpit. "How long do you think it will take them to find us?"

"I don't know. Soon, I imagine."

I went back to my original harebrained plan. "Can we swim to shore?"

"No. Two reasons that's a bad idea. One, it's a hell of a lot farther than it looks, and two, it's easier to spot the boat than it is to find a lone swimmer, particularly at night."

My teeth began to chatter. Connie explained that this was natural, the body's way of staying warm. For once I wished I had more insulating body fat, but I hadn't gained back the weight I'd lost during chemo.

"Shivering and chattering's normal, Hannah. I once took a survival course. They say what you have to watch for are the umbles—mumbles, stumbles, fumbles, and grumbles."

"Well, I'm certainly not going to stumble out here, but I might grumble."

Connie, whom I trusted to be experienced with such things, said we should huddle for warmth. She instructed me to wrap my clothes as tightly around myself as possible, then embraced me in a bear hug with our legs twined together.

"That was really brilliant what you did back there," Connie said after a moment.

"Thanks. I figured if the cancer was going to do me in anyway, I might as well go out in a blaze of glory! Sorry about taking you and the boat along with me."

Something brushed against my leg, and I freaked, breaking away from Connie with a shriek. "It's only a fish, silly! I felt it, too." She grabbed my life jacket by the straps and pulled me back. We floated there, bobbing in the waves.

"Tell me something, Connie. If we're going to die out here, I'd like to know. What's really going on between you and Dennis?"

"I think we're falling in love."

"But why keep it such a deep, dark secret?"

I felt Connie shrug. "It was too soon after his wife's death. And in addition to her other problems, his daughter, Maggie, is still grieving. She's made it very difficult for us to see each other."

I looked into my sister-in-law's eyes, just inches from my own. "Why didn't you tell me this before? What is there to be ashamed about?"

"I don't know exactly. Perhaps I was feeling disloyal to Craig. Dennis and he had been such pals."

"I still don't understand why you wouldn't share your feelings about Dennis with me, particularly when they were so obvious."

"It's silly, now that I think about it. But I thought I was protecting you."

I was incredulous. "Protecting me? From what?"

When Connie spoke again, her voice was husky with emotion. "I didn't tell you that Dennis lost his wife to cancer. I knew you weren't out of the woods yet, medically speaking, and I was afraid you'd think that the first thing a husband widowed by cancer did was to dash off into the arms of the nearest available lover."

"And you thought, because of Jennifer Goodall . . ." I squeezed Connie tightly and laughed. "And you think I'm wacky!"

We floated quietly for a while, still wrapped around each other, taking turns holding on to the mast. "You know, I was thinking back there, if we got shot or if we drowned out here, I'd never get to say good-bye to Paul. I'd never be able to tell him how much I really love him." I took a deep breath and let it out slowly. "I've decided that one benefit of dying of cancer is that you usually have time to get your affairs in order. You can prepare your spouse for the time when you won't be around anymore. It's like saying a long good-bye." Connie didn't say anything, but I thought I saw tears on her cheeks.

I was resting my head on Connie's shoulder and vice versa, trying to separate navigational markers and lights onshore from the lights of would-be rescuers or a tug towing a barge or another hot-dogging power-boater hightailing it back from dinner on the Eastern Shore. After a while it all seemed a kaleidoscopic blur.

I was cold, and I was tired, so very tired. The next thing I remember was Connie's voice, spiraling down to me from the end of a long tunnel. "Sing!" it was saying. "Sing!"

"What?" My eyes snapped open, and my head lolled back against the neck roll of my life jacket.

"Sing!" Connie threw her head back, eyes closed, and launched into song, her voice off key, but hearty.

> *Do your ears hang low*
> *Do they wobble to and fro*
> *Can you tie 'em in a knot*
> *Can you tie 'em in a bow*
> *Can you sling 'em over your shoulder*
> *Like a Continental soldier,*
> *Do your ears hang looooow!*

Just before she got to the last line, she punched me playfully on the arm and I joined in, a *looooow* in perfect two-part harmony that would sound to anybody hearing it from the distant shore like the mating call of a pair of lovesick cows.

"I haven't sung that song since Girl Scout camp in California!" I sputtered.

"I thought singing would help keep our spirits up."

In the next hour we warbled our way through every camp song known to God and man—"John Jacob Jingle Heimer Schmidt," "White Coral Bells"—with a few nursery school songs, like "Eensy Weensy Spider" thrown in for good measure.

I was trying to remember all the words to "Teddy Bears' Picnic" when a cool breeze fanned my cheek. Connie had raised her head. "I think they're coming!"

Keeping one hand on the mast, I turned to look. When I first clapped eyes on those flashing blue lights, I did the nautical equivalent of jumping up and down for joy, kicking my feet and bobbing like a Halloween apple. Connie and I screamed, "Help! Help!" and waved our cushions again, hoping they'd be picked up by the rescuers as flashes of white against the dark sky.

The beam of a powerful searchlight pierced the darkness, swept across the water, and passed over us. My throat was raw from screaming and the salt water I'd swallowed. "They missed us! They passed right over us!" Tears of despair ran down my cheeks. Suddenly the beam stopped, shuddered and swept back, focusing on the cushion that Connie held aloft. I kissed Connie on the cheek. "Thank God, thank God!"

The vessel approached at a high rate of speed, the roar of its engine the most beautiful sound I have ever heard. And to think I'd so recently consigned all motor-powered boats to low places in hell. The engine throttled down, and the boat slowed, circling, but the searchlight never left our bodies. As it drew within fifteen feet of where we clung to *Sea Song*'s mast, I could see that it was an inflatable inner tube–like boat about twenty feet long. The dark outlines of several crewmen moved about on board.

"Ahoy!" one of the crewmen called, and I thought what a quaint, old-fashioned thing to say, but every bit as effective, I supposed, as "Hey there!" "Sit tight. We'll get a line to you in a minute."

The boat crept fractionally closer, then stopped, its engine idling. "We can't get too close to your boat, ma'am. If we get tangled up in it, we might all be in trouble." Now I could see that the men wore uniforms and life jackets. One of them began to wind up like a softball player delivering a slow pitch. A line uncoiled from his hand, whooshing to our left. I heard a gentle plop as an orange, softball-size float landed not five feet from my head.

"You first, Hannah. Swim to it."

"How about you?"

"They'll throw one for me in a minute."

I dog-paddled to the orange ball and grabbed it with one hand, then wrapped the fingers of both hands gratefully around the plastic rope. Almost immediately a crewman began to pull me through the water, but I was in such a hurry to get aboard that although it hurt my chest like crazy, I hauled myself, hand over hand, along the rope until I reached safety. Panting and almost insane with relief, I grabbed one of a dozen or so white lines looped along the side of the rescue craft. My arms and legs trembled with exhaustion, and it was all I could do to hold on until someone's strong arms reached over and gently pulled me aboard. I flopped in the bottom of the boat like a stranded dolphin and tried to catch my breath.

"Thank goodness we found you!" said a familiar voice.

"Dennis! How'd you—"

"I'll explain in a minute." A towel appeared from somewhere; then I was wrapped in a blanket and hustled out of the wind. In less time than it took for me to sit down, Connie's white-clad legs appeared on deck. Dennis himself had pulled her aboard. Almost before her feet hit the deck, he had gathered her up in a fierce embrace.

"Oh, Connie, Connie! Thank God. Let me take a look at you." He held her at arm's length as if checking to see if anything was missing or broken, then cradled her face in both his hands and stared into it for a long minute. "I don't know what I would have done if I'd lost you." I saw Connie's arms lift from where they hung, dripping, at her sides, and wrap themselves around his neck. She kissed him then, long and hard, his arms snaked around her waist, and he lifted her feet nearly off the deck. Everyone but me was busily looking elsewhere.

"Where are the others?" a female crewman asked. I could see the beam of the searchlight she held sweeping the water around the mast in ever-broadening circles.

"He was on the boat," I cried. "We threw him a life

jacket. But I didn't see him come up after the boat went down."

"You radioed a man overboard."

"That was Liz Dunbar," Connie said matter-of-factly, as she, too, was cocooned in a blanket. "She got clobbered by the boom and went over about two miles from here."

Dennis settled Connie next to me, then turned to consult one of the crew. I snuggled deeper into my blanket, figuring we'd be stuck out there for hours while the coast guard searched the bay for Liz and Hal. I found myself nodding, unable to keep my eyes open. Might even have dozed off for a bit.

Suddenly I was aroused by a flurry of activity—motors, flashing lights, crew shouting back and forth—as another boat, this one from the Maryland Department of Natural Resources, pulled up alongside.

Once again Dennis seemed to take charge. "Call SMC," he told the crewman at the wheel. "Make sure they've got some divers on the way. Then let's get these women ashore."

This time when Dennis said we'd go to the hospital, I didn't argue. As we waited in separate cubicles under the bright lights of the emergency room with only a thin curtain between us, Connie and I learned that Frank Chase had been found and airlifted to University Shock-Trauma in Baltimore. No one could tell us how he was doing. Eventually we were examined, our temperatures taken, and an earnest young doctor from Poland, whose nametag had no vowels in it, pronounced we were suffering from mild hypothermia. Several hundred dollars later he sent us home with instructions to keep warm and drink plenty of hot liquids. Some thoughtful person even produced hospital scrubs for us to wear and returned our wet clothes, neatly folded, in a plastic garbage bag.

An hour later, at home, dressed like Christmas morning in flannel pajamas, Connie's terry-cloth robe, and a pair of fleece-lined slippers from L. L. Bean, I cornered Dennis in the living room.

"How did you know where we were, Dennis?"

"It's a long story."

I glanced at Connie, sitting next to him on the sofa. "I think we have time to hear it," she said.

Dennis rested his coffee cup on the arm of the sofa and balanced it there with two fingers. "I was at the nursing home, talking with my informant . . ."

"Your informant works at the nursing home?"

"Not exactly. He lives there."

"Lives there?"

"You bet! He's too frail to take care of himself, but there's nothing much wrong with his mind."

"Your father-in-law? I don't believe it."

"Oh, he's a clever old chap. Last October he overheard one of the orderlies discussing a drug deal, and naturally he told me. I'd been aware of Hal's involvement with drugs for almost a year, but the rascal's been careful. Supercareful. According to their records, the coast guard boarded *Pegasus* down in Florida last year, ostensibly for a routine inspection, but they couldn't find a thing. I've been keeping my eye on him ever since."

Connie plucked at Dennis's sleeve. "How much is it worth to you to break this case wide open?" She told Dennis about the hidden compartment on *Pegasus*, giving appropriate credit to me, I'm pleased to say, and I watched as his eyes widened in amazement.

"When we discovered the doctored keel, we called you at home, but Maggie told us you were at the nursing home. We were on our way there when—well, when we got diverted." She curled up on the sofa and rested her head in Dennis's lap, all pretense aside.

Dennis laid a gentle hand on her back. "I didn't know a thing about that. When Dad gave me the tip that a shipment was going out tonight, I rushed straight down to the marina to see what was what. When I saw your car in the parking lot"—he stroked the hair back over Connie's temple and smoothed it behind her ear—"I was surprised. Then I checked the office and found Frank Chase, lying in a pool of blood. He was alive, but barely. I called an ambulance, then went looking for you, fearing the worst. When I discovered *Sea Song*'s slip was empty . . ." He paused to clear his throat. "Well, I hot-footed it back to the office to call the coast guard. They had just received your May Day, so I asked them to swing by the marina and pick me up. The rest you know."

"Liz tried to kill us," I said.

"Because you found out about her involvement with the drug ring?" His fingers made little circles on

Connie's back, moving up and down the bumps along her spine. "I have to confess that I never suspected Liz of being involved with drugs. And certainly not Frank."

"I don't think Dr. Chase was. He was only involved with Liz and Hal in the cover-up of Katie's murder."

I told him what we had learned about Katie's becoming pregnant by Hal, about her plan to pass the baby off as Chip's and how, when that plan fizzled, she had tried to get rid of the child with disastrous results. "When they salvage *Sea Song*, I think you'll find that the gun that shot Frank Chase was the same one used to shoot Katie."

"Well, I'll be damned!" He shot me a wink. "Thanks to you, it looks like two cases got solved today. Maybe three. The orderly we arrested is David Wilson's brother. We've impounded David's van. I suspect we'll find traces of his encounter with your car on his bumper. If so, he'll be charged with attempted murder and reckless endangerment, in addition to any drug-related charges we can pin on him."

"Good!" Privately, I hoped Dennis would lock them up and throw away the key.

Dennis checked his watch. "It's midnight, sports fans. You gals will be wanting to get some sleep."

I had to ask him. "How about Hal?"

"If he's still in the boat, the divers should have found him by now."

"Do you think he's still alive then?"

Dennis gently lifted Connie's head off his lap and slipped one of the sofa pillows under it. She was fast asleep. He crossed to where I sat curled in the armchair and perched on the ottoman at my feet. "There's a chance, but slim. Sometimes there are air pockets." Clenching my fists until my fingernails left crescent-shaped impressions on my palms, I relived my panic in the car as the water from Baxter's pond closed in on me. "There's also a small chance he swam to shore," Dennis continued, "but I think that's one in a million."

"I can't excuse the drugs, but Hal wasn't a killer. Not really. He just got caught up in the crossfire between Liz and Frank."

"But he certainly seemed determined to get rid of you and Connie. I can never forgive him for that."

Neither could I.

Dennis startled me by taking my hand. "I hope you don't mind, but I've located Paul. I talked to him from the hospital. He's leaving the Cape now and should be down here by morning."

I was amazed. "But how did you find him?"

"Simple, really. Just called the local police, gave them Paul's license number, and they cruised around North Truro until they found his car parked somewhere along Beach Drive. You should join him up there, Hannah. Great house, I hear."

He patted my knee, then stood to go. "You girls going to be all right now?"

"Of course. And thanks, Dennis. Thanks for everything." I stood and gave him a hug, trying to ignore the pain that shot across my chest as I did so. "I'll make sure Connie gets to bed."

"Thanks. I've got some loose ends to tie up. University Hospital says Chase should be stable enough to interview by morning."

I walked him to the back door and held it open as he stepped through it onto the stoop. "Will you do me a favor?"

"Sure. What is it?"

I closed the screen door and studied Dennis's face in the porch light. Huge moths wheeled out of the blackness and made kamikaze runs against the screen. "If Dr. Chase is well enough to talk, will you ask him something for me?" And I told Dennis what I wanted to know.

I KNEW PAUL HAD ARRIVED WHEN HE CRAWLED INTO bed next to me, his face still cool from the early-morning air. He nestled against my back, fully clothed, and wrapped his long arms around my waist, pulling me close, until our bodies fitted together like spoons. I felt his warm breath on my neck, the bristles on his chin against my cheek, and then the softness of his lips.

"Ummmm. That's nice." I rolled over to face him. "Ouch!"

Paul recoiled. "Did I hurt you?"

"I don't think there's a single part of my body that doesn't hurt."

He kissed my ear. "There?" The tip of my nose. "There?"

Our silly game. I felt a surge of warmth and affection for Paul, glimpsed the ghosts of the carefree young couple who used to be so mischievously loving in this room. His lips found my mouth. *Oh, it had been so long!* I melted into him, my arms clasping his waist. His hand slid under my pajama top and caressed my breast so tenderly that I shuddered with delight. Suddenly my brain kicked in, unbidden and unwelcome. I envisioned Paul touching Jennifer this way, kissing her hair, playing our game. Gasping, I worked my hand up between our bodies and pushed him away.

"What's wrong?" In the dim light his face wore a worried frown.

"I don't know *what's* wrong with me! But every time you touch me, I think you're just being nice to me because you think I'm going to die. And I don't want your pity! I can't stand it." I buried my face in my pillow.

"Pity you? Hannah, I love you." His voice was soft against my ear. "I can't tell you how panicked I was when Dennis told me I'd nearly lost you. Again. I love you more than I can say."

I turned my head to look at him, his eyes, dark as chocolate, only inches from my own. "I love you, too, Paul. I do! But I keep picturing you with that—that child." The word just tumbled out of my mouth. I couldn't believe I'd said it.

"Hannah! How many times do I have to tell you it's not true?"

"I'm sorry. I just can't seem to help it. Why can't things be the way they were? I want you back. I want

Emily back. I want my breast back. Oh, God, maybe I need to see a therapist." I sat on the edge of the bed, my back to him, feeling ugly and vulnerable without my prosthetic bra and my wig.

Paul ran a finger down the nape of my neck, brushed my shoulder with his lips. "You've got me, Hannah. You've always got me. And if you want to see a therapist, I understand. We can go together if you want. I'll wait for you, Hannah. I'll do whatever it takes, but I won't lose you." I felt his weight shift on the bed and heard the creak of the bedsprings as he stood up.

"Katie's death has made me realize how important Emily is to me, Paul. I don't want to end up like poor Mrs. Dunbar. She'll never be able to hug her daughters again, tell them that she loves them. Never rock her grandchildren to sleep."

Paul walked over to the window and drew open up the curtains. Sunlight cascaded into the room. "Emily's not as far away as you think, Hannah." He bent and kissed the top of my head. "Take your time." Seconds later the door closed softly behind him.

I remained where I was, with the sun falling full on my body. I stretched in its warmth and felt as if the healing had already begun.

I took a shower and pulled on a pair of shorts and a T-shirt. After yesterday's adventures my wig looked like road kill, so I settled a hat on my patchy head, dabbed on some makeup, and padded downstairs.

In the kitchen the clock said nine, and Paul was

pouring a cup of coffee for his sister. I had just sat down to join them when there was a knock on the door and Dennis walked in, looking as if he hadn't had much sleep. He extended his hand to Paul, who took it in both of his and pumped it up and down enthusiastically. "Glad you made it. You made good time."

"Lucky I didn't get caught speeding on the Jersey Pike. Found a truck cruising along at seventy-five and dogged his tail. I tell you, though, when that trooper knocked on our door in North Truro, I nearly had a heart attack."

"Sorry, old man. Couldn't think of any other way to locate you."

"Glad you did." He looked at me with such affection that it nearly broke my heart.

I broke the spell. "Coffee?"

"Can't refuse." Dennis pulled out a chair and sat down. After he poured milk into his cup and stirred in half a teaspoon of sugar, he took a careful sip. "Chase is going to be okay. He's confessed to everything, implicating the others. Didn't want a lawyer, although I insisted one be called. Says he'll plead guilty to all charges."

"And?"

"And you were right, Hannah. Old Dr. Chase had prescribed herbs for Katie's cramps. Frank found the notations on her chart. He says she induced her own abortion by taking two tablespoons of pennyroyal. Dangerous stuff. The usual dose is five drops."

"Why didn't she just pay for the abortion with the money Hal gave her?" Connie's forehead wrinkled in confusion.

"I can guess," I said. "She spent it all on the dress she wore to the dance. It was meant to dazzle Chip into bed."

"How foolish and sad." Paul slumped in his chair, his coffee forgotten.

"How about Liz? And Hal?" Connie wanted to know.

"Still no trace of Liz. But the divers found Hal in the boat."

I set my mug down on the table, carefully, using both hands. My heart was thumping wildly. "Dead?"

"I'm afraid so. He had a life preserver on, but his foot was wedged in an opening in the bilge. Snapped his ankle."

I closed my eyes and took a deep breath. My hands trembled.

"And I think we'll need to talk about this." Dennis pulled a neatly wrapped package out of his pocket, placed it on the table, and unrolled it. It was the silver lure, its tail feathers ragged, but its barbed hook as bright, shiny, and sharp as the day Craig had bought it.

"It was the only weapon I had. I couldn't think of anything else." I looked Dennis in the eye. "Did I kill him?"

Dennis rewrapped the deadly lure and returned it to his pocket. "No, Hannah. Looks like he drowned."

But I felt responsible, either way. Even if the lure

hadn't killed him outright, I was still the one who pulled the plug on *Sea Song*. I'd have to learn to live with that.

Paul rose and stood behind me, a hand on my shoulder. "My God, that was brave."

"It didn't feel very brave at the time. I was scared spitless."

Dennis poured the coffee remaining in his cup down the sink. "You'll need to come down to make a formal statement." He handed the empty mug to Connie. "Both of you."

Connie looked down at her bathrobe and turned her fashion-critical eyes on me. I must have been a sight in my paint-spattered shorts and a sequin-decorated ball cap perched sideways on my head. "Later this afternoon?"

"That'll be fine."

I started to panic. "You're not going to arrest me?"

Dennis's face broke into a huge grin. "Don't be silly! We'll probably give you a medal."

Two weeks later, back in Annapolis, we learned that Liz's body had been discovered by a crabber, caught in a trotline near the mouth of the Patuxent River. I sent a silent prayer to the Dunbars; I could only imagine their anguish at losing both their daughters, and under such horrible circumstances.

At the same time I called my daughter, Emily, in Colorado. I spent an afternoon rehearsing what I was going to say, but when she came on the line, my script flew out the window, I was so relieved to hear her voice.

"Hi, how's it going, pumpkin?"

"Oh, hi, Ma. I've been meaning to call."

Daniel's business was going well, she told me. He'd hired another masseur and had completed a year's training at the Rolf Institute in Boulder. My son-in-law was a certified rolfer, some sort of high-class masseur, I gathered, who could get away with being called simply Dante.

"And, Ma?"

"What?"

"I got a job, Ma."

"That's good news. What are you doing?"

"Working in a bookstore. Not one of those big chains. A little store. You'd like it."

The old me would have mentioned all the money we'd spent on her Bryn Mawr education, just so she could follow some dropout to Colorado and work in a bookstore, but the new me bit my tongue. "I'm sure I would like it," I said.

"Even has a cappuccino bar."

"Now I know I'd like it." I paused. "I don't think the place where I'll be working has a cappuccino bar."

"Mother! I thought Dad said you were going to take it easy for a while."

"I'm temping. The job doesn't start until September anyway. I'll be working for a law firm somewhere out on West Street, filling in for a secretary on maternity leave."

"Funny you should mention that."

"Mention what?"

"Maternity leave." Emily giggled, then was silent. A light began to dawn.

"Emily! Are you pregnant?"

"Hold on, Ma. I've only just found out. Took one of those home pregnancy tests yesterday morning. Damnedest things. Pee on a stick and *voila*! If the double pink lines are to be believed, you and Dad are going to be grandparents."

I counted on my fingers. "December?"

"That's what I figure. A little Christmas package for the old parental units."

I thought I was saying words like *how wonderful* and *I'm so happy*, but what came out was babble. When I could finally put two words together, I said, "Emily, I'd like to come and stay with you, to help out when the baby is born. If that's okay."

"I'd like that very much, Mother."

Many minutes later, after we finally said good-bye, I levitated around the house, picking up newspapers, watering the houseplants, loading the dishwasher. Then I thought about Katie and the precious little life she had carried, both snuffed out before they had a chance to bloom, and I felt guilty about being so happy.

While I waited for Paul to get home so I could deliver the news that he was going to be a grandfather, I strolled down the block and around the corner to Maryland Avenue. At Aurora Gallery, I bought Emily an iridescent dragonfly pin, beautifully crafted by a local artist. As Jean was wrapping it up, I spotted a hand-painted tie. "And I'll take that, too," I told her.

Forty bucks. What the hell, I'd send it to Daniel. "To Dan, with love," I wrote on the card when I got it all to the post office. No way was I going to write "Dante."

On May 22 Jennifer Goodall was graduated with the rest of her class. Paul delivered this news upon returning from graduation exercises at the stadium where the reporters were busy snapping pictures of the Blue Angels, the navy band, the president of the United States, and the hat toss, ignoring my husband for a welcome change. Paul hung his academic regalia in a plastic garment bag, zipped it up so hard that the bag tore, then placed a long phone call to his lawyer.

I was suspicious when I heard the news. "Did you change her grade? Pass her after all?"

"Absolutely not."

"Well, how could she graduate then? Wasn't it a required course?"

"Apparently the academic board waived the requirement."

"Why? Was she a star athlete or something?"

"What a cynic you are! No, I suspect somebody browbeat the board. Maybe she cut a deal. Offered to drop the charges against me if the academy would allow her to graduate."

"How do you feel about that?"

"Outraged. A number of us are planning to write letters of opposition, for all the good it will do. But I'm enormously relieved, and disappointed, too. Relieved that it's over. Disappointed that the truth about her accusation will never be resolved." He grasped my shoulders, searching my eyes for understanding. "I wanted to be exonerated, Hannah! I wanted you to *know* I'd been faithful. Beyond all doubt."

Beyond doubt. My mother says I have to make up my mind one way or the other—either Paul slept with that woman or he didn't—and then deal with it on those terms. Better advice than I got from the therapist, and about two hundred dollars less expensive, too.

Speaking of therapy, that's how I ended up on the beach at Manchineel Bay, eating conch fritters out of a paper container resting on my stomach. Paul sprang the trip on me as a surprise. "I'm taking you to the Virgin Islands. No argument. I've chartered a sailboat out of Tortola."

"A sailboat! Ha! That's just what I need."

"It's therapy, Hannah, like getting back on a horse after you fall off."

So there I was, waiting for Paul to return from the Cooper Island Beach Bar with two piña coladas. He plopped down on the towel next to me and handed me my drink. I took a sip, moaned with pleasure, then set the glass into the sand next to me, twisting it back and forth, digging a little hole so it wouldn't fall over. Gentle waves licked at my toes. Another day in paradise. I watched our charter vessel, *Visage*, bob and sway at anchor in water so crystal clear that it seemed to be suspended in air.

"Paul?" He had returned to his paperback book.

"Umm?"

"After I finish my stint at the law firm, do you think I should go ahead and have that breast reconstruction?"

He laid his book open on the sand and turned to face me, sunglasses askew, propped up on one elbow, sand sugaring his knees. He looked adorable. "Do it for yourself, honey, not for me."

"I was looking in that little shop up there." I pointed toward an island boutique behind the Beach Bar where earlier I had spent nearly thirty minutes looking at tropical beach wraps and swimsuits. "There are a couple of bikinis I could wear if I had two decent boobs to hang them on."

"Hannah, you know I love you no matter what. I want whatever makes you happy." He reached up and touched my hair, which had blossomed, surprisingly, into a profusion of brownish gold ringlets. "Significant change in hair texture," Dr. Wilkins had written on my chart after my last examination.

I smiled at my husband, feeling waves of affection wash over me. With his finger, he traced a line along my shoulder and down my arm. When he picked up my right hand and gently kissed my fingers, I knew we wouldn't be sleeping in separate cabins anymore.